KU-127-900

A Scandalous Publication

A Scandalous Publication

Sandra Heath

ROBERT HALE · LONDON

© Sandra Heath, 1986, 2006
First published in Great Britain 2006

ISBN-10: 0-7090-8084-0
ISBN-13: 978-0-7090-8084-8

Robert Hale Limited
Clerkenwell House
Clerkenwell Green
London EC1R 0HT

The right of Sandra Heath to be identified as
author of this work has been asserted by her
in accordance with the Copyright, Designs and
Patents Act 1988.

2 4 6 8 10 9 7 5 3 1

for Charlotte McCaffrey
in the hope that
she approves of her namesake

Typeset in 11/15pt New Baskerville
by Derek Doyle & Associates, Shaw Heath.
Printed in Great Britain by St Edmundsbury Press,
Bury St Edmunds, Suffolk.
Bound by Woolnough Bookbinding Ltd.

1

'SIR MAXIM TALGARTH AND Lady Judith Taynton.'

The footman's voice rang out over the quiet drawing room, and the two lawyers paused as they sorted through the deeds and other legal documents about to be signed. They glanced across at the young woman in black, seated alone on the magnificent crimson velvet sofa. How would the outspoken Miss Charlotte Wyndham react to the unexpected and rather insensitive arrival of Sir Maxim's mistress, a lady whose gloating delight at the downfall and ruin of the Wyndham family had never been disguised?

Charlotte's heart sank as both names were announced, and her hands clasped among the folds of her black muslin mourning gown. She took a deep breath. She must remain calm and composed, and not give in to the anger that suddenly invaded her. The sale of Kimber Park had to go ahead without delay, and so she would have to try to ignore the prospective purchaser's incredible display of thoughtlessness in bringing Judith here today. Or perhaps it wasn't thoughtlessness at all, perhaps it was quite deliberate. . . .

The two visitors entered, pausing for a moment in the doorway. Max Talgarth was a tall man of very arresting appearance. Dressed in a dark-blue coat and close-fitting gray trousers, his intricate cravat graced by a costly diamond pin, he was not only a Corinthian of the first order, he was also extremely handsome, his looks somehow enhanced by the jagged white dueling scar on his left cheek, and by the streak of gray in his otherwise coal-black hair. There was something almost demonic about his dark good looks, an air of danger that had made many women other than his lovely, accomplished mistress yearn to submit to him. Women found him irresistible. Perhaps it was the dark whispers about him. His wife had died so mysteriously, driven, it was said, to the depths of jealousy and heartbreak by his unfaithfulness and cruelty. And then there were the duels, three bitter confrontations at which he had deftly consigned his opponents to eternity. He wasn't a man to cross; indeed the devil himself was said to have had a hand in his affairs, and sometimes, when a flash of anger blazed in his piercing blue eyes, it was only too possible to believe that all that was said of him was true.

As he bowed to Charlotte from the doorway, however, he was the epitome of breeding, refinement, and courtesy, the perfect and most elegant of gentlemen. 'Good afternoon, Miss Wyndham.'

She inclined her head. 'Good afternoon, Sir Maxim.' Her glance flickered coldly toward the clinging figure in golden yellow at his side. She and Judith had known each other all their lives, their families' estates adjoined each other, but a bitter quarrel had put an end to any semblance of friendship and now the two women cordially loathed each other. 'Good afternoon, Lady Judith.'

Judith's rosebud lips curved into a sleek smile, her green eyes glittering. 'Good afternoon, Miss Wyndham,' she replied, her drawling tone an affectation acquired from her many visits to Devonshire House, where such an accent was practically *de rigueur.*

Everything about her grated on Charlotte, who nevertheless managed to remain outwardly civil. 'Won't you please sit down?'

Judith's yellow skirts rustled as Max conducted her to a chair. She looked soft, fragile, and utterly feminine, an effect she had labored long to perfect. The youngest and most abandoned of the Earl of Barstow's three flighty daughters, she was also the most lovely, but she was cold and calculating, and there wasn't anything in the slightest bit yielding in her character.

Watching as the other woman took her seat, Charlotte wondered if Sir Maxim, for all his diabolical reputation, could see beyond his nose where his mistress was concerned. Judith Taynton was a snake, but she was a very beautiful snake, with an enviably willowy figure and a heart-shaped face framed by a short tumble of shining blond curls. Always clad in yellow, which color she had long since realized flattered her most of all, she was one of the undoubted belles of society, a beauty who knew she was beautiful and who constantly acted the part. Today she was wearing a primrose spencer over a high-waisted, décolleté gown of a yellow silk so sheer that it revealed every curve of her body. There was a little matching hat on her head, its flouncy ostrich plumes trembling a little as she tilted her chin at a most becoming angle, but the smile on her lips was hard, revealing the real Lady Judith Taynton to anyone who cared to look.

Glancing across at Charlotte, so dull in black, Judith couldn't conceal her delight with the way things had gone recently for the loathed Wyndhams. George Wyndham, Charlotte's father, was dead, his fortune lost at the gaming tables, and his daughter and widow were left to sell their beloved estate in order to meet his mountainous debts. How good it was to be here today, to watch Max become the new owner of their precious Kimber Park, and to know that Charlotte was cut to the very heart to know that a Taynton would soon be mistress of the house.

Max took up a position with his back to the immense white marble fireplace, and he too looked at Charlotte. Until recently he had never met her, although he had heard of her. Indeed, who hadn't heard of George Wyndham's startling daughter, the heiress who was reluctant to have anything to do with tiresome matters like the Season and the marriage mart, who kept her nose

7

far too much in books, and whose inclination to speak her mind when she felt like it had cost her more than one excellent proposal of marriage? She could have done so well for herself had she tried, but she had made no effort to obey the countless rules of etiquette and convention that bound the exclusive circle of which she was part, and so at twenty-three she was still unmarried, and likely to remain so, for what man in his right mind would want such an unpredictable, independent, stubborn wife?

He studied her for a moment. Dear God, how stiff and cold she was! She could almost have been fashioned from ice, except for the warmth in the dark-red hair piled up in a knot on the top of her head, a long tress hanging down to her shoulder, and except for the occasional fire he saw in her large gray eyes when something annoyed her. Her detached, cool manner irritated him, touching him on a nerve that pricked him constantly whenever he was with her. Today she was making an effort to conceal her feelings, but on previous occasions she had been so very transparent. She didn't like him particularly, and she positively loathed his mistress, facts that should not have been allowed to show. He had tried to make allowances for her, knowing that all that had recently happened had placed her under a great strain and had loaded her with responsibilities she had never known before; but none of that really excused the way she had so often allowed him to read her thoughts. She needed a lesson in manners, and he was just the one to do the teaching. She wanted this business over and done with as quickly as possible, but he intended to delay, to drag the meeting out and make her pay just a little for her poor conduct.

He smiled. 'I trust we haven't kept you waiting, Miss Wyndham.'

'Not at all, sir, you're always most punctual.'

'I've always considered punctuality to be a virtue, but perhaps you do not agree.'

Virtue? What would this man know of virtue? But she managed

a bland smile. 'Oh, I do agree, Sir Maxim, for to be prompt has the desired effect of hastening things to their conclusion.'

Not today it doesn't, he thought. 'Yes, it does indeed,' he murmured, his eyes veiled, 'provided one doesn't have to observe too many irritating niceties along the way. Is that not so, Miss Wyndham?' He was rewarded by the dull flush that stole into her pale cheeks. He wondered how much it would take to provoke her into a display of the fiery spirit for which she was known; he wondered too, as an aside, why it was that he found her so damned provocative.

She knew he was needling her deliberately, but she was determined not to rise to it. 'Did you have an agreeable journey from town, sir? I know it's only ten miles, but the summer has so far been so atrocious that the roads are more than a little dirty.'

'The journey was comfortable enough.'

'I'm so glad you weren't inconvenienced,' she murmured, glancing across at the lawyers. 'Perhaps we should proceed. . . ?'

'There was one stretch of road,' he continued as if she hadn't spoken, 'which was a positive mire; indeed it took some half an hour to traverse it.'

'How very disagreeable.'

'Yes, so close to the capital one expects so much more from the king's highway, does one not?'

She forced herself to smile, but not terribly successfully. She simply didn't like him, and his action in bringing Judith had made her dislike him all the more.

Judith sat forward then, a spiteful light gleaming in her green eyes. 'Yes, indeed, the journey was not an ordeal, but then we were in a very fine traveling carriage. When you leave with your mother in a month's time, you will not be so fortunate, will you? I mean, a hired chaise is hardly an agreeable mode of transport, and if the weather should continue as it has been . . . However, no doubt you will cope. Tell me, where is your new London abode to be? I did hear say that it was in Henry Street.'

Charlotte sighed inwardly, for Judith knew full well where it was; she was merely scoring unkind points. 'Henrietta Street,' she replied flatly.

'Not in Covent Garden?' Judith pretended to be shocked.

'No, near Cavendish Square.'

'Oh, *that* Henrietta Street. But isn't that rather a quiet area?'

'I sincerely hope so.'

'Well, it's certainly the wrong side of Oxford Street for all the whirl of Mayfair and the Season, isn't it? And it's hardly as grand as your Berkeley Square house. But, then, you've never taken to all that, have you? Just think, you'll be almost on the doorstep of Wyman's Circulating Library. All those books.' She gave a tinkling, false laugh. 'I've never indulged in reading to any great extent, books seem so very dull to me.'

'Yes,' replied Charlotte sweetly, 'I can well imagine that they would seem that way to you.' Then she looked up at Max. 'Shall we proceed with the matter in hand?' She deliberately rose to her feet, determined to conclude the interview.

He gave the faintest of smiles, inclining his head and offering her his arm. She accepted, but barely rested her hand on his sleeve as they proceeded to the table.

Judith's drawling tones carried clearly after them. 'Oh, Max, please don't forget to give especial attention to the boundary documents; you know my father is somewhat concerned to see there is no repetition of previous, er, discrepancies.'

A sharp anger rose in Charlotte as she sat down, and she was hard put to bite back the blistering retort. The discrepancies had all been the Earl of Barstow's doing, for he had some fifteen years earlier attempted to illegally annex some Kimber Park land adjoining his property at Taynton Castle. His double-dealing had ended a hitherto neighborly relationship and had resulted in the virtual feud that had existed between the two families ever since.

The lawyers, both clad in black and both wearing powdered wigs, had the papers ready. Mr Robards, the Wyndham lawyer, was a short, round man with bulging eyes and a nervous manner; his companion, Mr Berenson, the Talgarth lawyer, was tall, lean and stooping, with a beaky nose and spectacles. They stood back politely as Max took his seat. Charlotte immediately took up a quill and signed her name in all the relevant places, but Max made it clear straightaway that he was in no such hurry. He took his time, carefully reading through each paper as if it was the first time he had seen it.

The minutes passed and still he had yet to pick up a quill. Beside him Charlotte grew steadily more incensed, just as he intended she should. She knew that he had read everything before, that he and Mr Berenson had discussed all the details and had had various clauses inserted or removed, so there really wasn't any need at all for this studied caution. In fact, the more she thought about it, the more of an insult she found his conduct, for it was as if he was hinting there might have been some sly changes made without his knowledge or consent.

At last she couldn't bear it anymore. 'Sir Maxim,' she breathed coldly, 'do you intend to sign anything or not?'

He evinced a degree of astonishment at her chill manner. 'Why, Miss Wyndham, you seem angry. Have I offended you?'

'You begin to annoy me intensely, sir,' she replied, throwing caution and common sense to the four winds. She heard Judith's outraged gasp.

'Annoy you?' he replied. 'But how could I possibly have done that?' So, the famous spirit was to the fore at last.

'Sir, you've been endeavoring to do it, since the moment you entered the room, and now you'll undoubtedly be pleased to know that your efforts have been rewarded.' She got up. 'I think we may dispense with further false courtesies, for you like me as little as I like you, and I see no sensible reason for continuing with the pretense.'

He rose as well, his eyes still a little amused, but also bearing the faintest hint of anger. 'It seems to me, Miss Wyndham, that you are quite beyond redemption, after all. I had thought that all I'd heard about your temper must be exaggeration, but apparently it's all too painfully true.'

'Sir, I've wondered about your reputation as well and confess to having come to the same conclusion. I sincerely hope that I never have to come into contact with you again, and so I will bid you good-bye. I've signed all the papers and it only remains for you to do the same, if you still wish to possess Kimber Park. If my being beyond redemption has changed your mind, then I suggest that you go to hell, a place with which I'm given to understand you're very well acquainted. Oh, and if you do go there, pray take your, er, companion, with you.' With a disdainful glance in Judith's direction, she gathered her black skirts and walked from the room, closing the double doors behind her.

Silence reigned for a moment, the two lawyers glancing uneasily at Max, wondering how he would take such conduct. He remained motionless, a myriad of emotions showing fleetingly in his quick blue eyes; then he looked at the nervous, anxious Mr Robards. 'It seems to me, sir,' he said softly, 'that the late Mr Wyndham was singularly lacking in his duty.'

'L-lacking, sir?'

'He should have put his damned daughter over his knee long ago.'

'Sh-she's been under a great strain of late, sir,' replied the lawyer apologetically.

This caused Max to laugh briefly. 'My dear fellow, I wouldn't give much for your hide if she caught you making excuses for her.'

The lawyer cleared his throat uncomfortably. 'No, Sir Maxim,' he admitted with some feeling, 'nor do I. Will you still be going ahead with the purchase? Or has this perhaps changed your mind?'

'It will take more than Miss Wyndham's acid tongue and ill temper to deflect me, sir. I'm determined to have this house, and have it I will.' He sat down again and swiftly signed every document, not bothering to continue reading, now that Charlotte had gone. He didn't feel well pleased with himself for having goaded her into such a display, but she had been long overdue for a lesson. Maybe he'd been less than considerate in bringing Judith today, but was he expected to leave her outside when he was, after all, on his way to be a house guest at Taynton Castle? Why should he insult his mistress in order to placate a willful, opinionated, bad-tempered creature who seemed almost totally devoid of drawing-room manners? He tossed down the quill. Damn Charlotte Wyndham for so provoking him that his own drawing-room manners were for once less than perfect.

Mr Robards and Mr Bereson carefully sanded all the papers and gathered them together. Mr Berenson looked shortsightedly through his spectacles. 'You are now the new owner of Kimber Park, Sir Maxim. May I offer you my congratulations?'

Max looked around the magnificent room, with its gilded plasterwork, shimmering chandeliers, French furniture, and tall, elegant windows. From the ceiling gods and goddesses gazed down from heavenly clouds, as if intent upon all that passed in the room below. It was a beautiful room, a brilliant jewel set in a perfect crown, and he had coveted it all for a very long time. There wasn't a house in England that, in his opinion, could compare with this. He was tired of his exclusive gentleman's apartment at the house in Piccadilly known as Albany, and his estates in north Wales were too remote to be enjoyed at a moment's notice. Kimber Park, so very lovely and so conveniently close to London, was the ideal solution. 'May you offer me your congratulations, Mr Berenson? Yes, I rather think that you may.'

Judith, who with considerable effort had remained silent during Charlotte's outburst, now rose in a whisper of yellow silk to hurry across to him, slipping her slender arms about him as he sat at the table. 'And you have my congratulations too,' she murmured, bending to kiss him.

He got up quickly, pulling her into his arms and kissing her, ignoring the startled lawyers. But as he drew back, his glance moved thoughtfully toward the door where last he had seen Charlotte. He hadn't done with that young lady yet, but for the moment at least, she must remain unfinished business.

Charlotte was watching from the library window a little later as Max's carriage departed, its team of perfectly matched bays stepping high down the rain-soaked drive. The coachman's caped coat flapped in the gusts of wind that swept across the open park as he brought the horses up to a spanking pace, maneuvering them deftly around the curve at the foot of the knoll, where the lake wound its way through the wooded valley. The water was the color of lead as the carriage followed the drive along the shore, vanishing from sight for a while among the trees before reappearing on the open, rising land beyond. It climbed the long incline toward the lodge, driving out through the wrought-iron gates and turning west toward Taynton Castle, some two miles farther on. As the gates closed, she breathed out very slowly. It was nearly all over now; in a month's time she and her mother would be gone and Kimber Park would be part of the past.

She gazed out at the wet, windswept park she loved so very much. This summer of 1816 had been the worst she had ever known, with endless rain and low, scudding clouds. The house stood on a fine vantage point above the park, and usually it was possible to see right across the ten miles of rolling Surrey countryside to London, but today, as so often recently, it was all shrouded in mist and rain, like an afternoon in January, not July. Even the little white rotunda on the incline beyond the lake looked dismal and uninviting, when normally it was the prettiest of places, quite perfect for picnics on a sunny day. . . .

Her reflection stared back at her from the rain-washed glass. How pale and drawn recent events had made her. Her eyes seemed so very large and dark-shadowed, and her mouth more wide than ever. Oh, that mouth, it had been one of the banes of her life, robbing her of any real claim to beauty. Her father had fondly called it a generous mouth and had sworn that it gave her a wonderful smile, but she knew that it was simply another bad mark, for the fashion was for rosebud lips, like Judith's. Charlotte lowered her eyes, pondering all her other bad marks, from her undesirably red hair and freckled nose to her uncompromising character, her delight in books, and her refusal to suffer fools gladly. She was too spirited, too outspoken, and too bookish – what else need be said? Even with the prize of Kimber Park and the Wyndham fortune as an inheritance, she had put paid to her chances of an excellent match by being herself, and by being determined, like the heroines in her beloved books, to marry only for love; now, with her family ruined and her fortune lost, she was likely to remain unmarried forever more.

She glanced around the library, her favorite room with its dark-green brocade walls and countless shelves of costly volumes. Soon all the books would be gone, sold along with everything else at the auction Christie's was to hold in a week's time. Her jewels and wardrobes, and her mother's, had gone already, sold to meet the more immediate of her father's huge debts. What a sad irony it was that one of his few recent wins had been the horse that had thrown and killed him; and what a further sad irony it was that the horse had been won from none other than Max Talgarth. This, together with Max's association with Judith, had made him the very last man Charlotte wished to see as master of Kimber Park, but he had made such a very handsome offer that to refuse would have been the height of folly. Now at least she and her mother would have a modest house in a reasonably acceptable street in London, and they would have a small income upon which to live.

Tears suddenly filled Charlotte's eyes. Max Talgarth was wrong for this house, so very wrong, but now it was his, to do with as he pleased.

2

IT WAS STILL RAINING one month later on the day that Charlotte and her mother were to leave Kimber Park. The house seemed very empty now that most of the rooms had been cleared of furniture. Everything had been made ready for the new owner, the items sold at auction having long since gone, and those that Max Talgarth had purchased having been set aside. Those rooms no longer in use had been closed and shuttered, and the passages and staircases now echoed in a strange, hollow way that made everyone whisper. For the servants life was to go on as before, for although Max had yet to intimate when he intended to take up residence, he had let it be known that he wished to keep the entire complement of staff.

Mrs Wyndham's rather elderly maid, Muriel, was the only one accompanying them to Henrietta Street, and that last morning there were tears in her eyes as she dressed, pushing her sandy-gray hair beneath a fresh white mob cap and smoothing her clean apron and brown dress against her bony little person. She left her room on the top floor and went down to attend her mistress, following a routine that had been her very existence for the last twelve years.

When Charlotte and her mother had finished dressing, the housemaids were ready and waiting to strip the beds and remove the mattresses, then the footmen dismantled the beds and took them away to be stacked with all the other furniture Max had purchased at the auction. Then the bedrooms were shuttered and the curtains drawn.

The breakfast room was situated on the eastern side of the house, to catch the morning sun, but this morning, as on so many others this dreary summer, the weather outside was as wet and lowering as could be. The room's blue brocade walls and sapphire velvet curtains did little to create any cheer, and it was cold enough to warrant a fire in the hearth. The long mahogany sideboard, too heavy by far to be moved from the position it had occupied for some fifty years, had in happier times been laden with fine silver-domed dishes containing everything from cold roast meats to kedgeree, deviled kidneys, eggs of every description, mounds of delicious, crisp bacon, and a pleasing variety of fresh-baked bread; today there was only toast and coffee.

Mrs Wyndham had yet to come down when Charlotte entered the room, wearing her black muslin gown, her long red hair pinned up beneath a black lace cap. Sitting down at the table and pouring herself some of the coffee, she gazed out of the window at the terraced gardens, where the roses were weighed down by moisture and the dovecote was very quiet, only the occasional bird fluttering into the endless rain. She felt strangely calm now that it was almost over. Seeing the house gradually emptied of everything she had loved, and having to accept that although she and her mother were still beneath its roof, it was no longer theirs, had caused them both a great deal of pain; to leave it and start their new life would surely be a release.

The hands of her fob watch pointed to precisely nine when the door opened to admit Mrs Wyndham, her black bombazine gown and heavy petticoats rustling as she took her seat opposite her daughter. The former Miss Sophia Pagett, belle of the 1792 Season, was now a plump, rather anxious woman of forty-three, her pale, round face framed by wispy, reddish curls and a rather severe black biggin. She was quite haggard from the grief and anxiety of the past two months. Her gray eyes, so like her daughter's, were red-rimmed and tired, and her lips trembled a little now and then, as if she was fighting back a sob.

Charlotte looked fondly at her, her heart going out at the look of desolation on the face that had formerly been so happy and bright. 'Good morning, Mother.'

'Good morning, Charlotte.'

'Would you care for some coffee?'

'I couldn't possibly.'

'But you must have something or you'll make yourself ill. Please, at least have some coffee and a slice of toast.'

'Charlotte, I have no appetite whatsoever.'

'Ten miles in a hired chaise is not agreeable at the best of times, but it isn't to be considered at all if one hasn't eaten.'

'I have no wish to be reminded that we are now reduced to hiring vehicles.'

'What point is there in pretending otherwise?'

'The practical side of your nature can sometimes be quite insufferable.'

'Mother.' Charlotte looked reproachfully at her.

Mrs Wyndham looked a little shamefaced then. 'Forgive me, my dear, I don't mean to be sharp with you all the time, it's just that . . . Well, you know what it is.'

'Yes, of course I do.' Charlotte leaned across to squeeze her mother's hand. 'Now, then, will you have some coffee and toast?'

'You're quite a bully, aren't you?' Her mother smiled. 'Very well, I'll try.'

They sipped their coffee in silence for a while, Mrs Wyndham gazing out at the roses in the garden. 'Do you know,' she said after a moment, 'Richard and I planted those on the day before he left for America. It must be all of five years ago now. Oh, I do wish he was here now instead of the other side of the Atlantic, for I need him so very much.'

Charlotte said nothing. Richard Pagett was her mother's brother, but he was so much younger than his sister that Charlotte had always found it impossible to call him Uncle Richard. He had always been just Richard, and she too missed him a great deal.

Why, oh, why had he had to go and squander the Pagett fortune? But for that, he would never have taken himself across the world to seek his fortune anew. When he had first gone, she had written regularly to him at his New York address, and in the beginning he had replied, but he was a very poor correspondent and in the end his letters had stopped arriving. She'd continued to write, and she had informed him of her father's death, but so far no word had reached them. They didn't even know if he was still alive.

Mrs Wyndham looked sadly at her daughter. 'Well, I suppose yearning for Richard will do no good at all, he is as much part of the past as this house is about to be.'

'We may still hear.'

'That is a very faint hope and we both know it.' Mrs Wyndham took a deep breath then and continued in a more brisk tone. 'When is this wretched hired chaise to arrive?'

'Ten o'clock.'

'I trust it will be acceptable, with springs that perform their function.'

'Oh, I'm quite sure it will,' replied Charlotte a little mysteriously.

'I wouldn't be so sure, that rogue Job Rendell at the Three Tuns cannot be trusted in the slightest; he'll send whatever farm cart he chooses.'

'Not for an order placed by Sir Maxim Talgarth he won't.'

'I beg your pardon?' Mrs Wyndham stared at her.

'I ordered the chaise in Sir Maxim's name. Mr Rendell promised his very finest vehicle.'

'Charlotte! How *could* you!'

'Without any conscience whatsoever.'

'If Sir Maxim should ever discover your impudence. . . .'

'He can hardly call me out – even he cannot fight duels with women.' Charlotte was quite unrepentant. 'Now, then, I am determined to look over the house again before we leave. Would you like to accompany me?'

Mrs Wyndham shook her head. 'No, my dear, I would prefer to

try to remember it as it was before all this happened, but you go if you wish, I shall not mind at all.'

'If you're sure. . . ?'

'Quite sure.'

But as the door closed behind her daughter, Mrs Wyndham's eyes filled with tears again. Remember it as it was? That was all she could do now, for it was her memories that sustained her.

Charlotte's steps echoed in the dark, deserted rooms, and she pulled her shawl more firmly about her, as if cold. She walked slowly, savoring each well-loved door and passage, each cupboard and corner. The drawing room seemed vast without its furniture and paintings, and the chandeliers were oddly dull without daylight to enhance them. The gods and goddesses still gazed from their painted heaven, but now there was nothing for them to see in the earthly room beneath.

As she reached the shuttered room where the paintings Max Talgarth had purchased were being temporarily stored, she heard the chaise arriving outside. Glancing quickly at her fob watch, she saw that it had come much too early. She had time enough to glance through the paintings. She smiled at the first one, a scene by Mr Turner of a very stormy sea. The colors were very luminous and yellow, rather like Judith Taynton when seen in a bad dream, she thought uncharitably. She was reminded then of a dinner party some five years earlier, when a waggish guest had likened the painting not to Judith, but to the mulligatawny soup.

The next painting, to her great astonishment, proved to be the portrait of herself on her twenty-first birthday. Sir Thomas Lawrence, that most fashionable of artists, had stayed at Kimber Park while it was painted, and she well remembered wearing the beautiful lilac taffeta gown, her hair dressed up and adorned with the Wyndham diamond tiara. It was strange to see herself in so lovely a color, after two long months of nothing but unbecoming black.

She gazed at the portrait, and suddenly it occurred to her that it was very strange indeed for her likeness to have found its way into Max Talgarth's purchases. It was inconceivable that he had knowingly acquired it, and so it must be there by error. She picked it up to set aside.

'Please don't do that, Miss Wyndham, for I think it is very good.' Max himself suddenly spoke from the doorway behind her.

With a startled cry she whirled about, almost dropping the painting.

'Please be careful, I do not wish to see my unexpected acquisition damaged.' He smiled a little. He was leaning against the doorjamb, his cane swinging in his hand. He wore a light-green coat of superb cut and style, and tight gambroon trousers set off his manly figure to perfection. His waistcoat was striped in brown and white, his neck-cloth was of fine brown silk, and his starched white shirt was adorned by only the simplest of frills.

He came into the room, flinging open the shutters and placing his hat, gloves, and cane on the narrow sill. The pale daylight brightened the room immediately, and as he leaned back against the sill, his attention was drawn once more to the painting, which she had now replaced with the others. 'I cannot imagine how I managed to acquire you, Miss Wyndham, but no doubt you will grace my walls as elegantly as you once graced your own.' He glanced at her, for she had said nothing at all yet. 'I seem to have robbed you of your formidable tongue.'

'You startled me.'

'So it seems. However, I didn't feel the need to announce my approach with a drumroll,' he replied dryly.

'I didn't expect to see you again before we left.'

'Ah, yes, in *my* hired chaise, it seems. Perhaps I should explain that I rested my horses at the Three Tuns on my way here. You've been very free with my name, Miss Wyndham; that was naughty of you.'

Her cheeks reddened a little. 'What would you have done in my place, sir?' she countered. 'Would you have neglected the wits God

21

gave you by accepting Job Rendell's most wretched bone-shaker?'

He gave a brief laugh. 'If I was a proper, well-behaved, meek young lady, then no doubt I would submit to having my bones shaken. But since the question implies that I would be you, Miss Wyndham, then I must admit that I would then be unpredictable, and so I would probably sink to such regrettable deceit.'

'I don't think it regrettable if it means traveling to London in some degree of comfort.'

'No doubt.'

'Why have you come here today?'

'I do own the place, or had you forgotten?'

'Sir, forgetting such a fact would be quite impossible.'

'Even for the redoubtable Miss Wyndham?'

'I have a great many things to try to forget, sir, and I cannot be expected to succeed with them all.'

He smiled a little. 'Miss Wyndham, believe me, I'm not the monster I'm reputed to be, and my reason for coming here today is simply that I wish to say in person to you and your mother that if you should ever wish to visit Kimber Park, you will both be quite welcome to do so.'

She stared at him, quite taken aback at such an unexpected invitation. She wondered wryly if Judith knew anything about it. Accepting was quite out of the question, for even if Judith *did* know and was in agreement, which seemed highly unlikely, the thought of being a visitor in the house that had once been their home, and seeing as its mistress a woman who had always been an enemy, was disagreeable in the extreme. 'I, er, I thank you, Sir Maxim, but I do not think we can accept.' She tried to word her reply as tactfully as possible, but it still came out in a stilted, cold manner that left him with little option but to interpret her thoughts correctly.

A quiet anger stole into his piercing blue eyes. 'I confess to being overwhelmed by the graciousness and charm of your answer, madam.'

She was a little startled by the sharpness of his reaction. 'Sir . Maxim, I—'

'Are you always so damned rude?' he interrupted. 'I've tried to make allowances for your conduct, but try as I will, I cannot accept that grief can be constantly trotted out as an excuse for downright ignorance. My conduct toward you has at all times been correct—'

'At *all* times?' She was suddenly angry as well. 'Oh, come now, sir, aren't you conveniently forgetting your own sad lack of manners and sensitivity?'

'Whatever I've said or done, madam, has been the direct results of *your* behavior.'

'And that excuses you for bringing your mistress to this house at a time when even the devil might have shown more tact?'

His eyes were cold. 'Have a care, Miss Wyndham.'

She turned away. 'I refuse to cross swords anymore with you, sir, least of all today.'

'That is a great pity, for I'm in just the mood to take you on. I've heard it said that Sir Thomas Lawrence's portraits do not lie, but by God the one in this room does!'

'Are you presuming to form a judgment?'

'Oh, yes.'

'But you know nothing about the subject of that portrait.'

'Well, there you are wrong, madam, for I know sufficient to hold an accurate opinion. Until this minute I would have said that black doesn't suit you, that it does you no justice whatsoever, but now I've reconsidered, for it becomes your sour, disagreeable tempera-ment very well indeed. The creature I see smiling on that canvas no longer exists, her quite delightful smile is a figment of my imag-ination, and her excellent taste in clothes and the style with which she wears them is no more than a dream. Your father would be turning in his grave if he could see what has happened to his only daughter, for the Charlotte Wyndham he spoke of bears no resem-blance whatsoever to the one it's been my misfortune to know.'

'Have you quite finished?' she breathed furiously.

'I could go on, believe me.'

'Spare yourself the breath, sir, for I could not care less what you think about me.'

'That doesn't surprise me in the slightest. No wonder you have the reputation you have, for taking an interest in you is a singularly unrewarding exercise.'

'Then pray let me relieve you of any further tedium, sir, by relieving you of my presence.' She gathered her skirts and hurried to the door, where she paused to look back. 'Good-bye, Sir Maxim, I cannot say that making your acquaintance has been a pleasure.'

He sketched a mocking bow.

She turned on her heel and walked quickly away down the echoing passage, and when her footsteps had died away, he glanced down from the window at the drive in front of the great portico. His carriage had now been joined by the hired chaise, which two footmen were busily loading with the trunks that had been carried out of the house. When they had finished, Mrs Wyndham's little maid hurried down the wide steps, dashing through the rain to be helped in by one of the footmen. A moment later Charlotte and her mother emerged from the house. The final moment had proved too much for Mrs Wyndham, who was in tears again and needed much gentle assistance from her daughter.

When her mother was in the chaise, Charlotte paused for a moment in the rain, her black traveling cloak billowing in a sudden gust of wind as she gazed for a last time at the great white house that had been her home all her life. A stray curl of dark-red hair fluttered across her pale face, and then she turned away to climb quickly into the waiting carriage, which a second later pulled swiftly away toward the valley and the wind-rippled grayness of the lake.

3

T HE HOUSE IN HENRIETTA Street was three narrow stories high, and was built of red-and-gray brick, with a pale, distinctive band of stonework above the sash windows of the ground floor. There was a wrought-iron fence separating it from the broad pavement, and beside the front door there was a brass plate proclaiming it to still be the residence of the Reverend James Conway-Lewis, the unfortunate gentleman whose demise beneath the wheels of the Bath mail had brought the property so unexpectedly onto the market. The windows, with their small, rectangular panes, had an excellent view of the mansions and railed garden of nearby Cavendish Square, while to the rear of the house there was a narrow, secluded garden backing onto a disused alley and the buildings of Oxford Street, which ran parallel to the south and which, as Judith had taken such pains to point out, completely separated the new Wyndham residence from the elegance and grandeur of fashionable Mayfair.

After the magnificence of Kimber Park, the new house was at first almost claustrophobic, for the drawing room and dining room together were only half the size of the library at the country estate. The three bedrooms on the floor above were equally small, lacking the dressing rooms and immense wardrobes of those to which Charlotte and her mother had hitherto been used.

Apart from Mrs Wyndham's maid, Muriel, the only servants were the cook, Mrs White, who had previously been in the employ of the Reverend Conway-Lewis, and the timid housemaid, Polly, who burst into tears at the slightest rebuke, of which there were many from the rather particular Mrs White.

Henrietta Street itself was fairly quiet, but there was a constant noise from Oxford Street, where carriages, wagons, carts, and riders seemed to clatter past all the time. Throughout the night the watch called the hour, and the dawn was greeted by a chorus of street cries, each one seeming louder and more persistent than the one before. Charlotte lay in her bed at night, wishing with all her heart that instead of the sounds of the city she could hear the murmur of the breeze through the trees at Kimber Park and the cooing of the doves stirring at daybreak.

The wet summer gradually gave way to an equally wet winter, and Charlotte and her mother did their best to settle in, but it was very difficult because everything was so different now. From Richard Pagett in America there was still no word, although Charlotte wrote several times more. Each time the letter carrier's bell was heard in the street, Mrs Wyndham hurried hopefully to the window, but each time he walked on by.

Their new life was dull and restricted; at least Mrs Wyndham found it so, because she had always enjoyed a full social calendar. Charlotte found it less disagreeable, since a full social calendar was something she had always striven to avoid. She felt for her mother, however, especially as they had soon discovered the mettle of the so-called friends who in the past had sought their company. Now Devonshire House, Melbourne House, and so on ignored them. At first the lack of invitations had been put down to people's respect for their mourning period, but it soon became apparent that it wasn't this but their reduced financial and social circumstances that were uppermost in the thoughts of others. In the early weeks there were some callers, and a number of cards were left, but gradually even this contact dwindled to nothing. It seemed that no one wished to be encumbered with acquaintances whose low situation might prove embarrassing. Mrs Wyndham affected not to be concerned at the way they'd been excluded, but Charlotte knew how deeply her mother had been hurt by the concerted snub dealt so unfeelingly by those they had formerly regarded as friends.

Charlotte was determined to make the best of things, and as Judith had predicted so acidly, the first thing she had done on arriving in town had been to take out a subscription at Wyman's Circulating Library in nearby Wigmore Street, for books were one luxury she had no intention of relinquishing without a struggle. Losing herself in a book was a happy escape, but sometimes it had the very opposite effect, for it brought back a yearning for all that had gone. It was while she was curled up in a chair reading that her daydreams took her back to the library at Kimber Park, and it seemed that at any moment she would hear her father's tread at the door. . . .

The spring of 1817 was glorious, a succession of warm, sunny days that made the dreariness and horror of the previous year seem like a nightmare; that nightmare at last seemed to be a thing of the past when one morning in May, just one month before the anniversary of George Wyndham's death, the long-awaited letter arrived from Richard Pagett in America.

The day began ordinarily enough, with Charlotte and her mother taking their usual plain breakfast together. Mrs Wyndham disliked plain breakfasts, having in better times enjoyed the full range of delicacies provided at Kimber Park, and so she grumbled a little when Polly brought in the boiled eggs and toast.

'Oh, dear, not eggs again. No doubt they're as hard-boiled as they were yesterday and the day before.'

Polly eyes were wide, like a frightened rabbit's, and she gathered her skirts and fled before any blame could be attached to her for the condition of the eggs.

Mrs Wyndham looked disapprovingly after her. 'Foolish chit, why must she always take fright like that? I vow she would not have lasted a single week at Kimber Park.'

'Mrs White is rather hard on her.'

'Nonsense. Mrs White is exceeding tolerant, it's just her gruff manner. Now, then, where's the paper? Ah, yes.' She picked up the paper and began to glance through it.

'Your eggs will indeed be hard-boiled if you leave them for much longer,' Charlotte pointed out.

'Mm?'

'I said your eggs . . . Oh, it doesn't matter.' Charlotte could see that her mother was lost in the paper and would be for some time.

Mrs Wyndham looked up after a few minutes. 'Some good news at last, it was announced from Claremont House yesterday that Princess Charlotte is expecting her first child in October or November. There, isn't that excellent?'

'Yes, it is.'

'Let's pray that she keeps well and has a fine boy.' Mrs Wyndham read on. 'It goes on to say that the princess is at present sitting for her portrait by Sir Thomas Lawrence.'

'Then I pity her.'

'Why ever do you say that?'

'Sir Thomas is a dreadful man, all roving eyes and too-warm glances. And he lacks discretion.'

'That cannot possibly be so.'

'He gossips like an old hen.'

'Hens don't gossip.' Mrs Wyndham rustled the newspaper crossly, for Sir Thomas had been very charming and flattering when he had stayed at Kimber Park, and she didn't care to think that she had been fooled. 'Now, then, what else does it say about the princess? Ah yes, it seems that in view of her delicate condition, she will probably not now be among the royal guests attending the grand state opening of the new Waterloo Bridge on the eighteenth of June. Well, that I can understand, for no doubt she shudders at the thought of bobbing around on the Thames. As I recall, she suffers as much as I do from *mal de mer.*'

'Mother, I hardly imagine that the Thames will induce seasickness, especially not when one is in a vessel as large and comfortable as the royal barge.'

'The Thames can be positively stormy, Charlotte. Still, I must confess that although I'm a martyr to the waves, I would still move heaven and earth to attend such an occasion.' Mrs Wyndham gave a little sigh. 'If your dear father was alive, he'd see to it that we had a fine pleasure boat and he would secure us an excellent vantage point from which to view the ceremony.'

Charlotte smiled gently. 'Yes, he would, and you'd have adored every minute of it, even though you'd undoubtedly have turned a delicate shade of green before the day was out.'

Her mother smiled. 'Well,' she went on more briskly, 'it won't be happening, and society will have to struggle along without us as best it can.'

'I sincerely hope there's a gale and they *all* succumb to seasickness.'

'That's hardly charitable, Charlotte.'

'After the way they've snubbed us recently, I don't feel charitably disposed toward any of them. In fact, I feel so little sympathy that I'm positively *relishing* the thought of reading the book I'm collecting from the library this morning.'

'Book? What book?'

'*Glenarvon.*'

Mrs Wyndham pursed her lips disapprovingly. 'That book is a disgrace, and Lady Caroline Lamb should be ashamed of herself for writing it.'

'Why should she? Oh, I know it isn't the thing at the moment to speak up for her, but I believe she's been very shabbily treated by society, especially the Lambs and everyone else at Melbourne House.'

'You surely do not condone her conduct with Lord Byron?'

'No, of course not, I'm just saying that she isn't the only one to blame.'

'Her poor husband, William Lamb, did not deserve to be attacked in print like that; he's a positive angel. It was bad enough that she was so wildly indiscreet in her affair with Lord Byron, but to then further punish poor William by perpetuating the scandal in a *roman à clef* as ridiculously easy to decipher as *Glenarvon* puts her quite beyond the pale as far as I'm concerned. How *can* poor William be feeling when every drawing room he enters has a copy of his wife's literary stab in the back lying open on a table? That horrid scribble bares all the intimate secrets of his marriage to the world, and I for one am solely with him and not with his spoiled, hysterical, unprincipled wife.'

Charlotte sat back, smiling at such a long and fervent speech in William Lamb's defense. 'Well, what a tiger you are, to be sure.'

'I happen to like him, although I confess that he's the only person at Melbourne House I have any time for now.'

'Yes, I suppose I must concede that he has suffered unfairly because of the book, but the rest of his family and their odious friends have received their just desserts.'

'Maybe so, but I do not know that I approve of that book in this house.'

'You will not ban it, surely? Not when I've been waiting so wretchedly long for my name to reach the top of Wyman's list?' protested Charlotte.

'No, I won't ban it, for if I did you'd only take it out anyway and read it secretly.' Mrs Wyndham smiled. 'Well, it so happens that I already know a little about the book, enough to know that Lady Melbourne makes an absolutely horrid appearance as a character called the Princess of Madagascar, and that Lord Byron himself is the Glenarvon of the title.'

Charlotte poured herself some more coffee. 'Oh, I *am* looking forward to reading it and solving the key so that I know exactly who each character is really meant to be. I'm hoping against hope to identify Judith Taynton as someone perfectly loathsome, for she has insinuated herself at Melbourne House like a flea on a dog in recent years, and she and Lady Caroline cannot possibly have got on.'

'My dear, you are in an exceeding uncharitable mood this morning. It's quite unlike you.'

'Nonsense, it's very like me indeed, especially after the way everyone's ignored the very existence of the Wyndhams in recent months.'

'You cannot with any honesty say that *you've* minded,' pointed out her mother, 'for you've never liked socializing.'

'I know. I'm angry on your behalf. In fact, there have been times of late when I've been positively tempted to write a *Glenarvon* of my own.'

Mrs Wyndham was appalled. 'Charlotte, you wouldn't!'

'If one more of them affects not to have seen me in the street, I shall be giving the matter my deep and dark consideration.'

At that moment they heard the letter carrier's bell in the street, and Mrs Wyndham's breath caught as he knocked at the door. 'Oh, Charlotte,' she breathed, 'do you think it could possibly be. . . ?' She didn't dare to finish the sentence, for it seemed like tempting providence to say aloud that she hoped it might at long last be a letter from her brother.

Charlotte looked anxiously at her. 'Please, Mother, don't build up your hopes.'

They heard Mrs White go to the door, and a moment later she came hurrying into the room. She was a plump woman of about fifty, with a rosy complexion and shiny cheeks, and she wore a blue-and-white-checkered dress and an apron so crisp that it crackled when she walked. A large mob cap wobbled on her frizzy gray hair, and her brown eyes shone as she brought a letter to Mrs Wyndham, putting it quickly down upon the table. 'Begging your pardon for coming straight in, ma'am, but I know you've been waiting for it. It's a letter from America.'

Charlotte put her cup down quickly, staring at the letter, and her mother gazed at it too, so overcome that for a moment she couldn't move. Mrs White tactfully withdrew from the room, closing the door softly behind her.

Charlotte pushed the letter toward her mother. 'Please read it, I can't bear to wait.'

Mrs Wyndham broke the seal and unfolded the sheet of paper. Her hands were trembling and her voice was a little shaky as she began to read aloud.

My dear sister, Sophia,

It was with great sadness and shock that I read Charlotte's letter, and my heart goes out to you both in your sad loss. George was not only my brother-in-law, he was also my mentor and friend, and I grieve deeply that he has been taken from us all.

To tell you now that Charlotte's letter arrived on the very day I had decided to return to England anyway might seem to stretch coincidence too far, but it is the truth. Much as I've come to love America and its people, I've been missing England more and more, and recently I've yearned to come home. America has been good to the black sheep of the Pagett family, Sophia, with the result that he has had the opportunity to rebuild the fortune he squandered before leaving England. I am once again a very wealthy fellow, and very much in a position to take care of those most dear to me. You and Charlotte need me now, and if I am honest, I need you too, for I've been without my family for far too long. I will not fail you. Kimber Park may be gone, but there are other estates, and other town houses to take the place of the one you lost in Berkeley Square. I shall leave America as soon as I am able to put my rather complicated affairs in order, which might unfortunately take several months, my assets being scattered over three states, but I estimate that I shall be home in England some time next spring.

You will not hear from me again as I shall be quitting this

address and moving about the country attending to my business affairs, and anyway, you know by now that I'm the world's worst correspondent. I look forward with all my heart to being reunited with you both, and want more than anything to be able to restore you to your proper place in society.

Until next spring, I am, most affectionately, your loving brother,

Richard

Mrs Wyndham's cheeks were wet with tears as she put the letter down. 'I hardly dare believe it,' she whispered. 'Charlotte, he's coming home! Richard's coming home! And he's wealthy enough to put an end to all this.' She glanced around at the plain dining room. 'Oh, I've been hoping and hoping, and then, just when I'd begun to fear the worst . . . Oh, how I wish he'd written straightaway, and how I wish next spring wasn't so very far in the future.'

Something was puzzling Charlotte and she picked up the letter. 'But he didn't delay, Mother, he wrote immediately he received my first letter, look at the date. The first of August 1816. He then left his New York address and that's why all my other letters have gone unanswered; he never received them. I don't know what happened to this letter of his, but it went horridly astray somewhere between here and America; it's taken ten months to reach us.'

Her mother stared at her and then gave a squeak that was half-delight, half-horror. 'Then it's *this* spring he'll be arriving? Good heavens, he could be here at any moment! The spare room must be aired and cleaned from top to bottom, and all sorts of preparations must be made. I must speak to Mrs White immediately.' Without further ado, she got up, gathering her rustling skirts to hurry out calling the cook.

Charlotte smiled. How good it was to hear that sudden brightness in her mother's voice. And how good it would be to have

Richard with them again after all this time. She felt suddenly close to tears herself, for she too had really begun to fear the worst, that Richard Pagett was no more. But now all such fears could be forgotten, and with them their present reduced circumstances, for Richard would return a wealthy man.

She was lighthearted when a little later she left the house to go to the library in Wigmore Street to collect *Glenarvon*. Her black bonnet ribbons fluttered in the warm May sunshine and her tread was quick, and she had no inkling of the extremely interesting and rather shocking conversation she was about to overhear; nor did she know that before she returned to the house in Henrietta Street, she would have come face to face again with the subject of that conversation, Sir Maxim Talgarth.

4

Wyman's circulating library of Wigmore Street was second in size only to Hatchard's of Piccadilly, but in quality it considered itself London's foremost such establishment.

When Charlotte arrived, there were already a number of ladies and gentlemen browsing at leisure through the cluttered shelves, the low, discreet drone of their conversation almost muffled by the countless books. There were books everywhere, even piled on the floor, and the shelves rose so high toward the ceiling that those near the top could be reached only by using one of the tall ladders provided.

Assistance was given to all by a coterie of personable young men who ruled their domain from behind a grand circular counter in the center of the floor. These young men were helpful and polite, if a little haughty with those whose circumstances were not as fortunate as might be, when they were also inclined to be officious. Charlotte had to endure this latter treatment, but her determination to make full use of the library's facilities made her immune to their superior airs and graces; besides, she could now comfort herself with the thought of committing their sins to paper if and when she wrote her version of *Glenarvon!*

The book set aside for her took some time to find, at least that was what the particular young man who served her would have had her believe. He made a great fuss about searching, taking the opportunity to wipe his forehead with an elegant handkerchief, and fluff out the very intricate neckcloth burgeoning at his throat. He evidently thought himself very much the swell, and Charlotte was sure she could even smell cologne; it was as if he aspired to be Beau Brummell himself, not merely an assistant in a circulating library. At last he produced *Glenarvon*, which proved to consist of not one large but three very slender volumes beautifully bound in rich gilt and leather. She signed for them and tucked them carefully under her arm, feeling slightly disappointed as she prepared to leave, for the book promised to be shorter than she had anticipated. She hesitated, thinking that maybe she should select something else to take home as well, for Lady Caroline's publication, while very shocking, did not promise to occupy a great deal of time.

She went to the rear of the library, where in the past she had discovered several excellent volumes. It was a quiet corner, perhaps because it was dark and shadowy, and she was quite alone as she began to look along the shelves. If she hadn't knelt down on the little mat provided in order to inspect the bottom shelf, and if the reading table hadn't been positioned quite where it was, the two ladies would have seen her immediately and their conversation would never have taken place within her hearing. As it was, they had no idea she was there and consequently thought themselves at liberty to speak as indiscreetly as they pleased; and by the time Charlotte realized who they were and what they were talking about, she did not dare move or draw attention to herself in any way whatsoever. She knelt motionless where she was, unwillingly eavesdropping upon every word that passed between Lady Judith Taynton and a certain Miss Sylvia Parkstone, who proved to be Max Talgarth's former sister-in-law and who liked him rather less than she would an insect.

Charlotte couldn't see their faces; she saw only their silk-stockinged feet clad in the latest patent-leather shoes, and the hems of their elegant walking gowns, richly adorned with the heavy embroidery and rouleaux, which were all the rage this year and which made everything Charlotte wore so very out-of-date. Judith was, as usual, wearing yellow, and equally as usual she was displeased, this time about having to accompany her companion to somewhere as dull as a library, and also because their conversation had taken a turn she most definitely did not care for. The other lady's gown was a pale-pink muslin sprigged with silver-gray, and its beautifully decorated hem was trimmed with pink satin bows and a delicate edging of vandyked lace. She was evidently a little irritated, for the hem swung crossly as she moved, and she put down the books she was carrying with quite a bang on the table close to Charlotte's hiding place.

Judith was so antagonized that she forgot her Devonshire House drawl. 'You're quite wrong, my dear Sylvia. In fact, you've no idea at all what you're talking about.'

'Haven't I? You're the end in fools if you think Max Talgarth is about to make an honest woman of you. I think you believed that the moment he purchased Kimber Park he'd give up his apartment at Albany, which, after all, is exclusively for bachelors or widowers, but here we are, all this time later, and he still has his apartment.'

Judith's rather petulant shrug was audible in her reply. 'You're too prejudiced for words, and really, Sylvia, it's becoming quite tiresome.'

'You'd be prejudiced too if he'd done away with your sister.'

'Anyone would think you and Anne were close, but you most definitely weren't. She was your half-sister, Sylvia, and she gave herself airs and graces because of the immense fortune she inherited from her mother.'

'Anne wasn't like that and you know it.'

'Do I? Oh, come on now, Sylvia, stop being so stubborn, and stop overdramatizing everything. You were obsessed with theatricals when you were a child and you don't seem to have changed at all. You're the only one fanning the flames of suspicion against Max; even your own father doesn't seem to share your views. He doted upon Anne, so if anyone could be expected to hold a grudge against Max for her death, it should be him. But, no, Admiral Henry Parkstone still welcomes Max to his house, still calls him his son-in-law, and still shows every sign of holding him in as much regard as he did on the day Anne married.'

Charlotte felt rather than saw the angry flush these words brought to Sylvia's cheeks. 'Taunt me as you wish, Judith, but if you're honest with yourself, you'd admit that there was something very odd about Anne's death. She was an expert with a horse and gig, yet for no apparent reason lost all control of an animal that was known to be docile enough. And then, while she was struggling to rein in, the wheel just happened to sheer off a brand-new vehicle! Don't you think it strange? I know I do, especially when the gig was a gift from Max, at a time when the world knew they'd been at bitter odds. How can you pretend there's nothing suspicious about it? And how can you say that I'm the only one fanning the flames when *everyone* whispers secretly about it?'

'They only whisper because *you* persist in bringing the subject up!'

'Do you expect me to hold my tongue about something as important as this? It matters very much, Judith, because whatever you say, Anne and I *were* close. Can you imagine how I felt watching her change at Max Talgarth's hands from a vital, sweet-tempered creature into a sour-faced, jealous woman consumed with suspicion about everything? He did that to her; he was unfaithful, harsh, and thoughtless, and in the end he destroyed her. He married her because of the immense fortune she inherited from her mother's family, and when it suited him, he rid himself of her.' She paused. 'Accidents seem to have a peculiar way of turning to Max Talgarth's benefit, don't they?' she added quietly.

'And what exactly do you mean by that?'

'Surely it's struck even you by now that George Wyndham's death was immensely convenient for Max?'

Charlotte felt a sudden cold finger move down her spine. Her heart was beating so loudly that she was sure they must hear it at any moment, but they remained completely unaware of her presence.

Judith gave a brittle laugh. 'Convenient for Max? My dear, *I* found it even more so, for his demise meant one less Wyndham to plague us.'

'Can't you forget petty family quarrels for once? Forget what George Wyndham meant to you and think instead what he signified to Max.'

'Signified? What do you mean?'

'I mean that he was the obstacle between Max and Kimber Park. Max had long coveted that estate, Judith. He'd tried on a number of occasions to purchase it, but George Wyndham wouldn't countenance selling.'

'How do you know all this? No doubt it's as much an invention as all the rest of it.'

'It's no invention. As you so eloquently pointed out, my father doesn't share my views about Max, who is a frequent visitor to our house. Max told my father himself about his desire for Kimber Park and his attempts to acquire it. It wasn't a secret.'

Charlotte was shaking now, and her heart was positively thumping in her breast. A sliver of ice seemed to enter her at what Sylvia Parkstone was suggesting. Please, don't let it be true, don't let it be true. . . .

Judith was alarmed now. 'Sylvia, I know that you feel justified in loathing Max, but really, you go too far now if you start saying that he was responsible for George Wyndham's death.'

'Too far? Are you sure? Just remember, the horse that threw George Wyndham to his death had been won only a day or so before from Max, and that I find too much of a coincidence. Just think, another convenient "accident," and dear Max gets exactly what he wants. Oh, I admit that he offered a very handsome sum to the grieving family, but it doesn't alter the fact that in the end he gained the prize he had desired for so very long, and in Max's eyes, the end always justifies the means.'

Judith was quite uneasy. 'You're wrong about it all, Sylvia, and I think you're despicable. If Max is supposed to think that the end justifies the means, then the same and more can be said of you, for there's no depth to which you wouldn't sink in your vendetta against him. I begin to think you want him yourself, that all this is nothing more than jealous spite because he's never cast so much as a single appreciative glance in your direction.'

Sylvia gave a dry laugh. 'I always wondered if you really were the fool you seemed to be, Judith Taynton. Now I know beyond a doubt that you are. You'd be better employed forgetting if I harbor secret desires for him and turning your foolish thoughts to wondering what *his* desires really are – and I don't mean that I think he desires me.'

'What do you mean, then?'

'Well, since we've been together today, you haven't once mentioned the Westington duel.'

'Westington? *Lord* Westington?'

'The same.'

'But what on earth has he to do with this?'

Sylvia was enjoying her advantage. 'Oh, simply that he's yet another injured husband, one of the many Max Talgarth has left strewn behind him over the years.'

There was a long silence, and when Judith next spoke, her voice was much less sure. 'If you're suggesting that—'

'That dear Max has been unfaithful to you? Yes, I rather think I am. But you shouldn't be so surprised, my dear, after all he's merely running true to form; he simply isn't capable of being steadfast to one woman.'

'It's a lie,' breathed Judith. 'A horrid, horrid lie!'

'If it is, then the whole of society is perpetuating it. Westington has called Max out for seducing his wife, and it's a scandal that is rattling the teacups with a vengeance at the moment, but then, you might not have heard because you've only just come up from obscurity at Kimber Park.' Sylvia's voice was as smooth as silk. 'You know what they say: while the cat's away, the rat will play.' She laughed a little. 'I shrink from referring to Max Talgarth as a mere mouse.'

'You're only saying all this because I'm your cousin and you cannot stomach the fact that I've become his mistress.'

'Oh, I admit that that does make your fall from grace a little difficult to accept, but I'm not acting out of malice, I'm acting out of concern because you *are* my cousin and I want even at this late point to try to make you see him for what he really is.'

'I refuse to believe anything you say about him.'

'Really? Well, that does surprise me, for you were eager enough once to believe what was said of him. Indeed, as I recall it, you were positively *thrilled* by the stories of his wickedness. It excited you to think that he'd killed three men in duels, and you were attracted like a pin to a magnet by his reputation with women. You didn't care at all that he was on the point of marrying Anne; in fact, you sank so low as to try to take him from her. You were, and still are, the most conniving, spiteful, immoral creature it has ever been my misfortune to know, but God help me, you're still my cousin, and for that reason alone I sought you out today to try to make you see sense. This Westington business must surely make some impression upon you.' There was a pause as Sylvia was quite evidently faced with Judith's stubborn refusal to accept anything she'd been told. 'Oh, very well, think as you please. You're a lost cause, Judith Taynton, and you were even before you fell under Max Talgarth's spell. I wash my hands of you.' Flicking her pale-pink skirts, she picked up her books and walked away, her patent-leather shoes tap-tapping angrily across the floor. She slammed the outer door so loudly that it momentarily silenced the low buzz of background conversation from all the other people using the library.

Judith remained where she was, and for a dreadful moment

Charlotte thought her presence had been detected, but then she too walked out, closing the door much more softly behind her.

Slowly and very shakily, Charlotte got to her feet, leaning her hands weakly on the table and bowing her head, which was spinning with confused thoughts. Sylvia's voice seemed to echo close by: 'Forget what George Wyndham meant to you and think instead what he signified to Max . . .' 'He was the obstacle between Max and Kimber Park. Max had long coveted that estate, Judith. He'd tried on a number of occasions to purchase it, but George Wyndham wouldn't countenance selling . . .' 'Just think, another convenient "accident", and dear Max gets exactly what he wants. Oh, I admit that he offered a very handsome sum to the grieving family, but it doesn't alter the fact that in the end he gained the prize he had desired for so very long, and in Max's eyes, the end always justifies the means . . . justifies the means . . . justifies the means. . . .'

In something of a daze, she walked slowly from the library, the three volumes of *Glenarvon* clutched tightly in her hands. In the doorway, she halted in sudden surprise, for the warm sunshine had gone and a heavy spring shower had taken its place. People were hurrying by, umbrellas aloft, and already there were puddles in the gutters.

A carriage was passing, but it drew to a sudden halt by her and the solitary occupant lowered the glass. 'Good morning, Miss Wyndham, may I be of assistance?'

She found herself staring into Max Talgarth's piercing blue eyes.

5

H E ALIGHTED, IGNORING THE rain. He had on a dark-brown coat
and beige trousers, and there were spurs at the heels of his
Hessian boots. Removing his top hat, he inclined his head. 'May I
convey you anywhere in this rain, Miss Wyndham?'

She was so shocked to see him again, especially after all that
she'd just heard, that she froze, quite unable to reply. Her reaction puzzled him.

'Are you all right?'

She found her tongue then. 'Yes, quite all right. Thank you.'

'Is there any assistance I can offer you? If you're returning to
Henrietta Street, it's quite on my way.'

'No. Thank you. I'll wait until the rain stops.'

'You may have a long wait. It seems to me that this is something
more than a short shower.'

She wished he would leave her, for exchanging idle pleasantries with him was never easy. 'Are you an expert on the
weather, Sir Maxim? I can see blue sky approaching, and to me
that signifies an imminent end to the rain.'

He studied her for a long moment. 'London doesn't seem to
have improved your manners, madam.'

'My manners are not at fault, sir,' she replied coolly.

'No? Well, if that's the case, the implication must be that there's
something about me that is at fault, and since I know that it's not
my manners, it has to be something else. Have you been listening

to scurrilous rumors, Miss Wyndham?' He was looking at the three volumes she still held so closely. 'So, *Glenarvon* is your taste in literature. That explains a great deal.'

'About what, exactly?'

'Your willingness to appreciate the finer points of scandal. That *is* the reason for your cold manner now, isn't it?'

An angry flush stole into her cheeks. 'What constitutes scandal, sir? I'm not a connoisseur of the subject, never having caused any myself.'

'How very dull of you.'

'Possibly, but then I wouldn't presume to judge, since I've always been content with my dullness.'

'You do not strike me as being satisfied with your lot, Miss Wyndham; indeed, far from it.'

This was too much. 'Please, Sir Maxim, will you leave me alone? I have no desire whatsoever to speak to you.'

'I know, and I find the fact extremely vexing, since I know full well that at the moment it's based on nothing more than hearsay. You don't really know anything about me, madam, but you're woefully prepared to believe the worst anyway.' He still ignored the rain, which had soaked his costly coat as he stood there, his steady, shrewd gaze upon her as she sheltered in the doorway.

If he was vexed, however, she felt the same. Glancing deliberately at the scar on his cheek, she replied scornfully. 'Are you suggesting, sir, that you are completely innocent and misunderstood?'

'Hardly, since that would of a certainty lay me open to ridicule, but I *am* saying that I'm not as black as some have seen fit to paint me.'

'No doubt the devil himself has been heard to make the same claim.'

'I wouldn't know,' he said softly, 'since I've never presumed to think myself in his confidence.'

The flush was still hot on her cheeks. 'Please go, sir, for this conversation serves no purpose.'

44

'I have no intention of going until you've at least allowed me the courtesy of a fair hearing,' he replied, very deliberately offering her his arm. 'Now, then, are you and Lady Caroline Lamb going to accept my offer, or shall we stand here in public until full attention is drawn to us?'

She glanced around, seeing that several people were already looking a little curiously in their direction. 'Sir, I don't wish to accept anything from you.'

'Then we stand here.' He folded his arms, still holding her gaze.

'I seem to recall,' she said coldly, 'that you once boasted that your conduct toward me had at all times been correct.'

'I also said that my conduct was always the result of yours, which it is at this very moment. Be sensible, Miss Wyndham, my carriage would be much more convenient for you right now, and I promise you that whatever you may have heard to the contrary, it is not my habit to molest ladies in broad daylight in the middle of London. Your chastity is perfectly safe, you may be perfectly assured of that.'

She felt she had no choice, for she did not like the attention they were attracting. Reluctantly she accepted his arm, stepping from the shelter of the library doorway and across the rainswept pavement to the waiting carriage. He handed her inside, instructed the coachman to drive to Henrietta Street, and then climbed in as well, slamming the door behind him. The noise of the rain and the busy London street were immediately muffled and more distant.

He sat on the seat opposite, his long legs so close that they brushed against her skirts. His blue eyes were almost lazy then as they rested speculatively on her. 'Now, then, Miss Wyndham,' he said reasonably, 'are you going to tell me to what tittle-tattle you've been paying foolish attention? Or am I going to have to guess?'

'Has it not occurred to you that my manner is born purely and simply from an instinctive dislike?'

'Yes, that had indeed occurred to me, but I dismissed it immediately because I did not think a daughter of George Wyndham's would be so foolish as to allow such a thing to completely color her views.'

Hearing her father's name on his lips so swiftly after the revelations in the library forced her to look quickly away. A sudden rush of mixed emotions beset her and she had to look out at the rainy street to hide her reaction as best she could.

He watched her, a slight frown creasing his brow. 'Very well, since you will not tell me, I'm forced to arrive at the answer by a process of elimination. I shall begin with the furore aroused by this idiocy of Lord Westington's. Ah, I see that I have hit the bull at first shot.'

She was looking at him in disgust. 'How can you speak so sneeringly of it? You've gravely injured Lord Westington's honor, and now you have the gall to call his reaction idiocy. You're beneath contempt, sir.'

A cold fury leapt into his eyes. 'Damn you for saying that! If anyone's honor has been injured in all this, it's mine.'

'I fail to see how.'

'No doubt, but it so happens that I'm not and never have been—' He broke off sharply as something outside caught his full attention.

The carriage had come to a temporary halt in a crush outside the fashionable haberdashers, Messrs. Clark & Debenham of 44 Wigmore Street, and a young woman was just emerging into the rain. She was dressed in a deep-rose spencer and there were matching ribbons on the dainty hat on her dark, curly hair. She had wide brown eyes and an oval face of quite breathtaking sweetness, but it was her walking gown that held Charlotte's gaze, for it was of pale-pink muslin, sprigged with silver-gray, and its hem was adorned with satin bows and vandyked lace. The young woman could be none other than Sylvia Parkstone.

At that moment, as if she sensed the close scrutiny to which she was being subjected, she looked directly at the carriage. She met

Max's eyes, her expression cold.

Charlotte was very aware of the atmosphere that suddenly pervaded the carriage, and when she looked at Max, she saw how inscrutable his face had become, and how still. As the carriage jerked forward once more, Charlotte looked out again and for a fleeting moment her glance met the young woman's, but then the carriage had carried them apart and she could see no more.

Max remained silent for a while, and she couldn't tell what his thoughts were, but then he looked at her. 'As I was saying, Miss Wyndham, if anyone's honor has been injured in all this, it's mine. I am not and never have been Lady Westington's lover, although she has long wished that I was. Oh, no doubt you regard that as the ultimate in male arrogance, but it happens to be the truth. She pursued me without success and now wreaks her vengeance by accusing me of having vilely seduced and maltreated her, which fairy story her fool of a husband chooses to believe. I promise you, Miss Wyndham, that I've given him every opportunity to retract, but he persisted in reiterating his accusations very publicly indeed, in the end leaving me little choice but to pick up the gauntlet. *That* is the truth about this duel, madam, not the idle gossip to which you've apparently been lending your gullible ears.'

She said nothing. He sounded so very plausible, but how could she really believe a man whose reputation with other men's wives was as notorious as Max Talgarth's? The carriage entered Cavendish Square and at last turned into Henrietta Street, halting at her door, but as she quickly made to alight, he leaned across to prevent her.

'Miss Wyndham,' he said softly, 'what other tales you may have given credence to I shudder to think, but this much I ask of you: in future, please allow that there are two sides to every story, and that maybe, just maybe, my side is occasionally the more creditable.' He opened the door then, stepping down to the wet pavement and turning to hold out his hand to her.

47

She slipped her fingers into his as she alighted, but then quickly snatched her hand away and made to hurry into the house without another word, but his voice detained her.

'Isn't there something else apart from your manners that you've forgotten, Miss Wyndham?'

She turned coldly. 'I don't think I've forgotten anything at all, sir.'

'Oh, but there is.' He leaned into the carriage and took out the volumes of *Glenarvon*, which she'd left on the seat. 'Please don't leave me alone with Lady Caroline, for she is a lady whose word you simply cannot trust.'

Only too aware of the mocking light in his eyes, she hurriedly took the books and then went quickly into the house. When she glanced out from the drawing-room window a moment later, she saw his carriage pulling away. He sat gazing straight ahead, not looking back once.

She made up her mind not to say anything to her mother about what had happened, for it didn't seem right or necessary to ruin the happiness aroused by the arrival of Richard's letter. It wouldn't help her mother in the slightest to know that someone suspected foul play in her husband's death. Such news would only cause deep distress. It was all better left unsaid, especially as there was no proof at all that Sylvia Parkstone, who was undoubtedly Max Talgarth's avowed enemy, was being anything other than malicious when she'd suggested what she did in the library.

In spite of this resolution to say nothing, Charlotte's own doubts were very unsettling, and rather than let her mother see that something had upset her, she spent most of the rest of the day in her bedroom, ostensibly to commence reading *Glenarvon*, but really to try to come to terms with what she'd overheard.

Her bedroom, at the front of the house, was a soothing place with green-and-white-striped walls and green velvet curtains with golden tassels and fringes. The plain bed had a coverlet of the same green velvet, and the dressing table was draped with frilled white muslin. Beside the plain fireplace was a single comfortable chair, and in the far corner stood a table with a bowl and water jug, and the small wardrobe, which was more than adequate for the few clothes now in her possession.

She sat in the fireside chair, the first volume of *Glenarvon* open on her lap, but she made no attempt to read it; she just sat there, gazing at the raindrops meandering slowly down the window-panes. The blue sky was still close by, but could not quite push the clouds aside. A rainbow arced across the heavens to the north of Cavendish Square, its colors brilliant against the reluctantly retreating storm.

For a long, long while she thought about Max Talgarth and what he had said. He had accused her of being woefully disposed to believe only ill of him, and perhaps he was right, for her opinion had been swayed long before she'd met him; he had his reputation and his liaison with Judith to thank for that. And today she'd been further swayed by the words of a woman who'd made no secret at all of her loathing for him. Was that right or fair? One should never believe *all* one heard, for if one did, then one would honestly think Bonaparte to be a hideously deformed dwarf who ate only frogs' legs, and the Prince Regent to be a monster toward his poor, defenseless, virginal wife, Caroline of Brunswick, whose present antics on the Continent proved her to be the very opposite – if, indeed, one could believe *those* lurid tales either! No, anyone must be considered innocent until proven guilty, and that included Sir Max Talgarth, against whom there was not one shred of proof, no matter how much Sylvia Parkstone may plead.

Charlotte took a deep breath then. Her mind was made up: she would do her best to forget what she'd so unwillingly eaves-dropped upon; indeed, she would do her best to forget everything about Max Talgarth, for there was nothing she could do about him anyway. Settling back as comfortably as she could, she applied herself to *Glenarvon*.

6

MRS WYNDHAM WAS STILL in high spirits the following morning at breakfast, rattling on at great length about the very cheering prospects opened up by her brother's letter. As she thought about some of the very grand town houses she knew were available in Mayfair, there was a sparkle about her that had been absent for nearly a year.

Charlotte was quiet. Try as she would, she couldn't put the previous day's events from her mind, and after a while her mother noticed her withdrawn mood. 'Is something wrong, Charlotte? You're unusually quiet this morning.'

'I'm quite all right, truly I am,' replied Charlotte, hurriedly rousing herself to look brighter.

'Did you sleep well?'

'Yes.'

'You weren't up too late reading that dreadful book?'

'Not too late.'

Mrs Wyndham studied her for a moment. 'But you *were* reading it?'

'Yes. Why do you ask?'

'It's just that your answer seemed less than enthusiastic. You waited for so long for the wretched thing, and now that you have it, you haven't said anything about it. Wasn't it worth the wait?'

'Well, Lady Caroline isn't the world's most talented writer, and her plots are so wildly improbable that they're positively ridiculous.'

'With all due respect, Charlotte, you knew that before you started, and on your own admission your sole reason for acquiring the book was because you wished to read its attacks upon society.'

Charlotte smiled. 'Yes, and in that respect it measures up to expectations. Lady Melbourne is caricatured most horridly as the Princess of Madagascar, your poor William is positively pilloried as the heroine's far-too-worldly husband, Lord Avondale, and Lord Byron is suitably monstrous as the cruel lover, Glenarvon. Lady Caroline herself, needless to say, is the sweet, innocent, misunderstood heroine Calantha, whose ruin is brought about by anyone and everyone but herself. The whole thing is a vitriolic attack on Melbourne House *et al.* and I'm thoroughly enjoying it, my only quibble being that Judith Taynton fails to make an appearance. If the book had been mine, she wouldn't have slipped through the net.'

'So, you can quite understand why it was reprinted three times in as many weeks when it was published last year.'

'Yes, and I can well believe that there were some very red faces in some very important drawing rooms. No one comes out of it very well, but then, as far as I can see, none of them deserves to.'

Her mother looked shrewdly at her. 'You believe that you'd have written a much better book, don't you?'

'I like to think I could,' admitted Charlotte.

'Well, I'm glad that you haven't put pen to paper, for if we're destined to reenter society, I wish to be able to look them all in the eye.' Mrs Wyndham folded her napkin and rose from her chair. 'I mustn't sit here chitter-chattering any longer, I've far much to do before Richard arrives.'

Alone, Charlotte poured herself another cup of coffee and then sat back. Her mother's remark about writing a book like *Glenarvon* had set her mind working. How very satisfying an exercise it would be. If Lord Byron was the perfect model for Glenarvon, how much more splendid model would Max Talgarth be for a similar story . . . The thought slid into her head almost before she realized it, and then the more she thought about it, the more excellent a notion it seemed. The terrible things she'd heard said of him the previous day provided plots in plenty, and Max himself, so darkly handsome, satirical, and infamous, was surely a villainous hero second to none.

Oh, how tempting a thought. Slowly she put her cup down. It was *too* tempting – how could she possibly resist? And what harm would there be? It wasn't as if, like Lady Caroline, she ever intended trying to publish her scribbles. . . .

She glanced outside, where the rain of the previous day had gone and the sun was shining warmly from a clear May sky. She would go for a walk in Regent's Park and give the matter of a book of her own some very careful thought.

Mr Nash's magnificent new thoroughfare, Regent Street, now stretched as far north as the old royal park at Marylebone, where it ended in the gracious curve of Park Crescent. The royal land was being laid out at Regent's Park, a fine, landscaped area to be a fitting end to the new road, which started at the Prince Regent's residence, Carlton House.

There were originally intended to be at least forty elegant villas in the park, including one for the prince himself, set among groves of specially planted trees and beside the three-branched, serpentine lake, but now it seemed that very few of them would be built. The lake was there, however, glittering brightly beneath the sun, and the only sound, apart from the background noise of the city, came from the workmen on nearby St. John's Lodge, one of the few buildings to have been begun.

It was just after midday when Charlotte entered the park, strolling at a very leisurely pace as she enjoyed the scenery and thought about her book. After a while she began to sense that someone was watching her. It was an uncomfortable feeling, making her glance around. Away to her right there were two gentlemen riding toward some trees, while down to her left by the lake a laughing party of ladies and children were seated on the grass. There didn't seem to be anyone paying particular attention to her, but as she walked on again, the feeling that she was being watched became more and more strong. At last she couldn't bear it anymore and turned around to retrace her steps.

A short while before, she had passed a little pavilion set among flowering shrubs, and as she walked back toward it, a lady suddenly appeared, strolling in the direction Charlotte had been taking herself but a moment before. She was tall and stylish, with short dark hair. Her pelisse was of sapphire-blue velvet, and her ruffled gown of the sheerest cream lawn, its hem enviably stiffened in the very latest fashion. Her shoes were particularly pretty, their cream satin slashed to reveal blue beneath, and she carried a frilled pagoda parasol that she twirled a little as she walked. There was something oddly familiar about her.

The distance between them lessened, and then quite suddenly the lady halted a few feet away. 'Good morning, Miss Wyndham.'

Charlotte gave a start as she realized abruptly who the other was: Sylvia Parkstone. 'How do you know who I am?' she asked, so caught by surprise that the rather lame inquiry was all that sprang to mind.

'When I saw you with Max Talgarth yesterday, I made it my business to find out.'

Charlotte didn't care for the thought of someone making secret inquiries about her. 'Did you, indeed?' she replied a little stiffly.

'Please don't be angry,' said the other quickly, 'for I mean no insult or impertinence. I'm just deeply concerned that you, of all people, should not fall under that man's influence. You mustn't see him again, Miss Wyndham, for it's my firm conviction that he deliberately brought about your father's death.' She hesitated, putting out an anxious hand. 'Forgive me for saying such a dreadful thing, but I felt I simply had to approach you. You don't seem surprised by what I say.'

'No, because I already know your feelings on the matter, Miss Parkstone. I was in the library yesterday and heard everything that passed between you and Lady Judith.'

'You were there? But where?'

Charlotte explained the circumstances. 'So you see,' she finished, 'your conversation was not as private as you imagined it to be.'

'Forgive me if this sounds a little rude, but I find it amazing that after all you'd just heard, you should accept a seat in his carriage.'

'Yes, it does sound a little rude, since you do not know exactly what happened.'

'I've offended you, and I really didn't mean to.' Sylvia's face was crestfallen and her cheeks red.

Charlotte found herself unexpectedly liking her new acquaintance. 'I'm not really offended, Miss Parkstone, for I can quite understand that my action does seem a little unlikely. The truth of it is that he didn't give me much choice. He was very angry indeed because he guessed that I'd been listening to rumors about him. And before you ask, no, I didn't broach the subject of my father's death or your sister's. All that was mentioned was the duel he is soon to have with Lord Westington, a duel which he insists was forced upon him and in which he claims he is the injured party. He was as eloquent in his own defense as you are for the prosecution.'

'And you believed him?'

'I don't know what to think, and that's the truth.'

'Are you in love with him, Miss Wyndham?'

Charlotte's lips parted in astonishment. 'Certainly not! Why ever do you ask?'

'You seemed a little ... Well, you seemed as if you were defending him.'

'I can hardly defend him since I don't know anything about it. Sir Maxim and I do not see eye to eye, Miss Parkstone, so love is one of the last things I feel toward him.'

'Forgive me for having asked such a thing, it's just that I know how very winning Max can be when he chooses. My sister continued to adore him, even when he treated her abominably, and my cousin Judith . . . Well, Judith is beyond redemption.'

'Oh that I will agree with you.'

Sylvia smiled then. 'And I hope that you will agree with me on everything else before much longer. Miss Wyndham, would it be too much to hope that you and I might become friends? Or am I being too presumptuous?'

'You aren't being presumptuous at all, Miss Parkstone. I would very much like us to be friends.'

'Then let us begin by continuing our walk together, and then perhaps you would take tea with my father and me at our house in Cavendish Square?'

'Cavendish Square? You live so close to me?'

'Yes, that's how I found out who you were. I'd already seen you going to and from your house in Henrietta Street, so when I saw you with Max I knew exactly how to find out about you.' Sylvia looked a little rueful then. 'I don't often go around poking and prying into other people's affairs, you know; it's just that I'm determined to one day expose Max Talgarth for the monster he is. Still, enough of him for the moment . . . Shall we continue our walk?'

Charlotte smiled and nodded.

The Parkstone residence was a fine, balconied building on the eastern side of Cavendish Square, facing Henrietta Street. It was a house Charlotte had often noticed before, having many times walked past its jutting stone porch.

The grand drawing room on the first floor had rose brocade walls and a ceiling decorated with very ornate gilded plasterwork. The satinwood furniture was upholstered in gray figured velvet, and there were gold-fringed velour curtains at the tall windows overlooking the square. Dominating the room was the immense white marble fireplace, above which hung a portrait of Sylvia by Mr Hoppner. Charlotte was silently critical of the portrait, which she did not consider to be a particularly good likeness.

Admiral Henry Parkstone was a tall, personable gentleman of military bearing. His brown hair had not receded or even faded, and his face was that of a man much younger than his sixty or so years. He dressed plainly but fashionably, and he walked with the aid of a stick, having been wounded in the leg at the battle of Trafalgar. There was something very agreeable about his smile, and Charlotte took to him as easily as she had to his daughter.

Sylvia poured the tea from an exquisite Sèvres porcelain teapot, and the admiral settled himself comfortably, leaning his walking stick against the sofa. 'Tell me, Miss Wyndham, are you by any chance one of the Wyndhams of Kimber Park?'

'Yes, at least we *were* of Kimber Park. Mr George Wyndham was my father.'

'Ah, yes, a very sad loss indeed. Such a terrible accident.'

Sylvia abruptly put the teapot down. 'Accident?'

Her father looked warningly at her. 'Sylvia, this is neither the time nor the place—'

'Maybe it isn't, but I cannot sit meekly by accepting your description of Mr Wyndham's death as an accident.'

The admiral was appalled at such an indiscreet statement. 'Sylvia, that's quite enough! Your private views must be kept private, and certainly should not be aired in front of Miss Wyndham.'

'Miss Wyndham already knows what I think.'

'Which can only mean that you wasted no time at all in telling her. I'm quite ashamed of you, my girl, and I think that you should apologize to her immediately for causing her unnecessary distress.'

Charlotte was embarrassed. 'Oh, please, there's no need.'

He looked apologetically at her. 'You're being too kind, Miss

Wyndham. I'm afraid that Sylvia is quite unreasonable where my son-in-law is concerned.'

Sylvia flushed then. 'He isn't your son-in-law,' she said stiffly.

'He was married to Anne, and as far as I'm concerned, that makes him my son-in-law.'

She pointed at the portrait above the fireplace. 'Anne would be with us now if it wasn't for Max Talgarth, and she'd still be the happy, laughing person we once loved so much.'

Charlotte stared at the portrait. So that was why it wasn't a good likeness; it was a picture of Anne Talgarth, not Sylvia.

The admiral took a long, patient breath. 'Sylvia, I've had quite enough of all this. I forbid you to say anything more on the subject, is that quite clear?'

Sylvia looked rebellious for a moment but then lowered her glance. 'Yes, Father.'

'I suppose I've this duel with Lord Westington to thank for your renewed enthusiasm for blackening Max's character?'

'The duel merely proves that I was right about him all along.'

'Does it? Come now, Sylvia, you no more believe Georgiana Westington's tale than I do; you're simply saying you do because it suits you. She's one of the most immoral and conniving women in London, and has invented the whole story out of spite. What her foolish nonentity of a husband chooses to believe is his business, but I know that *I* believe Max's side of it.'

Sylvia said nothing more, but the defiant set of her chin showed only too clearly that she did not accept her father's point of view.

The admiral turned to Charlotte. 'You must forgive us, Miss Wyndham, for we are very wrong to foist our family disagreements upon you like this.'

'Please don't apologize, sir, for there isn't any need.'

'But there is, my dear, there is. However, let us talk of something more agreeable – our summer ball in July perhaps? I do hope that you will be able to attend, or will you still be in mourning then?'

'July? No, we will not be wearing black then, sir.'

'We?'

'My mother and I.'

'The invitation will naturally extend to include your mother as well.'

'Thank you.'

'We like to pride ourselves on our summer balls. They are considered to be quite important social occasions.'

'I know, sir, although I've never been fortunate enough in the past to attend.'

'We'll make up for that sad omission this year,' he said, smiling.

She looked at the long-case clock standing against the wall between two of the windows. 'Goodness, is that the time? My mother will be wondering where I've got to.'

'Allow me to escort you home, Miss Wyndham.'

'That's very kind of you, sir, but please do not trouble yourself.' She glanced at the walking stick.

'My dear young lady, you cannot spare me, for my leech has instructed me to walk as often as possible. I shall take a stroll this afternoon with or without your company to make it more agreeable.'

She smiled. 'Then I should be glad to make it more agreeable, sir.'

Sylvia assisted him to his feet, and when the two young women had made arrangements to see each other again the following day, the admiral and Charlotte left the house in Cavendish Square and walked the short distance to Henrietta Street.

Just as Charlotte was about to go inside, her mother happened to look out of the drawing-room window. The admiral's lips parted in surprise. 'As I live and breathe, it's Sophia Pagett! Miss Wyndham, your mother was Miss Pagett, wasn't she?'

'Why, yes, sir. Are you acquainted with her?'

'I was, my dear.'

'Then please come inside, sir, for I'm sure she would be

delighted to see you again.'

Mrs Wyndham was indeed delighted. 'Henry Parkstone,' she declared. 'I thought you'd long since gone to perdition.'

He grinned, drawing her hand to his lips. 'My dear Sophia, you haven't changed a bit; you're still horridly cruel to me. I've a good mind not to pay my respects.'

'You wouldn't be so ungentlemanly.'

He looked fondly at her. 'Well, well, after all these years . . . I had no idea at all that you married George Wyndham. To tell the truth, I thought you'd married some high-up in the East India Company and had gone to live in Madras.'

'Good heavens,' she replied, 'what a terrible thought! Still, our paths wouldn't have crossed, would they, not when you had the poor taste to be related to the Earl of Barstow. How is the old wretch? His gout is making him suffer, I trust?'

'As much as ever.'

'Good.'

'You always were a heartless creature, Sophia.'

She smiled. 'Oh, Henry, do say you can stay awhile, for we have so much to talk about.'

'Stay? I'd be honored.'

Charlotte left them to reminisce. Going up to her room, she took some sheets of paper and a pencil and settled down at the dressing table. She gazed at the blank paper for a moment before beginning to write the first sentence of her secret exposé of Max Talgarth.

7

IT WAS A MATTER of conjecture what Max Talgarth would have
said had he known about the odious *alter* ego Charlotte
created for him over the next few weeks, but she doubted very
much if he would have appreciated his other self. Rex Kylmerth
was too obviously meant for him, from the deliberately similar
name to the scarred cheek and flash of gray in his hair, and he was
very wicked indeed, carving his way through the pages, seducing,
dueling, cheating, and murdering with ruthless abandon. The
whole thing was an extremely libelous parody of Max's supposed
career, and Charlotte knew that what she was doing was very
reprehensible indeed, especially as anyone happening to read it
would know straightaway that Rex and Max were one and the
same. But she was very careful to keep the book a secret, hiding it
away at the back of her wardrobe where no one would find it.

Max himself was very much in the public eye, the Westington
duel having divided society into two very distinct camps, those
who sided with the injured husband and those who believed Max.
The affair excited interest among the general public as well, and
the gentlemen residents at the exclusive Albany were much irritated by the noisy crowd that gathered outside on the eve of the
duel.

The duel itself took place one fine June morning on Putney
Heath, and from all accounts the whole of the *beau monde* traveled
there at dawn to watch. The great attendance meant that the

confrontation was very reliably reported, so that Charlotte was left in no doubt that of the two protagonists, only Max came out of it with any credit. He had again declared himself innocent and had requested his opponent to call a halt to the proceedings, but Lord Westington had not only refused, he had also been far too precipitate, turning to fire before the command was given. Fortunately his shot had missed its mark, but he had then had to summon every last vestige of courage to stand there while Max slowly and at his leisure took aim for his heart. The watching crowd had held its breath, giving a loud gasp when at the last moment Max had fired his pistol into the air before tossing it scornfully to the ground and turning away. Lady Westington, who had been unable to resist the temptation to be present, had received a very reproachful and accusing glance from Max as he walked to his carriage, and those who saw her exceedingly guilty reaction had no doubt at all that her whole story had been a fabrication, invented out of pique. That night Lord Westington, much reviled for having fired early, had taken his erring wife away to their country seat in Northamptonshire, intending to stay there until the whole sorry incident was forgotten. For the moment, however, it was talked of in all the drawing rooms, including that at the Parkstone residence, where a very reluctant Sylvia had in the end to admit to her father that she had been wrong about Max and Lady Westington and that Max had conducted himself very well indeed throughout the whole affair.

Charlotte's friendship with Sylvia became very firm over those weeks, and they were frequently to be found in each other's company. The renewed friendship between Mrs Wyndham and Admiral Parkstone flourished too, the admiral often taking tea at Henrietta Street, at which occasions he and Mrs Wyndham sat chattering for hours, driving their respective daughters to the point of ennui with their recollections of events long since past and people long since gone.

Of Richard Pagett there was unfortunately still no sign. The house sparkled like a new pin in readiness for him, and poor Polly was dispatched each morning to clean his waiting bedroom anew.

Richard's arrival was not the only event toward which Charlotte was looking forward; there was also the Parkstones' summer ball. Her enthusiasm for it took her completely by surprise, for in the past such functions had never appealed to her, but now it was somewhat different. However, it was one thing to eagerly anticipate it; it was quite another to feel entirely happy about what she would wear. Her wardrobe was very sorry now, lacking all the beautiful gowns created for her by Madame Forestier, that most-sought-after of couturières, and even if she had still possessed them, they would have been two summers out-of-date. Only one of the gowns she had retained offered any possibilities, and that was a plain white muslin with a fairly high neckline and long, puckered sleeves. It needed a great deal of alteration to be suitable for a ball, and so in the evenings she divided her time between writing *Kylmerth* and attending to the gown, which soon sported a desirably low décolletage and a shortened skirt with a stiffened hem. She adorned it with hundreds of tiny silver sequins, some taken from a rather ornate reticule which had somehow been overlooked when she had sold her things at Kimber Park, and some purchased from Messrs. Clark & Debenham at considerable cost to her small allowance.

Planning the ball and making all the arrangements naturally occupied a great deal of Sylvia's time, and when she was with Charlotte, it was a frequent topic of conversation. It was to discuss some minor catering difficulty that she called one afternoon at Henrietta Street, and was shown through to the sunny garden, where she found not only Charlotte and Mrs Wyndham seated on the white-painted, wrought-iron furniture beneath the cherry tree, but also her father, who was paying yet another of his lengthy visits.

While they were talking and sipping their tea, a carriage drew up at the front of the house. It was a post chaise, dusty from the long journey from Falmouth in Cornwall, and as the postboy dismounted and began to unload the many trunks, a young gentleman alighted, pausing for a moment to glance up at the house. He was elegantly attired in a pale-green coat and white trousers, and there was a handsome gold pin in his voluminous neckcloth. His hair was the same dark red as Charlotte's, and his eyes the same gray, and at just twenty-nine Richard Pagett could have been taken for her brother, not her uncle. He had a very agreeable face, with laugh lines at the side of his mouth and eyes, and there was something about him that made others always feel at ease in his company. As he looked up at the little house, remembering the grandeur and style of Kimber Park, he decided that he would attend to the matter of more suitable residences as quickly as possible.

When he knocked at the door, Mrs White came immediately, her face lighting up with a smile. 'Mr Pagett?'

He was a little taken aback. 'Yes, but how—'

'How do I know you, sir? Oh, I'd know you anywhere, you're so very like Miss Charlotte. Please come in, and I'll take you through to the garden.'

He stepped inside and followed her. 'Don't announce me, Mrs—?'

'Mrs White, sir, I'm the cook and housekeeper.'

'I'm pleased to meet you, Mrs White. I'd like to surprise them, so please don't let them know I've arrived.' His voice bore traces of an acquired American accent, and it was very pleasant, soft and unhurried.

'Oh, of course, sir, if that is what you wish. If you just go through that door there, you'll see them in the garden.'

'Thank you.'

'Would you like some refreshment, sir?'

'That would be most agreeable.'

The cook beamed and hurried away, determined to give such a winning gentleman the very finest repast she could muster.

Richard pushed open the door and looked down the garden at the little group beneath the cherry tree. They were completely unaware of his presence, so he could observe them at leisure. His sister, Sophia, did not seem to have changed a great deal, except perhaps that she was more plump. It suited her, he thought, for she now had that round rosiness that can be so very becoming. He surveyed Charlotte next. Ah, Charlotte, as pretty as a picture still, and with that splendid smile he remembered so well. How rueful she had always been that her mouth was too wide; she had never seemed to realize that it gave her a smile so glorious that she could seem the most beautiful of creatures. Had she been less independent, less determined to indulge in her virtual worship of the printed word, she would undoubtedly have long since made an excellent match, but it was her misfortune that her would-be suitors had been a timid bunch, too lily-livered to dare take on a wife who might have the temerity to think for herself and speak her mind.

He glanced at the admiral, wondering who he was. A military gentleman, that much was for sure, for he had the bearing that spoke of either the army or the navy. Whoever he was, Sophia was most certainly well disposed toward him, for she positively dimpled at every word he uttered.

At last his glance rested on Sylvia, lingering appreciatively on the dainty figure in its peach lawn dress. How beautiful she was, with her pale, flawless complexion and delicate profile, and how lustrous her dark hair was in the afternoon sunlight. His gaze was so intense that at last she sensed it, looking around directly at him, her face framed by the mock-Tudor ruff adorning the neck-line of her dress.

Charlotte saw her glance and turned as well, her face breaking into that wonderful smile he had missed so much as she got quickly to her feet and ran across the grass, flinging herself gladly into his open arms. 'Richard! Oh, Richard, you're here at last! I've missed you so! You're never to go away like that again. Never.'

He laughed, hugging her tightly. 'I've no intention of going away again, sweetheart.' He kissed her warmly on the cheek. 'How are you?'

'Well.'

'I can see that you are.' He took her left hand and inspected her fourth finger. 'So you're still unattached. I'll have to see what I can do about that, I can't have spinster nieces cluttering up my grand new house.'

She laughed. 'Come on, Mother's been in a positive lather ever since your letter arrived.'

He went to his sister then, taking both her hands and drawing her to her feet and into his arms. 'Hello, Sophia,' he said softly. 'It's so very good to see you again.'

Her voice was a little shaky, for she was almost weeping with joy. 'Richard Pagett, five years is an unforgivable eternity, quite unforgivable.'

He squeezed her. 'Forgive me all the same.'

'I shall endeavor to, but I cannot promise,' she replied, dabbing her eyes with her handkerchief and smiling foolishly at him. 'If ever a sister was more fiendishly tormented by an unthinking brother . . .' She allowed the sentence to die away unfinished. 'I'm forgetting my duties. Allow me to present Admiral Henry Parkstone, an old friend whose acquaintance it has recently been my good fortune to renew. Henry, this is my brother, Mr Richard Pagett.'

The admiral had struggled to his feet the moment Richard appeared, and now he bowed. 'Sir.'

Richard returned the bow. 'I'm delighted to meet you, Admiral Parkstone.' His inquiring glance then moved to Sylvia, who seemed even lovelier now that he was close.

Mrs Wyndham hastened to effect the introduction. 'This is Henry's daughter, Miss Sylvia Parkstone. Sylvia, my brother, Richard.'

Richard took Sylvia's hand, raising it slowly to his lips. 'I'm very pleased to know you, Miss Parkstone.'

'Mr Pagett.' She smiled up at him.

He looked deep into her dark eyes and was lost.

There was so much talking to be done and so much lost time to be made up that it was well past midnight before the residents of the house in Henrietta Street at last retired to their beds. As Charlotte undressed and sat by her dressing table brushing her long hair, she could hear her mother in the adjoining bedroom, chattering brightly to Muriel, just as she had done in times gone by at Kimber Park.

Charlotte extinguished the candle and then went to the window to look out for a while. She could see the watch in Cavendish Square with their staves and lanterns, and she could just hear their call on the hour. There was very little traffic; in fact, it was so quiet that she heard the carriage approach long before she saw it. It drove slowly along the street toward the square and at first she didn't recognize it, but then with a jolt she realized that it was Max Talgarth's. She couldn't move away from the window; it was as if she was transfixed, even though she knew that she was clearly visible from the street below.

He was seated on the side nearest her, looking as superbly elegant as ever in black velvet evening clothes, his arm resting along the window ledge so that the moonlight flashed on his diamond ring. She wasn't expecting him to glance up, so that when he did, he saw her immediately and knew that she had been watching him. She was embarrassed at the amused directness of his shrewd gaze, but still she couldn't draw back. The carriage drove on, turning the corner into the square and vanishing from sight, and only then could she manage to step back into the shadows of the room.

It was a long time before she fell asleep, and when she did, she was transported in her dreams to Kimber Park. The sun was warm on her face and she was walking past the lake toward the little white rotunda, its domed roof topped by a statue of Mercury. It was a favorite walk, one she had taken countless times in the past, and she was lighthearted. As she neared the rotunda, a man appeared from inside it, a tall, handsome man with a scar on his cheek and a flash of gray in his coal-black hair. She halted, her breath catching. He smiled, holding out his hand, and suddenly she was running to him. He swept her into his arms, pressing her close as his lips sought hers in a kiss that seared through her like a flame. Her senses responded to him, and she wanted to surrender, to give in completely to the wild, rushing desire he aroused in her . . . But as he bore her to the ground, his body hard against hers, her eyes suddenly flew open and she was awake.

She lay there in the dark room, her heart still thundering as if his lips had indeed been on hers a moment before. A bewildering wave of emotion was still coursing through her, emotion such as she had never known before. The desire lingered, leaving a yearning so sweet and clear that it was like a pain.

She stared up at the shadows thrown by the streetlamp. Was it true that dreams made one know oneself? If so, she now knew that far from despising Max Talgarth, she was drawn to him as to no other man before. He had awakened her slumbering emotions, and those emotions would still be there when daylight came. She didn't want to want him, but she couldn't deny it. But how could it be right to be so strongly drawn to the man who might have deliberately caused her father's death?

8

SEVERAL DAYS LATER THE anniversary of George Wyndham's demise came and went, and a day or so after that Charlotte and her mother ceased wearing black.

The first day of this change dawned hot and humid after a sultry night of distant thunder without any rain to refresh the air. Charlotte awoke with a dreadful headache, so much so that she simply couldn't contemplate putting her hair up and wearing a bonnet. She brushed her hair loose about her shoulders, wishing that her head would stop thumping, and then she looked at herself in the dressing-table mirror. The gown she was wearing for the first time in over a year was a simple gray spotted lawn with a demure, not too high neckline and dainty puffed sleeves. It was a little long, not revealing her ankles, and its hem wasn't padded in any way, but it was light and cool and it made a very welcome change after the stifling black she'd been wearing for so long now.

Richard and her mother weren't alone at the breakfast table, for the admiral had called, having obliged Richard by calling upon several estate agents with whom he was personally acquainted. He had acquired the details of a number of very desirable properties in Mayfair and it was the plan for them all to go to inspect them in the admiral's barouche. Mrs Wyndham was very excited and full of praise for the houses before she'd seen them, and she was very disappointed when Charlotte very apologetically declined to accompany them because of her headache.

Charlotte felt a little mean, for she knew how much her mother wanted her to be there, but the thought of clambering in and out of a hot carriage, looking over house after house and listening to an agent extolling the virtues of each one was simply too dreadful.

When they set off at just before noon, she remained behind, going to sit in the garden in the shade of the cherry tree. She took her manuscript with her, intending to glance through it in a little while, but first she just sat there, her eyes closed as she savored the coolness of the leafy shadows. Overhead storm clouds were creeping across the sky. Her thoughts turned inevitably to Max Talgarth, who had been on her mind constantly since she had dreamed about him. She wished that she could be indifferent to him, but it was no use; he lingered at the edge of her thoughts, forcing her to acknowledge that he had irrevocably aroused her very unwilling heart.

She had been there for some time and her headache had eased when suddenly Mrs White announced that Sylvia was calling. Looking very pretty in a strawberry wool spencer and white silk gown, her strawberry hat adorned with bouncy little plumes and bright golden chains, she hurried excitedly across the grass and sat down. 'Charlotte, I've had such a glorious morning, I vow I've managed to purchase every single tartan accessory in the world! I heard last night that Osmond's warehouse had had a new delivery and so I was up practically at dawn this morning to be there before everyone else, and I had the place virtually to myself. It was wonderful; I've bought so many scarves, sashes, and hats that I think I should send the bill to Sir Walter Scott for writing his wretched Waverley novels and making tartan *the* thing.' She paused. 'You're not wearing black.'

'Full marks for observation.'

'And your hair is loose! Aren't you feeling well?'

Charlotte couldn't help laughing. 'I'm not quite sure how to answer that. Do you mean, am I not well because I'm not wearing black, or because my hair's loose.'

'Because of your hair, silly.'

'I had a headache, but it's nearly gone now.'

'Are you sure? I mean, I'll toddle along if you're feeling wretched.'

'No, it's gone – truly it has.'

'I suppose Richard and your mother have gone with Father to look at houses?'

'Yes.'

'I'd forgotten all about it when I called.'

Charlotte glanced at her, wondering if this was entirely true, for Sylvia's conduct in recent days had been a little hard to understand, and Richard was quite obviously the reason. He had fallen head over heels in love with her at first sight, and he made no secret of the fact, but what Sylvia's feelings were could not be easily judged. Sometimes she seemed relaxed and happy in his company, but at other times she drew back and became almost cold. Charlotte was inclined to doubt that Sylvia had forgotten anything about the arrangements made for today; indeed, it was quite probable that from the house in Cavendish Square she had seen who had departed in her father's barouche and had therefore known full well that Charlotte was still at home. Maybe the guess was wrong, and for Richard's sake Charlotte hoped it was, but she had grave doubts that he was going to be fortunate enough to have his love returned.

At that moment there was an unexpectedly strong gust of wind that snatched the sheets of manuscript from the chair where Charlotte had put them, and scattered them all over the grass. With a gasp, Charlotte got up to gather them in. She'd forgotten all about them, and now Sylvia might see what she had been engaged upon in recent weeks.

Sylvia hurried to retrieve them as well, and as she was about to return those she had managed to gather, she glanced down at the top sheet. She paused, her eyes widening and then she slowly looked at Charlotte, who was looking very guilty indeed.

'Charlotte? What's this?'

'Nothing,' came the quick reply. 'Just a little scribbling I've done.' Embarrassed color had flooded into Charlotte's cheeks and she tried to take the papers.

Sylvia stepped quickly aside, looking at the writing again. 'Nothing? How can you say that? My eyes don't deceive me and I have to confess intense curiosity about a character named Rex Kylmerth, who just happens to have a scar on his cheek and a streak of gray in his hair. Don't expect me to believe this has nothing whatsoever to do with Max Talgarth, for I simply will not believe you.'

Charlotte hesitated. 'If I tell you, you must promise not to say anything to anyone else, for if you do I'll never forgive you. Oh, dear, I feel so very foolish, because it's all a nonsense really. I'd been reading *Glenarvon* and something my mother said set me thinking, and I just started to write a *roman à clef* of my own.'

'Based on Max?'

'Yes.'

Sylvia's eyes shone. 'Please, may I read it?'

'I'd rather you didn't.'

'But why? I'm *bound* to approve.'

'Yes, you probably would, but I'd be mortified to think of anyone reading it, even you. Besides, it's extremely libelous and I should never have written a single word of it.'

'But *I'm* hardly likely to go and tell him, am I? Oh, please, Charlotte, let me read it.'

'No.' Charlotte at last managed to take the sheets from the other's hands. 'No one's going to read it, and I want your word, Sylvia Parkstone, that you won't breathe a word about this.'

Sylvia gave a sigh. 'Oh, very well, you have my word.' She sat down again a little crossly. 'I'd have adored reading Max's wickedness set down in black and white, though. But tell me, how have you managed to write all that without anyone knowing?'

'I write in my bedroom and keep the manuscript at the back of my wardrobe.'

Sylvia grinned then. 'Good heavens, what a scandal I could make of it – Charlotte Wyndham hides Max Talgarth in her wardrobe at night! My goodness, what a titillating rumor *that* would set in motion.'

'Sylvia Parkstone, you gave me your word.'

'I know. I'm only joking. Oh, don't look so put out, your secret's safe. Look, I don't want to fall out with you, so let's talk about something else, like the state opening of Waterloo Bridge in a few days' time.'

Charlotte had to smile. 'Whatever makes you think of that?'

'Well, Father and I will be going and he intends inviting you all to join us in our pleasure boat. I believe he's going to broach the subject today. You'll be able to come, won't you? It should be very pleasant, at least it should if the weather is fair.' She glanced up at the sky; the thunder clouds that had been threatening since the night had begun to burgeon over the city.

'Oh, I should love to come,' replied Charlotte eagerly. 'It's very kind of you to think of us.'

'Kind? Well, my father's motives are all too clear; he'd do anything to secure your mother's presence at his side. I believe he's very smitten indeed. He'd also do anything to – to. . . .'

'Yes?'

'To place me in Richard's company.'

'Oh.'

Sylvia glanced away. 'My father is an inveterate matchmaker at times.'

'You dislike the thought of being with Richard?'

Sylvia lowered her eyes and said nothing.

Charlotte had no chance to pursue the matter, for it began to rain and they had to hurry inside, and by the time she'd hidden her manuscript away in her wardrobe again, the admiral's barouche had returned and everyone was in the drawing room talking about the houses that had been viewed.

Mrs Wyndham was full of praise for one house in particular, in

Hanover Square. It was, she declared, the most delightful property in Mayfair and she was determined to have it, even though it
needed a complete refurbishing. The admiral was in agreement
with her, and Richard, who was torn between this house and
another in Piccadilly, was eventually forced to accede that the
latter property would be exceeding noisy, Piccadilly being such a
busy thoroughfare. The admiral mentioned a friend of his, Mr
Algernon Green, who was considered very fashionable indeed for
decorating grand houses, and he offered to approach him on
their behalf. Mrs Wyndham was overjoyed and Richard acknowledged that the Piccadilly property no longer stood a chance and
that therefore Hanover Square was the victor.

It was four o'clock and still raining hard when the admiral and
Sylvia at last prepared to return home. Before they left, the matter
of attending the opening of the Waterloo Bridge was raised, and
everyone agreed that it was a splendid idea and they would all be
delighted to go.

Richard accompanied Sylvia to the door, with Charlotte a little
behind them. The admiral had already gone out into the waiting
barouche, but Richard spoke again to Sylvia on the doorstep. 'I
trust you will not think me too forward, but Charlotte and I are to
attend a firework display at Vauxhall Gardens tomorrow night,
and I would very much like it if you would come with us.'

Charlotte looked at him in astonishment, for this was the first
she'd heard about the visit.

Sylvia hesitated. 'Vauxhall Gardens? I had not realized they had
opened yet.'

'Yes. Tomorrow night is the first main event of the season.
Please say you'll join us.'

Her dark eyes moved fleetingly to Charlotte and then she
nodded. 'Thank you, I would like that.' Then she was hurrying
out through the rain before he had time to put up the umbrella
he had been intending to protect her with.

The barouche drove away through the puddles and a low

rumble of thunder echoed over the lowering skies.

Charlotte and Richard turned back into the house, closing the door on the storm, and Richard put his hand on his niece's arm. 'Charlotte?'

'Yes?'

'Forgive me for using you like that, but I couldn't think of anything else and she was about to leave.'

She smiled. 'Don't be silly, you know I don't mind.'

'I love her to distraction.'

'I know.'

'I only wish I could be certain of what her feelings are. She gives no hint; sometimes I feel as if I'm taking one step forward and two back.'

'You haven't known her for very long, Richard. Give it time.'

'But I knew the moment I saw her. It was love at first sight.'

'That doesn't mean that she will necessarily fall in love as quickly.'

He looked away. 'I feel. . . .'

'Yes?'

'That she already loves someone else.'

'Oh, Richard, I'm sure I would know if that were the case. Besides, the admiral quite obviously wants to further your suit with her, and he wouldn't do that if he knew her heart was given elsewhere.'

'No, I suppose not.' His voice was still doubtful.

'Richard? Is there something else?'

'I was just thinking that the admiral might behave as he does if he didn't know about her true feelings. What if she's keeping them secret, even from him?'

'I'm sure you're wrong.'

'Am I? Charlotte, you would tell me if you knew something, wouldn't you?'

'Of course I would. Richard, Sylvia's heart isn't given anywhere, I'd swear it wasn't. She and I have become very close, she'd have told me before now if there was someone else. I'm sure it's just that you're rushing things a little. You've fallen so completely in love that you're impatient.' But as she said it, she knew she was sounding more optimistic than she felt. Quite unbidden, an echo of the conversation in the library returned to her, and she could quite clearly hear Judith's angry voice taunting Sylvia about Max Talgarth: '. . . I begin to think you want him yourself, that all this is nothing more than jealous spite because he's never cast so much as a single appreciative glance in your direction. . . .'

9

IT WAS PARTICULARLY FINE the following evening as Charlotte, Richard, and Sylvia set off for Vauxhall Gardens in the landau Richard had hired for the occasion. The coach-man wore green, the carriage itself had gleaming brown panels, and the horses were a perfectly matched team of four bays. There was a crush at Hyde Park Corner and the Duke of Wellington's mansion, Apsley House, known simply as Number One, London, but then they were driving southwest along a broad new boulevard toward the river.

It was the first time in more than a year that Charlotte had gone out in something other than black, and the experience was quite strange, as if she had forgotten something important. She wished that she were a little more fashionable, but she knew she looked well enough in her pale-green muslin dress, white cashmere shawl, and straw bonnet tied on with green-and-white-checkered ribbons. But glancing across at Sylvia, so very bang up to the mark again, she longed for a new gown so that she too could cut a dash among the elegant crowds who would be thronging the pleasure gardens.

Sylvia was in pink and white, a dainty, fringed parasol twirling prettily above her head as the open carriage drove through the warm June evening. Her spencer was unbuttoned to reveal the frilled square neckline of her white lawn gown, and her Leghorn bonnet was adorned with artificial rosebuds and shining satin ribbons. She looked almost ethereally beautiful, the paleness of the pink spencer setting off her dark coloring to absolute perfection.

At her side Richard could hardly keep his eyes off her. He was nervous, having decided to take Charlotte's advice about not rushing Sylvia, but the only result was that he made himself edgy and uncomfortable, and far too aware of watching everything he said or did. He wore a dark-blue coat with a high standfall collar, and his starched muslin cravat sported an enviably complicated knot. He had taken a great deal of care with his dark-red hair, which was teased into fashionably disheveled curls, and he had spent an unconscionable length of time polishing his Hessian boots, which gleamed so much that Charlotte was sure she would be able to see her face in them. He crossed and uncrossed his beige corduroy legs, fidgeted with his ebony cane, adjusted the angle of his top hat, and continually flexed his fingers to tighten his already tight kid gloves. He had hardly uttered a word and looked quite wretched, and Charlotte felt desperately sorry for him.

Sylvia seemed almost oblivious to him as the carriage swept past the new villas of the Vauxhall Bridge Road, which, like the bridge itself, had only been completed the year before. To the south of them the land was laid out to market gardens and osier beds, with only a few scattered cottages dotted here and there. There were more houses the closer they came to the river, and now there were other carriages as society sallied forth to enjoy the famous pleasure gardens' first grand display of the summer.

There was a toll to pay at the nine-arched iron bridge, and then they were crossing the glittering, broad expanse of the Thames. Downstream, beyond the span of Westminster Bridge, were the gleaming new arches of Waterloo Bridge, so soon to be opened with the great pomp and ceremony they were to witness at first hand.

Vauxhall Gardens stretched up from the riverbank, the trees, avenues, and glades illuminated by thousands of little colored lanterns, their light as yet barely discernible in the brilliance of the setting sun. There were fountains and cascades, and temples in the Baroque, Gothic, and Chinese styles. Statues in plenty adorned the paths and grottoes, with particular admiration being accorded to a fine likeness of Mr Handel, whose music so often graced the proceedings. Elegantly dressed crowds strolled between the trees, while from the depths of the trellised, overhung path known as the Dark Walk, the squeals and giggles of young ladies could be heard as they ventured inside with their beaux.

Close to the main entrance was the magnificent Gothic rotunda, a huge building where an orchestra played on one of the balconies, and as the landau drew to a standstill, there was laughter and conversation mingling with the music in the warm evening air.

The shadows were lengthening by the minute as Richard escorted his two ladies toward the rotunda, where he had reserved a private supper box so that they could eat and enjoy the music while waiting for the fireworks to begin once darkness had fallen. It was very agreeable indeed to sit there taking iced champagne with a delicious roast-beef salad, followed by a particularly light ginger syllabub.

Richard was beginning to recover a little from his attack of nervousness, but he was still far from his usual witty, charming self, and he knew that his attempts at conversation were not having the desired effect upon the object of his love. Sylvia was attentive enough, laughing and smiling, but the reserve was there constantly. Time and time again Charlotte noticed him glance at the beautiful young woman in pink and white, and it was quite obvious that he was wondering if her heart was given elsewhere. Charlotte tried not to think about the one possibility that had so suddenly occurred to her.

It was while they were lingering over their supper that Charlotte saw Max Talgarth. He was strolling with Judith on his arm. He looked very handsome in formal evening wear, and he did not appear to be in a very good mood, for his face was dark and his eyes cold. Beside him, Judith was in an equally poor humor, her rosebud lips set in a thin line, her fan wafting busily to and fro in that angry way so eloquent of irritated ladies. She was wearing her usual yellow gold, her gown made of shining satin, and there were topazes at her throat and in her ears. A golden fillet rested across her forehead, and from it sprang tall ostrich plumes. Her costly, fringed cashmere shawl dragged carelessly along the ground behind her, and a shimmering, sequined reticule swung from her slender, white-gloved wrist. She looked very lovely, but her obviously sour temper detracted quite considerably from the otherwise impeccable effect of complete beauty.

Charlotte's heart was beginning to rush as she watched them walk by. It was with only half an eye that she noticed how bad things seemed between them, she was too startled at seeing Max again after what seemed like an age; and she was too taken up with the realization that her dream had not lied to her, she did indeed feel more drawn to this man than to any other.

As she watched, they halted suddenly, Judith snatching her hand from his arm, two spots of high color leaping to her pale cheeks. She looked up at his impassive face and then gathered her skirts to hurry away, her plumes streaming and her shawl still dragging in the dust.

Max didn't follow her; indeed, it was hard to tell what his reaction was. His eyes seemed almost veiled and his face was as inscrutable as it was possible to be. Knowing that he had no idea she was there, Charlotte could study him without fear of being caught. He looked manly and elegant in his charcoal velvet coat, which was so tight-fitting that it could not be buttoned and thus conceal the excellence of the tucked, frilled shirt beneath. He wore white knee breeches, silk stockings, and black, buckled shoes, and there was a *chapeau bras* tucked under his arm. Where was he going after this? The opera house perhaps. It had to be somewhere rather superior to warrant such formal clothes. He turned away then, walking slowly until he vanished from her sight among the crowds.

Charlotte lowered her gaze for a moment and then returned her attention to Richard and Sylvia, who had not noticed anything.

At last it was almost time for the fireworks display. They left their box to stroll with the waiting crowds on the lawns by the river. The shadows were so long and dark now that they had almost blended into one, and the lights among the trees were suddenly bright and clear, twinkling like fairyland. As the fireworks began, Charlotte found herself glancing around at the sea of illuminated faces for another glimpse of Max, but she could not see him anywhere. Perhaps he had already left because of his argument with Judith.

The fireworks were breathtaking, a dazzling extravagance of brilliant colors flashing in an indigo sky. There were girandoles and jerbs, Roman candles and Chinese fire, *pots de brin* and clusters of rockets, and with each successive wonder, the watching crowds gasped and clapped with delight.

Richard had gone to procure a glass of water for Sylvia when Charlotte knew instinctively that Max Talgarth was somewhere close by. She turned quickly to see him walking toward her, obviously quite intent upon speaking. Her heart thundered and she looked quickly at Sylvia, who was still engrossed in the fireworks. Should she say something to her? But even as the indecision seized her, he was there, bowing.

'Good evening, Miss Wyndham.'

'G-good evening, Sir Maxim.'

Sylvia turned with a sharp gasp, her face growing pale.

Max's expression was impenetrable as he inclined his head to her as well. 'Good evening, Miss Parkstone.'

She did not reply.

He feigned not to notice, addressing himself to Charlotte once more. 'I'm glad to have seen you again, Miss Wyndham, for you've been on my mind a great deal of late.'

'I have?' She was taken aback.

'I intend making certain improvements at Kimber Park, and it occurred to me that before any such work commences, both you and Mrs Wyndham might care to visit it once more.' He smiled a little, as if he were remembering the last time he had mentioned something similar to her, and the fireworks reflected in his eyes. 'It so happens that I must go there myself in two days' time, and I would be more than pleased to convey you there and back. That is, if you wish, of course.'

Sylvia's angry silence was almost tangible, and Charlotte simply didn't know what to say. She was torn, part of her desperately wishing to accept and part of her knowing that to refuse would be by far the wiser decision.

At that moment Richard returned with the glass of water for Sylvia, and it fell to Charlotte to introduce him to Max. 'Richard, allow me to present Sir Maxim Talgarth. Sir Maxim, my uncle, Mr Richard Pagett.'

Richard bowed. 'Your servant, sir.'

'And yours, sir.'

'Your name is familiar to me. Are you not the new owner of Kimber Park?'

'I have that honor. As a matter of fact, it was about Kimber Park that I was speaking to Miss Wyndham.'

'Indeed?'

'I plan some improvements there and I thought that maybe she and her mother would like to see the house again before any work begins. Maybe you would like to see it as well, since you are a member of the family?'

'You're very kind, sir,' replied Richard, smiling, 'but Kimber Park did not mean so very much to me, and I know that my sister would prefer to remember it as it was. However, I know that Charlotte would love to see it again. Is that not so, Charlotte?'

'Oh. Well, I. . . .'

Richard looked at her in surprise. 'You surely do not hesitate? Come now, you *know* you're always saying how much you'd like to go there again.'

She could feel embarrassed color creeping into her cheeks, and she was increasingly aware of Sylvia's stony face and angry silence.

Richard looked reprovingly at her. 'Charlotte, I'm surprised at you. Of course you must accept, especially since Sir Maxim has put himself out on your behalf.'

She felt quite dreadful, but really she had no choice now but to accept. 'Forgive me if I seemed less than enthusiastic, Sir Maxim, it's just that the generosity of your offer took me by surprise. Of course I would like to accept. Thank you.' She could feel Sylvia's disbelieving eyes upon her and steadfastly kept her own gaze upon Max, whose thinly veiled amusement at her predicament was plain enough to her, if not to anyone else present. He must have realized that Sylvia would have regaled her with the full list of his misdemeanors, both great and small, and as on occasions in the past when her manner toward him had provoked him into toying with her, so it happened again on this occasion.

'I'm so pleased you accept, Miss Wyndham, for I'm sure you will find the visit most agreeable.'

'Yes. I'm sure.' She could feel the color deepening on her cheeks.

'As I said earlier, I will be setting off the day after tomorrow, and it my intention to leave at about eleven in the morning. Will that be convenient?'

'Perfectly.' She met his mocking eyes again. 'Excellent. Until that time, then.'

'Until then.'

'*Au revoir*, Miss Wyndham.' He bowed.

'Good-bye, Sir Maxim.'

He inclined his head to Richard and Sylvia and then turned to walk away.

Richard looked at Charlotte then. 'You would seem to have an admirer.'

She gave a brief, embarrassed laugh. 'That I doubt very much.' No, he had just been amusing himself at her expense. . . .

'Why are you so certain I'm wrong?' Richard studied her for a moment. 'Are you convinced someone like Sir Maxim would not glance at you because you aren't attractive enough? If that is the case, then you are definitely wrong.'

'Richard, apart from many other considerations, I'm hardly the fashionable sort of young lady gentlemen like Sir Maxim seek out. Nor am I. . . .'

'Yes?'

'Meek and mild enough.'

'Ah, well there you might have a point,' he replied, grinning. 'But as to the matter of fashion, well, something can be done about that, can't it?' He gave Sylvia the glass of water, glanced once more at his niece, and then returned his attention to the fireworks display.

Sylvia immediately took Charlotte's arm, drawing her aside a little. 'You mustn't go to Kimber Park, Charlotte. Please change your mind.'

'But, Sylvia, it would look so very obvious if I did that.'

'Cry off. Plead illness.'

'No, Sylvia, I must go.'

'You mustn't become involved with him.' Sylvia's dark eyes were anxious and pleading.

'Involved?' Charlotte hoped that her voice sounded as light and unconcerned as she wanted it to. 'Sylvia, I'm only going so that I can see Kimber Park again.'

Sylvia searched her face and then nodded. 'Then go, if that is what you really want, but beware of him, Charlotte. He doesn't do anything without good reason. He can be the personification of charm, as my sister found out to her cost. I couldn't bear it if you fell under his spell as she did.'

Fell under his spell? Charlotte looked away. She was already under his spell . . . But she would steel herself against it. She gazed up at the brilliant colors bursting in the velvet sky above. How much of Sylvia's concern was the result of true friendship? And how much the result of her own love for Max Talgarth?

10

T HE FOLLOWING MORNING CHARLOTTE awoke wishing that she
hadn't accepted the invitation to Kimber Park, especially as
her mother was quite adamant about not going herself. After
breakfast Richard suddenly announced that he had an appointment at the new house in Hanover Square with the admiral's
fashionable decorator friend, and to Charlotte's astonishment he
virtually insisted that she accompanied him to offer her advice.
Her advice? To a gentleman as famous as Mr Algernon Green? But
Richard simply wouldn't take no for an answer, in fact he was
mysteriously determined that she went with him, and so at half-
past ten they set off in the same hired landau of the evening
before.

Hanover Square was very quiet and gracious, much more exclusive and elegant than Cavendish Square. Built on gently sloping
land, it had a central garden containing trees and bushes, and an
equestrian statue of George I. The house that had so entranced
her mother occupied a site close to the northeastern corner, and
was built of mellow red brick. It was a beautiful building, almost
one hundred years old, its main entrance approached up a
shallow flight of steps and sheltered by a magnificent columned
stone porch.

Mr Green's carriage was already waiting as they arrived, and he
was in the oval entrance hall with several builders and an archi-
tect. Sheaves of papers and plans lay on the black-and-white-tiled

floor, and the men's voices echoed around the blue walls, black marble double staircase, and the soaring columns lining the balcony of the floor above. After the little house in Henrietta Street it was palatial, the splendor of the entrance hall being worthy of Kimber Park itself.

The sought-after decorator was a round little man, evidently enjoying to the full the fruits of his popularity. He was rosy-faced and beaming, and his portly figure was tightly laced to give him a semblance of a waist, which effect he promptly ruined by wearing a quilted waistcoat of such sumptuousness and of such a bright crimson brocade that he appeared as spherical as a ball on legs. His dark-blue coat was quite obviously the work of one of London's finest tailors, but even the genius of a Weston could not make him elegant. He was full of ideas for the refurbishing of the house, and as Charlotte trailed around from room to room in his and Richard's wake, she wondered why on earth Richard had been so insistent that she was there to offer her opinion. It was quite obvious that Mr Green was not the sort of gentleman to heed the advice of amateurs, and it was equally obvious that Richard and her mother had already made the necessary basic decisions upon which the decorator would base his plans.

As she followed them through the property from cellars to attic, she had to admit that it was a very beautiful house, and she could quite understand why her mother had so swiftly become set upon having it. The reception rooms were very spacious and magnificently proportioned, offering the approving Mr Green a great deal of scope for some very grandiose plans; and since Richard asserted that money was indeed no object, the little man was busily making notes all the time, measuring this corner, then that, and exclaiming that he had the very Chinese silk, the very shade of lavender, the most skilled plasterer to achieve this and that effect.

After a while Charlotte became quite overwhelmed by it all, paying less and less attention to what they were saying and thinking instead about her forthcoming visit to Kimber Park. She was alternately thrilled and uneasy, literally torn about how she felt. One half of her wanted so very much to spend what amounted to a day alone with Max Talgarth; the other half was only too aware of what he might have been guilty.

'Charlotte?'

Richard's voice at last aroused her from her thoughts. 'Yes?'

He grinned. 'We've reduced you to ennui, have we not?'

She colored a little. 'No, of course not.'

Mr Green was very gallant, drawing her hand to his lips. 'Forgive us, dear lady, for we've been less than considerate, dragging you around without any thought. I trust only that my sins will be forgiven when you see the result of my work.'

She smiled. 'Oh, I'm sure that you're forgiven already, sir, for it's most kind of you to assist us when I know that society is constantly at your door.'

He beamed. 'My dear, it is a pleasure to be of assistance to friends of Henry Parkstone. I am his oldest friend. I trust that from this moment on I will be regarded as your friend also.'

She smiled, liking him. 'I'm honored, sir.'

He patted her hand, still beaming. 'Nonsense. But now, to work.' He turned back to Richard. 'I will attend to all that we have agreed, sir, and in the unlikely event of there being any queries or problems, I will contact you straightaway.'

'Very well, Mr Green.'

The two men shook hands and a moment later Charlotte and Richard emerged into the sunny square once more, where the landau was waiting.

Charlotte halted on the pavement, facing him. 'Why did you want me to be there? I know that I hadn't seen the house, but if that was your reason, why didn't you simply say so? What are you up to?'

'A niece ain't supposed to quiz her uncle!' he protested, grinning a little sheepishly. 'All right, I admit to an ulterior motive.'

'What motive is that?'

'Clothes.'

She stared at him. 'I beg your pardon?'

'Clothes. Or at least, your lack of them.' He took her hands, smiling into her puzzled eyes. 'Charlotte Wyndham, I may have been away for five years, but I can still read you like a book. You're fretting about your unfashionable wardrobe, aren't you? Don't deny it, I can see it in your eyes each time you're with Sylvia. She looks bang up to the mark all the time, whereas you feel dowdy and unmodish. Am I right?'

She nodded. 'Yes, I suppose you are.'

'Am I also right that that is the real reason why you hesitated about accepting Sir Maxim's invitation?'

She looked quickly away. 'Well, not exactly. . . .'

'But it has a great deal to do with it, doesn't it? Don't deny it, Charlotte, for I know I'm correct. So, I've made it my business to find out what can be done about the situation in so short a time. In fact, I was out very early this morning, while you were still asleep. Actually it was something Sylvia said in passing that gave me the notion. I've heard all about the duel Sir Maxim had with Lord Westington, and it seems that his lordship is so displeased with his errant wife that he canceled a substantial order for a new wardrobe she had been expecting from Madame Forestier. I was so bold as to steal a gown from your room while you were asleep, and I took it to Madame's premises in Oxford Street to see if by any good fortune you and Lady W. were the same size. You are; in fact, you are perfectly matched in that respect, and if you wish it, the whole wardrobe can be yours within the hour.'

Her breath caught. A whole wardrobe by Madame Forestier? Just as she had had at Kimber Park. Why, it was a dream come true! 'Oh, Richard,' she breathed, her eyes shining, but then her delight faded and she bit her lip. 'But it will cost a small fortune. No, I couldn't possibly impose upon you to that degree.'

He still held her hands and now he squeezed her fingers.

'Charlotte, when I wrote to you about returning from America, I said that I was in more than a position to return you and your mother to the status you had enjoyed in the past. I meant every word. I'm a very wealthy man, and the cost of a wardrobe from Madame Forestier is a drop in the ocean to me. I want you to be happy, and if a few fashionable rags will help achieve that, then I will be happy too. Now, then, do you want Lady Westington's lost prizes or don't you?'

She smiled. 'Of course I want them.'

'Then it's settled. We'll go there straightaway.' He escorted her to the landau and instructed the coachman to drive to the couturière's premises almost opposite the Pantheon in Oxford Street.

It was a short drive, and Charlotte felt quite strange to be once again drawing up outside in a handsome carriage, and to be welcomed into the exclusive rooms by Adam, the dressmaker's liveried black footman, who showed them both up the red-carpeted stairs to the rooms on the first floor where Madame Forestier herself waited to greet them.

The showroom was just as cluttered as Charlotte remembered, with a number of cheval glasses set at strategic points, and count-less beautiful garments hanging from the picture rail. There were bolts of cloth, cards of lace, trimmings, and other fashionable bits and pieces scattered everywhere. Only one chair was left clear, and Richard was conducted to this.

The couturière was French, as her name suggested, which was a little unusual, since it was quite the thing for English dress-makers to adopt French names. She was a petite person with olive skin, and her dark hair was tugged back into a knot at the back of her head. Her eyes were the darkest of browns and her accent very heavy indeed. She wore gray taffeta that rustled almost as much as Mrs White's aprons crackled, and she used a rather heady scent that wafted over Charlotte in waves as she led her into an adjoining room to commence trying on the first garment.

For the next hour or more Charlotte was in the seventh heaven of delight as gown after gown was slipped over her. There were sheer muslins, sprigged, spotted, and spangled for evenings, soft lawns, delicate silks, rich taffetas, and brightly colored tartans, all as up-to-date as any lady of fashion could desire. The hems were short to reveal her ankles, and stiffened to make the skirts stand out in the A shape that had become all the rage this summer. The dressmaker also showed her pelisses, spencers, and mantles, and an array of millinery, bonnets, and hats to satisfy any need, and there were even shoes, little bottines, evening slippers, and ankle boots for every occasion imaginable. The wayward Lady Westington had evidently been most thorough about her new wardrobe, but it was to be Charlotte Wyndham who benefited.

She gazed at herself in the cheval glasses, watched by a smiling Richard as she came out, turning this way and then that to show each gown off to best advantage. Now the gown she had so painstakingly altered for the forthcoming ball could be set aside, for she had a breathtaking choice of dazzling ball gowns from which to choose. And the state opening of Waterloo Bridge could be enjoyed far more if one were clad in clothes perfect for the occasion, as were so many of the combinations of gowns and pelisses or spencers she had been shown today.

But it was the visit to Kimber Park the next morning that was of more immediate importance. She had already decided what she would wear: a particular cream muslin dress was the ideal choice. Made of very fine Indian cloth, sprigged with little flowers the identical shade of dark red as her hair, it had a dainty mock-Tudor ruff and full sleeves gathered at the wrists. Its hem was padded and deliciously stiff, and its waist very high and trimmed with dark-red satin ribbon. With it she would wear a wide-brimmed gypsy bonnet tied on with satin ribbons again of the same dark red; and if the weather was uncertain, there was a dark-red pelisse of a close-enough match to be more than satisfactory. If the weather was fine, then she would content herself with one particular cashmere shawl that had caught her eye, for it too was patterned in dark red. Yes, that was what she would wear, and in such togs she would feel so much more able to carry off the day.

She looked at herself in the mirror again. Carry off the day? Could she do that? Could she really push to the back of her mind all the things she had heard Max Talgarth accused of? She wanted to, she wanted to be able to ignore all that and simply enjoy herself.

Richard was glancing at his fob watch. 'Charlotte, I realize that this is paradise to you, but we really should be on our way. Mrs White's luncheon will not wait an eternity.'

She smiled at him, twirling once more in the lilac-and-white silk evening dress she was wearing. 'Forgive me, I hadn't realized how long I was taking. I'll go and change straightaway.' She hurried back into the little room where Madame Forestier's assistant was waiting. The thought of putting on her old clothes again was not to be borne, and it was with great delight that she chose a frilled blue lawn dress and white spencer in which to drive back to Henrietta Street.

As the assistant helped her to change for the last time, she could hear Richard and Madame Forestier in the show-room, settling the financial side of things and arranging for the entire wardrobe to be delivered. Suddenly the assistant gave a startled gasp, stopping what she was doing. Puzzled, Charlotte turned to see what was wrong. Her heart sank and her skin felt suddenly cold, for the door into the little changing room from the outer passage was open: Judith stood there, her green eyes ice cold. The dyed yellow plumes springing from her golden velvet hat streamed angrily as she jerked her head at the assistant to leave them. The assistant hastened to comply, scuttling out and closing the door behind her, leaving Charlotte and her enemy alone.

Judith's yellow clothes were dazzling in the poorly lit room, and her skirts hissed a little as she came closer, her eyes glittering with that frozen dislike Charlotte knew so well from all the occasions in the past when they'd come face to face.

Charlotte raised her chin a little challengingly. 'Yes, my lady?'

'No doubt these fripperies are for tomorrow. Oh, you think you're so clever, don't you? Well, let me warn you, *Miss* Wyndham, Max Talgarth belongs to me, and I'm not about to relinquish him to the likes of you. Go to Kimber Park tomorrow and you'll be sorry. Is that clear?'

'You don't frighten me, and since I have been invited by Sir Maxim, who is the owner of Kimber Park, and since you are his mistress, not his wife, I don't see why I should take any notice at all of what you say.'

'Because your uncle has returned and brought his wealth with him, you think you are returned to favor, don't you? You're wrong, Miss Wyndham. The Wyndhams are nothing, and you are the least of them. Stay away from Max, and stay away from Kimber Park. Defy me and I'll make you pay.' She turned and walked out, leaving the door open so that Charlotte could hear the swish-swish of her skirts.

Richard and the couturière were approaching from the adjoining showroom, and Charlotte took a deep breath to steady herself. Hastily doing up the final buttons on the gown and donning the white spencer, she was tying on a bonnet and smiling as she bade them enter.

Madame Forestier was all smiles; indeed, she had had as excellent a morning as Charlotte, not only at last ridding herself of an expensive wardrobe that had seemed likely to remain on her hands indefinitely, but also acquiring a further lucrative order to clothe Mrs Wyndham. The dressmaker was well-pleased with herself, promising to bring several items to the house in Henrietta Street for Mrs Wyndham to inspect.

As the landau conveyed them back to the house, Charlotte tried not to think of Judith, but of her new clothes instead. It was as if she'd been reborn. She felt a little foolish for having taken such a delight in trying everything on, but she had enjoyed it all so much that even now she couldn't stop smiling. She glanced at Richard. 'I don't know how to thank you for this.'

'Your happy smile and bright eyes are reward enough for me. You looked lovely in everything you tried on today, Charlotte, I don't think you've any notion at all how beautiful you are.'

'Beautiful?' She gave a rueful laugh. 'Now you're being too flattering, for no one with a mouth as wide as mine—'

'That mouth gives you a smile quite beyond compare,' he interrupted gently. 'You don't do yourself justice, Charlotte. You're a very lovely young woman, and I'm right when I say that Sir Maxim Talgarth admires you.'

She looked quickly out of the window and said nothing more.

When they reached the house, she went upstairs to put her new white spencer away in her wardrobe. Her glance fell on her manuscript, hidden away at the back; tomorrow she would be spending the day with the man who was the original of Rex Kylmerth ... Quickly she closed the wardrobe and hurried downstairs again, for her mother was more than a little cross that luncheon had been delayed for such a disgracefully long time, although she was mollified by the news of Madame Forestier's impending visit.

As Charlotte neared the foot of the staircase, she paused, for the door to the kitchen had been left ajar and she could hear Mrs White and Polly talking as they prepared to serve the meal.

'Well, now, Polly Jenkins,' the cook was saying, 'and who was that fine lady I saw you talking with on the corner earlier?'

'Fine lady?' The maid's reply was very guarded.

'Oh, don't come the innocent with me, my girl, I saw you chitter-chattering away as if you had all the time in the world, when in fact you'd been far too long already purchasing those vegetables from the Oxford market. What was it all about, then, eh? Wanted you for her personal maid, did she?' This last was uttered with heavy sarcasm.

'No, of course she didn't,' replied the maid, 'for who'd want someone like me for a lady's maid?'

'Who indeed?' agreed the cook dryly. 'Well? Who was she?'

'I-I don't know.'

'Well, whoever she was, she was a lady of rank, that's for sure. Only someone very rich could have afforded clothes like that, all so beautifully matched in the same shade of yellow, and her carriage, so magnificent and so startling in the same color. Oh, yes, a lady of rank and of fashion, and she chose to halt her carriage to speak to the likes of you. What did she want?'

'Nothing.'

'Really,' declared the cook, 'you must take me for a nitwit at times, Polly Jenkins. Do you honestly expect me to believe that she went to the trouble of stopping her carriage and addressing you so that she could say nothing?'

'She only wanted directions to Regent Street,' said the maid quickly, and more than a little lamely.

The cook gave an irritated sigh and said nothing more.

Charlotte remained where she was at the foot of the stairs. The lady in yellow with a yellow carriage could only be Judith Taynton, who most definitely knew the way to Regent Street and to every other thoroughfare of importance in London. Charlotte had to admit to sharing Mrs White's curiosity about the incident. Why, indeed, had Judith gone to the trouble of speaking to Polly? And why wasn't Polly prepared to admit to what really happened? Quite suddenly Charlotte recalled Judith's words of warning at Madame Forestier's: 'Stay away from Max, and stay away from Kimber Park. Defy me and I'll make you pay. . . .'

11

WHEN IT WAS ALMOST time for Max to arrive the next morning, Mrs Wyndham and Richard suddenly realized the impropriety of allowing Charlotte to spend so much time alone with him. To solve the problem, Mrs Wyndham's maid, Muriel, was hastily dragooned into service, being sent scuttling to her room on the top floor to change into her best clothes in order to be Charlotte's chaperone for the day. Charlotte felt unaccountably embarrassed by all this. Had she been spending the day with any man other than Max Talgarth, she would have accepted that a chaperone was indeed necessary for the protection of her character, but somehow the fact that it was Max made a subtle difference. Perhaps, she reflected as she waited nervously in her room for him to arrive, it was because she knew he was bound to wonder if the maid was there as much because of all the rumors Sylvia had been spreading about him as because of the accepted need to at all times observe the proprieties where a lady's reputation was concerned.

Last-minute doubts and uncertainties beset her, and her heart almost stopped when at last she heard his carriage outside. Looking discreetly from the window, she saw him alight. He wore a rust-colored coat and Bedford cord trousers. His neckcloth was of brown silk, and his waistcoat a similar shade. A tasseled cane swung in one gloved hand, while with the other he tipped his top hat back on his tangle of dark hair. She could see the scar on his cheek and the penetrating blue of his eyes.

He made no comment about Muriel's presence; indeed, he hardly seemed to notice she was there. As he and Charlotte emerged from the house to climb into the waiting carriage, she was conscious of a sense of disappointment, for when he had seen her in her fashionable new clothes, there had been nothing in his glance or words to signify that he was particularly aware of the change in her.

The carriage set off at a smart pace, with Muriel pressed into a corner seat as if she was trying to appear invisible. Very little was said as they left London behind and drove along the road that had once meant going home to Charlotte. She had not driven along it since leaving Kimber Park the previous year, and how different things were now. Then she and her mother had been in the depths of grief and despair, and the weather had been more than a match for their sorrow; now the future again looked bright, and the weather matched this optimism. The sun shone down from a cloudless sky, and the air was warm and still, with hardly a breath of breeze to stir the hedgerows as London faded farther and farther into the distance behind them.

Because the day was so warm, she had decided against wearing a bonnet and had chosen instead to follow the pretty fashion of draping a lace veil over the back of her head. A shawl rested lightly over her arms and she carried a marquise parasol tilted back to shade her head just a little from the sun while at the same time revealing her face. The steady pace of the carriage fluttered the parasol's fringe and made her gown's cream-and-dark-red muslin sleeves move softly against her arms. She could smell honeysuckle and wild roses in the hedgerows, and there was something almost lulling about the carriage's gentle rhythm.

Judith's threats and actions the day before were a great deal on her mind, and she wondered what Max would say if he knew about them. She wondered too exactly what it was that Judith would do now that her warning had been so deliberately disregarded. The ultimatum delivered at Madame Forestier's had been unpleasant enough, but the secret approach to Polly was disturbing. What did she have in mind? And what was there anyway that Polly could possibly tell her? Charlotte took a deep, slow breath. Polly didn't know anything, because there wasn't anything to know. She tried to reassure herself with this, but somehow the deep unease continued.

Opposite her, Max lounged with his usual grace. He seemed oddly withdrawn today, she thought, and there was obviously something on his mind. He spoke when spoken to, but made no attempt to keep any form of conversation flowing. She tried once or twice to break the lengthy silence but after a while gave up. They traveled the last few miles to Kimber Park in absolute silence.

At last they reached the lodge, and her heart tightened at the well-remembered sound of the wrought-iron gates swinging open. As the carriage turned onto the drive, she at last saw across the lake and the valley to the great white house on the knoll opposite. Something like a pain passed through her as she gazed at it. How she loved this place and how she missed it! Suddenly she wished that she had taken her mother's attitude and refused to come, for seeing it again made her realize anew that no other house would ever take the place of this one, and no other house would ever be really home.

She gazed out at every well-loved feature: the trees, the sparkling waters of the lake, the little Mercury rotunda ... She stared at this last for a long time, remembering her dream, and she felt the hot color stealing inexorably across her cheeks. She couldn't help glancing at Max, her eyes lingering for a moment on his firm lips. So real had that dream been that now, when she was actually by the lake and the rotunda with Max seated so very close, it was as if the dream had been no dream at all, but had really happened. She looked quickly away, fearing that if he had met her gaze in that moment, he would have been able to read her every thought.

The carriage came to a standstill before the great portico of the house, and Max alighted first, turning to extend his hand not to Charlotte, but to a rather astonished Muriel. For the first time that morning he smiled a little as he handed down the diminutive maid. 'No doubt you have many friends here that you are longing to see, and I'm sure Miss Wyndham doesn't require your services. Is that not so, Miss Wyndham?'

Charlotte was as astonished as the maid, for it was a very transparent move to see that there was little chance of a chaperone. When she didn't immediately reply, his blue eyes swung quickly toward her. 'Do you require her, Miss Wyndham?' he asked again.

There was something so compelling in his gaze that she could only shake her head. 'No, of course not.'

He smiled a little, nodding at Muriel. 'You may go, then. You'll be sent for if you're needed.'

'Yes, sir. Miss Wyndham.' Muriel bobbed a hasty curtsy and then hurried thankfully away in the direction of the stables, and thence to the rear of the house and the kitchens, where she knew most of the servants would be found.

Only then did Max extend his hand to Charlotte. 'Propriety isn't about to be mortally wounded, Miss Wyndham, you have my word on that.' There was a noticeable edge to his voice.

She was embarrassed, but managed to meet his gaze. 'I didn't for one moment imagine it would be, sir.'

'I'm relieved to hear it, for I'd hate to think a chaperone was deemed necessary because of my dastardly reputation.'

So he had been irritated. 'No, sir, it was deemed necessary because of *my* reputation, dastardly or otherwise,' she explained quickly.

A slight smile reached his lips then. 'You've a way of saying the unexpected, haven't you? I could certainly never accuse you of being dull.'

She looked at him for a moment. 'Unlike you so far today.'

'The unexpected yet again? I confess to being quite bewildered by the lightning darts of your personality.'

'Do you? Come now, sir, you aren't in the least bewildered.' She didn't quite know why she was saying all this; it was all just slipping from her lips as if she had no control over her tongue.

'You evidently have your forthright hat on today, Miss Wyndham.'

'I was merely remarking that during the journey your conversation was less than scintillating.'

'I rather thought that idle pleasantries irritated you considerably, Miss Wyndham.'

'That was quite uncalled for.'

He nodded then. 'Yes, it was, and I apologize.'

'If you would prefer not to proceed with this visit, I shall quite understand.'

'It isn't that at all, I promise you. I was indeed a little surly on the way here, and for that too I apologize. I'll endeavor to improve from now on.'

'Sir, you really do not have try on my account.'

He smiled again. 'I know, and you may take that as a compliment. Miss Wyndham, I know very well that you've been told all manner of things about me by my former sister-in-law, and I realize that you must be wondering how much of it is true. Whatever conclusion you've reached, today I wish to forget all that. Rumor names me a monster and a rake, and it blames you as a hot-tempered, uppity bookworm. Now, I'm sure that I can be agreeable enough; in fact, I flatter myself that I've been occasionally known as good company, and I'm equally sure that you have the same excellent qualities, so I suggest that we are at our angelic best today and make the occasion do our bidding – in the most proper and polite way, of course.'

She smiled too. 'Are you suggesting a fresh start, Sir Maxim?'

'Something of the sort.'

'Perhaps that would be the most civilized approach.'

'Civilized? I don't know about that; it's certainly the *best* approach, in my opinion.' He offered her his arm then. 'Shall we proceed?'

She slipped her hand over his sleeve and they went slowly up the almost majestic steps beneath the great columned portico toward the huge double doors, which opened as if by magic as they came near.

It was strange to enter the house again, for it was at once the same and yet very different. The echoing vestibule and the sweeping double staircase had not changed, but now there were elegant crimson upholstered sofas and chairs arranged along the cream-and-gold walls, instead of the green-and-white-striped furniture that had been there in her father's time.

Throughout the house the story was the same, with strange furniture and paintings taking the place of all that she could still remember so clearly from the past. Some things were the same, however, like the immense side-board in the breakfast room, the long mahogany table presiding over the dining room, and her father's silver brocade four-poster bed in the principal apartment. There were other items Max had purchased at the auction, and the faces of the servants were as she remembered, and of course the rooms themselves had not yet been physically altered; it was very strange indeed to stroll through it all, as if she were observing it all from a great distance.

They had completed the circuit of the house and were descending the staircase to the hall when suddenly they heard a carriage arriving outside. Max halted, his face suddenly very still, as if he knew who it was. Charlotte looked inquiringly at him, but he merely remained where he was, gazing expectantly at the main doors.

Someone knocked, and after a moment one of Max's footmen hurried to open it. Charlotte's heart almost froze as she saw Judith standing there, looking as gloriously beautiful as ever in a daffodil-yellow silk gown, a gossamer light yellow-and-white shawl and a dainty, flower-adorned straw bonnet tied on with yellow ribbons.

The footman hesitated, looking uncertainly at his master, still absolutely motionless on the staircase.

The undercurrents that had so suddenly sprung into being were almost tangible, and Charlotte could only stand there, wondering with a dreadful sinking feeling what was about to happen.

Judith stepped into the vestibule, the fresh brilliance of her clothes making a startling splash of color as she stood on the gray-and-black-tiled floor, her green eyes shining as she looked up at the two on the staircase. 'Well, well,' she murmured, 'how very cozy. I do hope I'm not intruding.'

Again Charlotte looked at Max. His face was dark with anger now. 'Madam,' he said coldly to Judith, 'you were asked not to come here.'

'So I was. Put my presence down to base female curiosity; I simply had to know how you were proceeding with the little Wyndham.'

Max stiffened noticeably, turning quickly to Charlotte. 'Please wait in the walled garden. I will come presently.'

'But—'

'Don't choose this of all moments to show your independent spirit, I beg of you. Please, just do as I ask.'

She stared at him for a moment and then gathered her skirts to hurry on down the staircase. As she crossed the vestibule and passed Judith, the other's low voice halted her momentarily.

'Charlotte Wyndham, if you thought I was your enemy before, it is as nothing to the enemy I am now. Be on your guard, for I'll claw you down, you have my word on it.'

Charlotte said nothing, hurrying on and out into the warm sunshine.

Her mind was racing as she reached the peace and solitude of the walled garden, a place well away from the confrontation that was evidently taking place between Max and his furious mistress.

Was it over between them? Had the argument she'd seen take place at Vauxhall Gardens been evidence of a much more serious split than she had hitherto realized? She gazed around at the beautiful, sun-soaked gardens and at the house beyond. Oh, she hoped it was, for she still couldn't endure the thought of Judith Taynton living here. Nor could she bear to think of Judith lying in Max's arms, close and cherished, sleeping at his side throughout the night and waking to feel his lips upon hers in the morning. . . . Charlotte closed her eyes, turning sharply away from the house. Such thoughts were so very wrong.

The minutes passed, and still there was no sign of him. She walked slowly along the neat gravel paths between the sweet-smelling flower beds. The doves cooed softly in the dovecote, their wings white against the blue sky as now and then they rose in a cloud. The roses her mother and Richard had planted all those years before were at their best now, their colors almost vibrant against the warm stone walls. Sitting on a seat beneath a bower of purple-blue wisteria, she listened to the remembered sounds of the park she loved so much, and at first she didn't hear the sound of Judith's carriage leaving. It wasn't until the coachman's whip cracked to bring the team sharply up to speed that she was roused from her thoughts. Hurrying to the arched doorway in the wall, she looked across the open park to see the eye-catching yellow carriage driving at almost breakneck speed down toward the lake. As it reached the valley, the whip cracked again, urging the team to even greater effort, and it almost flew along the shore toward the rising ground beyond.

She heard Max approaching and turned quickly. His face was a little pale and she could see the lingering anger in his blue eyes.

He halted. 'I trust I haven't kept you waiting too long, Miss Wyndham.'

She was a little, surprised at such a bland statement after the bitterness of the confrontation in the vestibule. 'Too long? Why, no, sir.'

101

He glanced past her toward the distant lodge and main gates, where Judith's carriage was just passing out of sight onto the main London highway. 'Then let us continue,' he murmured. 'I was about to suggest luncheon. I do hope you are in good appetite.'

She stared at him. Not a word about what had just happened?

He seemed not to notice her surprised reaction. 'I thought that such a fine day called for enjoyment of the great outdoors, and I've taken the liberty of having a picnic sent out in readiness. My phaeton awaits.' He offered her his arm.

Hesitantly and still a little taken aback, she accepted. 'Where are we going?' she inquired as they walked back toward the house, where she could see his high red phaeton waiting, a groom holding the bridle of the leader of the team of six grays.

'I thought the Mercury rotunda on the far side of the lake, if that's agreeable to you.'

Her breath caught and her eyes flew toward the little white building.

12

THE SPEED WITH WHICH he drove the highly sprung phaeton was even faster than that previously attained by his mistress's carriage. On his little perch behind the seat, the little groom clung tightly to his place, holding his beaver hat on firmly. Charlotte's lace veil streamed in the air behind her, and the hem of her gown, even though it was padded and stiffened, lifted now and then in the breeze caused by the vehicle's pace. It was as if by driving so recklessly, Max was exorcising the dark mood that had been with him at the outset of the day and that had returned when he had come face to face with Judith. By the time they reached the rotunda, he seemed almost himself again, driving the team at a spanking but not foolhardy speed across the smooth open grass.

It was pleasantly cool in the shade of the little marble building, which seemed larger now than Charlotte remembered. Memories of the dream that had awakened her to the way she really felt about Max were very strong as the phaeton came to a standstill and she gazed up at the statue of the god Mercury on the top of the domed roof. There was a slight breeze now, she could hear it whispering through the trees and among the rotunda's six Ionic columns. From here she could look across the bright water of the lake toward the house, and beyond that the Surrey hills stretching away into the beautiful green infinity of the hazy, indistinct horizon. It was a peaceful, idyllic place, but for her charged now with a secret atmosphere that made her shiver a little, even though she was far from cold.

The groom jumped lightly down from his position and hurried to steady the team, while Max fastened the reins and then alighted, coming around to her side and holding his hand up to assist her. Her fingers trembled imperceptibly as she stretched down to him, slipping from the high vehicle and down to the grass. She almost lost her balance, and he caught her quickly, his hands firm about her waist, their warmth quite plain through the soft material of her gown. She was so aware of his touch that she felt sure he must guess how she was feeling.

A rug and some cushions had been laid on the grass beside the rotunda, and he led her there now. As she made herself comfortable, the groom brought the hamper from the phaeton and then withdrew to a discreet distance. The food was delicious, but then, didn't even the most ordinary fare always taste exceptional out of doors? And this was no ordinary fare: there was cold turkey and spiced ham, crisp salad and feather-light salmon mousse, tasty cheeses and fresh-baked bread. The butter had that subtle flavor she associated only with Kimber Park, and the various pickles were exactly as she always remembered them; one thing was clear: the kitchen staff had indeed continued as if nothing had changed.

The wine had been chilled with ice taken from the lake during the winter and stored in the icehouse deep in the woods, and as Max opened the bottle, he glanced, as if for the first time, at her new clothes. 'So, Miss Charlotte Wyndham is restored to elegance. I confess I approve of the transformation.'

'Thank you.'

'And you are not only fashionably elegant once more, I understand you are on the point of reentering society.'

'We are fortunate that my uncle is in a position to provide for us.'

He smiled a little. 'Will you be honoring society with your full presence? Or must we be grateful for the occasional glimpse at selected occasions?'

'Since I cannot be present at every single occasion, sir, I'm not quite sure how to answer that.'

'I think you know perfectly well what I mean. Does the advent of your uncle and his wealth mean that you will scuttle off to some new library and shun the Season as you have done hitherto?'

She thought for a moment. 'My attitude has changed,' she admitted. 'I know that before I was indeed always distancing myself from society, but this last year has made me see things differently. I'm truly looking forward to attending the opening of Waterloo Bridge, and I'm delighted to be going to the Parkstone summer ball.'

'I'm glad to hear it, for your previous attitude was a positive waste. You have a great deal to offer, Miss Wyndham, and your light should not be hidden under the proverbial bushel.'

'You have your complimentary hat on today, sir.'

'It must be the country air – and the excellent company.'

She studied him for moment. 'You haven't found me excellent company in the past, Sir Maxim.'

'Perhaps because you haven't *been* excellent company in the past.'

'Ah, now *that* sounds a little more like the real Sir Maxim Talgarth,' she replied with heavy irony.

He smiled. 'And *that* sounds like the real Miss Charlotte Wyndham.'

She smiled too. 'Leopards and spots, sir.'

'No doubt.'

She looked across the lake at the house, deciding to change the subject. 'What alterations do you intend to make? Nothing too drastic, I hope.'

'Hardly anything at all.'

She stared at him. 'But, you said. . . .'

'Perhaps I've changed my mind.'

105

'Oh.'

'Maybe the addition of a ballroom, but that's probably all now.'

'What made you change your mind?'

'Seeing your delight in being here once more. If you find it so perfect – and quite obviously you do – then, who am I to find fault with it?' He gazed at the house. 'I found it perfect in the past as well, that was why I was so anxious to possess it.'

She lowered her eyes quickly, reminded suddenly of what she had heard Sylvia tell Judith in Wyman's library. He was still looking at the house. 'Do you think a ballroom would put the finishing touch?'

'I suppose so, if you intend holding balls.'

'That would be the general idea,' he replied, his shrewd blue eyes swinging toward her as he detected the subtle change. 'Am I to take it that you think the addition of even a ballroom would amount to sacrilege?'

'No, of course not. I'm sure such a thing could only be an asset, especially when you have someone like Lady Judith to preside over things. She and I may loathe each other, but I have to acknowledge that she is a very accomplished hostess and will be ideal for. . . .'

'For what, Miss Wyndham? It can hardly have escaped even your notice that things are not exactly sweet between Lady Judith and myself; indeed things are nonexistent. Whatever may have been the case in the past is not the case now, and the, er, liaison is at an end.'

'It's none of my business, Sir Maxim.' A secret surge of gladness passed through her.

'No, it isn't, but you were the one to bring her name up, and in such a way as to require an explanatory answer. So, you see, Lady Judith will *not* be presiding over any future ball, masquerade, rout, or assembly here at Kimber Park. And please don't murmur empty words of condolence, for I know damned well that you're highly delighted.'

She flushed a little. 'I haven't any opinion on the matter, sir.'

'No? Well, you certainly have done in the past, and you've left me in no doubt about what you think.' He grinned suddenly. 'And you were right.'

She didn't know how to take him. One moment he was sarcastic and almost cutting, the next he seemed to be mocking himself.

His smile became a little more soft then. 'Have a sip of your wine, Miss Wyndham, you look a little ruffled.'

'Perhaps because I don't understand you.'

'No one understands me, least of all myself.'

'Then there's little hope for you, sir.'

'Do you understand yourself, Miss Wyndham?' he asked very softly. 'Or are there some things that defy explanation?'

The warm flush deepened a little on her cheeks. Yes, her love for him defied explanation. She couldn't help loving him, and that was something about herself which she didn't understand at all. . . .

His glance rested speculatively upon her. 'You seem almost ashamed of some dark secret, Miss Wyndham, but I cannot imagine you being guilty of anything shameful.'

Her cheeks were positively aflame now. 'There isn't any dark secret, sir.'

'If you say so, then of course I am mistaken,' he murmured, his eyes at once amused and thoughtful.

She felt hot and uncomfortable, fearing that at any moment he would realize the truth. She got up quickly. 'Shall – shall we walk awhile by the lake?'

'If you wish.' He got up too, pausing for a moment and then putting a hand on her arm and turning her toward him. 'If my conversation has embarrassed you. . . .'

'No, of course not.'

'You're an execrable liar, Charlotte Wyndham.'

'I haven't had much practice.'

He smiled a little. 'Maybe not, but your tongue is practiced enough in other directions.' He drew her hand through his arm and they walked slowly down the sloping grass toward the lake.

They strolled in silence for a while, and then she halted, taking a deep breath of the sweet air, perfumed by the fragrance of a nearby balsam tree. 'Oh, I do so love it here,' she whispered, half to herself.

'Then you must forgive me.'

'Forgive you?'

'For having what you have lost.'

Again intrusive memories passed over her, reminding her of what she'd heard said of him. Had her father's death really been an accident? Or had it been something more?

Suddenly he put his hand to her cheek, an intimate gesture that made her pulse quicken and sent her doubts spinning into confusion. 'What is it, Charlotte?' he asked softly. 'Why are you sometimes open and natural with me and then abruptly reserved and withdrawn?'

'Please. . . .'

'If I'm being too forward addressing you by your first name, then that is something else I shall have to trust I'm forgiven for, but I make no apology for overstepping any damned rule of propriety. I've seen today that you and I can get along very well, and yet you constantly step back. Why?'

She couldn't reply. His fingers seemed to set her skin on fire and her heart was thundering so much that she was sure he must hear it, or see its frantic throb in her breast.

'Why, Charlotte?' he repeated, his piercing gaze holding her eyes with a compulsion from which she couldn't break free.

His thumb moved softly against her cheek, and for a breathless moment that stopped her heart in its wild racing she thought he was about to kiss her. The dream was coming true . . . An intoxicating elation swept through her, but it was accompanied by a morsel of doubt. She broke away from his touch, her senses alive to everything about him, but alive too to the uncertainty within herself.

He still held her with his eyes, and she saw a cool awareness settling over him. 'Charlotte,' he said softly, 'there is only one question I will ask you now. Do you believe me when I say I'm innocent of everything evil of which I'm accused by certain people?'

She stared at him, her lips moving but no sound passing them.

'Do you believe me, Charlotte?' The coldness spread from his eyes to his voice.

'I don't know what to believe,' she said at last, her voice very low.

'Damn you,' he breathed, taking a quick, angry breath and half-turning from her. 'Damn you to hell and back, Miss Wyndham. I was indeed mistaken to think I saw anything in you. You're a hollow vessel, madam, a vacuum, and I was a fool to think you were anything more. I think it's long past time to call a halt to this farcical visit, don't you?' He turned on his heel and walked quickly back to the phaeton, where the startled groom began to hastily prepare the drowsing team.

She felt as if he had physically struck her. The day's spell was shattered, gone as irretrievably as wood smoke before the bitterest of winter winds. She was utterly shaken by the fullness of his fury and contempt, but she could not unsay what she had said. Slowly she followed him. Her heart felt as if it were breaking within her, but her face was a protective mask, shielding her from outward vulnerability. He could not read anything as he coldly assisted her onto the high seat and then climbed up beside her.

He drove back to the house at the same wild, breakneck speed with which he had set out for the ill-fated picnic, and the gravel scattered as he reined the sweating team in before the main portico. Grooms came hurrying from the stableyard, and he alighted quickly, peremptorily ordering that his traveling carriage be brought immediately, and Miss Wyndham's maid told to prepare to leave straightaway.

His hand was cold and unfeeling as he helped her to climb down from the phaeton, and he avoided her eyes, saying absolutely nothing as they waited the few minutes for the carriage to be brought around. Muriel came quickly from the direction of the kitchens, her bright glance fleeing from Max's angry face to Charlotte's.

The journey back to London was accomplished without a word passing between the three occupants of the carriage. To Charlotte it seemed that those ten miles of broad highway took a lifetime to pass, and all the time she kept her eyes averted, staring out at the lengthening shadows of the summer evening.

It was twilight when at last they reached Henrietta Street, and Muriel hurried from the carriage and into the house before Max had time to alight. He stood on the pavement, holding his hand out to Charlotte. She couldn't accept it, and stepped down without assistance. The utter misery of her breaking heart was still masked from him as she made to walk past into the house, but suddenly he caught her arm.

'I haven't finished with you yet, madam.'

'Please, let me go. There doesn't seem to be anything left to say.'

'But there is,' he replied icily. 'When first I met you, I thought that you needed teaching a lesson; indeed, I was determined to be the one to teach you, for your manners and general conduct left far too much to be desired. Then I had second thoughts and I wondered if I had misjudged you. Those second thoughts were extinguished today, madam. You're beneath contempt. You seem almost eager to give credence to all that you've been told about me, and you haven't the wit to think and judge for yourself. Very well, if that's how you wish to think of me, I'll act the part and really give you something to believe.' He pulled her roughly into his arms, his lips harsh over hers as he forced her to submit to a kiss that was almost brutal in its intensity. There was no gentleness in him. He pressed her body against his, caressing her as if she were naked in his arms, and all the time his lips moved over hers, hurting her, enticing her, drawing an unwilling response she was powerless to deny. The ferocity of the embrace aroused her, stirring a warm, rich ecstasy more potent than the dream that had first warned her of the truth about herself. She ceased to struggle, holding him close and giving herself to the kiss, but as she did so, he thrust her scornfully away. He gave a bitter, derisory laugh. 'Your dark secret isn't so secret now, is it, Miss Wyndham? Well, I wish you well of your upright, self-righteous falsehoods, for you are indeed worthy of them.'

She was frozen as he turned and climbed back into the carriage, the door slamming behind him. It was as if she had been on fire but was now plunged into ice. Numb and dazed by the cruelty of his actions, she turned slowly to go into the house.

13

Mrs white opened the door to her. 'Why, Miss Charlotte, I didn't think you'd be home first.'

'First?' Charlotte struggled to compose herself.

'Yes. Mrs Wyndham and Mr Pagett have accompanied Admiral Parkstone to the theater.'

'Oh.'

The cook looked curiously at her pale face. 'Is something wrong, Miss Charlotte?'

'No. No, everything's quite all right.'

'Would you care for some refreshment? Some hot chocolate perhaps?'

'Thank you.'

'I'll see to it immediately.'

At that moment there was an urgent knocking at the door behind them. Charlotte turned quickly, hope leaping into her heart. Was it Max? Had he relented? But as the cook hurried to open it, the hope died away as she saw Sylvia standing there.

Mrs White beamed. 'Why, Miss Parkstone, you must be feeling better. Do come in, Miss Charlotte is at home.'

'I know.' Sylvia came in, clutching her shawl around her. She was wearing a flimsy silk gown and looked a little flustered, as if she had hurried all the way from Cavendish Square.

Mrs White glanced uncertainly at her, for her face was as pale as Charlotte's. 'Shall – shall I bring chocolate for two, Miss Charlotte?'

'If you please,' replied Charlotte, going through into the

candlelit drawing room.

Sylvia followed her, carefully closing the door so that they were quite alone. 'Did you enjoy your day?' There was a noticeable edge to her voice.

'Enjoy it?' Charlotte hesitated. 'No.'

'You do surprise me. You seemed to be enjoying things well enough when I looked out and saw Max taking his leave of you.'

Charlotte lowered her glance. 'Oh.'

'Such a passionate embrace, and in so public a place.'

'It wasn't what it may have seemed.'

'No?'

'No.'

'So you were only going to see Kimber Park again, were you? Well, it's quite obvious that the day became something more than that, isn't it?'

Charlotte turned quickly away. Was this genuine concern on Sylvia's part? Or was it something much more. . . ? 'Please, Sylvia, I feel miserable enough without you adding to it.'

'Miserable? That wasn't how you seemed to me.'

'No, I don't suppose I did.' Charlotte's voice was empty. 'As I said before, it wasn't what it seemed.'

'What was it, then?'

'I was being taught a very salutary lesson, one I will never forget.'

Sylvia looked a little puzzled. 'I don't understand.'

'1 learned the lesson that although I love Max Talgarth with all my heart, he feels nothing but contempt for me.'

Sylvia recoiled. 'You – you *love* him? You can't mean it.' Her face became even more pale.

'I only wish I didn't.'

'Charlotte, you mustn't! You can't love him, he ruined your father.'

'Please. . . .'

'Didn't you hear what I said? He ruined your father.'

'If you're going to say again about the horse. . . .'

'No. Your father wasn't only in debt to moneylenders, Charlotte, he owed a vast amount to Max as well, and Max was pressing for payment.'

Charlotte stared at her then. 'What do you mean?' she asked.

Sylvia took a piece of folded paper from her reticule. 'Look at this.'

As Charlotte took it, she immediately recognized her father's writing. It was an IOU, dated January 22, 1816, only a few months before his death. '*Mr George Wyndham owes Sir Maxim Talgarth the sum of twenty-five thousand guineas, and promises to pay within one calendar month.*' Her heart became suddenly cold within her, and her doubts about Sylvia's motives died. Sylvia was driven now by concern, not jealousy.

Sylvia watched her. 'Within one calendar month, Charlotte, and that can only mean that Max was pressing him.'

'How did you come by this, Sylvia?'

'Does it matter? What matters is that you now believe once and for all in Max's guilt.'

'Have you known about this for long?'

Sylvia avoided her eyes. 'No, not long.'

'Where did it come from?'

'I'd rather not say. Suffice it that it exists and isn't a forgery.'

Charlotte nodded. 'Yes. I know.'

'I've already accused Max of having deliberately caused your father's death through that horse, but now I think he's guilty of much more. I believe he deliberately set out to ruin your father, because he wanted Kimber Park and your father wouldn't sell. He ruined him and then brought about his death, leaving your mother no choice but to sell the estate. Max then made an offer he knew she wouldn't be in any position to refuse, and so he succeeded in getting what he wanted. Maybe it's farfetched, but I think it's the truth. You must see it, Charlotte; for your own sake you must. He's master of Kimber Park, don't let him be your master too.'

The IOU fell from Charlotte's fingers as she turned away. 'My master? Oh, I don't think that that will ever arise, Sylvia. I told you, he despises me.'

'What happened?'

'I don't want to talk about it.'

Sylvia looked closely at her. 'You still love him, don't you? Nothing I've shown you has changed that.'

'Yes, I still love him.'

'But how can you, after reading this?' Sylvia retrieved the IOU from the floor.

Tears sprang to Charlotte's eyes. 'There are some things,' she whispered, 'that defy explanation.' She could see Max again, lounging back looking at her as they sat on the grass in the shadow of the rotunda.

'You mustn't have anything more to do with him, Charlotte.'

'I know. My common sense is in complete agreement with you, Sylvia, it is my heart that betrays me constantly. But whatever my foolish heart wishes, he's made it perfectly clear he has no desire to even see me again, so I don't think there is any need for warnings.'

'He shouldn't be allowed to get away with what he's done, Charlotte.'

'Maybe not, but there isn't a great deal I can do about it, is there?'

'You can hurt him.'

Charlotte looked quickly at her. 'Hurt him? Sylvia, there's absolutely nothing I can do, or wish to do. I don't want to hurt him, I love him,' she finished, taking out her handkerchief and beginning to wipe away her tears as she heard the admiral's carriage arriving outside.

'You're wrong when you say there's nothing you can do,' said Sylvia. There was a strange note in her voice.

'I don't know what you're talking about, Sylvia. I only know that I don't intend to do anything. I just want to forget him, and that will be impossible enough without anything else.'

Sylvia lowered her eyes. 'That is up to you, but . . .' She said no more for at that moment the drawing-room door opened and the

115

others came in.

'My dears, we've had an absolutely splendid evening,' cried Mrs Wyndham. 'I don't remember enjoying the theater so much before. So many people came to the box to pay their respects.' The tall plumes in her hair bounced and trembled as she sat down.

Charlotte whispered quickly to Sylvia. 'Please don't say anything to them, my mother would only be distressed.'

Sylvia nodded.

Both the admiral and Richard were dressed very formally and looked very dashing. In spite of her unhappiness, Charlotte couldn't help thinking how well such attire became Richard, and she hoped that Sylvia would think so too.

Richard's face lit up as he saw Sylvia, and he quickly crossed the room to take her hand. 'I'm delighted to see that you're better now.'

She was still a little distracted from her conversation with Charlotte. 'Better?'

He was puzzled. 'Why, yes, your headache. That was why you couldn't come to the theater with us.'

'Oh yes. I'm quite well now. I was at the window and saw Charlotte returning, so I came to see her.'

He turned to Charlotte then. 'Ah, yes. Kimber Park. And how did it go?'

'Well enough.'

'Is that all you have to say?'

'There isn't much else to say.'

He looked in her gray eyes, so like his own. 'Isn't there?' he asked thoughtfully.

'No.'

Before he could say anything more, Sylvia drew his attention away. 'We haven't made final arrangements for the day after tomorrow.'

Mrs Wyndham looked up quickly. 'Dear me, so we haven't.'

Richard gave a rather self-conscious laugh. 'Forgive me if I'm being particularly dense, but what is happening the day after tomorrow?'

His sister tutted a little crossly. 'Shame on you, it's the grand opening of the bridge.'

'Oh, yes, it had quite slipped my mind.' He glanced at Charlotte again but didn't say anything more, for Mrs White brought the chocolate tray, laden now with five cups.

Charlotte endured another hour of conversation before at last Sylvia and her father departed. For a moment Charlotte feared that Richard was about to press her again about her visit to Kimber Park, but then his sister asked him to go up to her bedroom door with her and so Charlotte remained deliberately behind, knowing that in a moment he would be asked to sit with her mother while Muriel unpinned and brushed and plaited her hair for the night. She listened, and sure enough, he had to go in and talk all over again about the theater.

Mrs White came to clear away the chocolate tray, and at last Charlotte went softly up to her room, tiptoeing past her mother's door. She undressed in darkness, knowing that if Richard saw a light under her door, he would be bound to speak to her again.

She lay in the bed, listening to the voices in the adjoining room. After a while Richard left his sister. He paused outside his niece's door and then tapped softly. Charlotte didn't reply and a moment later he went on to his own room.

The house was suddenly quiet. The shadows across the ceiling from the streetlamps seemed strangely oblique as she stared up at them, and when the watch went past calling the hour, his voice seemed harsh and almost alien. Nothing seemed right tonight, because nothing *was* right. Her happiness, resting so very tenuously upon Max Talgarth's smile and charm, had been dashed to the ground by his anger and loathing. She turned away from the shadows then, burying her face in her pillow as she wept.

14

BEFORE NOON ON WATERLOO Day, the eighteenth of June, huge crowds had gathered on the banks of the Thames for the opening of the new bridge. Every possible vantage place had been taken, and the murmur and laughter of so many people seemed to fill the air like the drone of a colossal beehive. There was a fair on one shore, with swingboats, wheels of fortune, booths of all description, and many other amusements and diversions associated with such events. On the river itself bobbed an armada of barges, wherries, pleasure boats, and countless other small craft, their bunting flapping gaily in the summer breeze. The new bridge was decked with flags and streamers, and a military band was playing, the brisk martial music vying with the noise of the crowds and the fair.

Admiral Parkstone's private barge was a very elegant vessel, its high prow graced by a figurehead of mermaid with long flowing hair. There were cushioned seats amidships, shaded by a very fine blue-and-white-striped canopy; very few craft could claim to be superior, although many were larger. As became so distinguished a naval officer, the admiral took command himself, taking up his position at the stern and maneuvering her to an excellent place close to the bridge. From here his small party of guests would be able to view the entire proceedings, from the very first moment the royal barge appeared from the direction of Whitehall.

Richard stood beside the admiral, having earned that

gentleman's praise by proving a more than. adequate sailor himself after learning a great deal during his years in America. Wearing a gray coat and white trousers, the unstarched folds of his large neckcloth lifting now and then in the breeze sweeping upriver from the distant sea, he glanced frequently at the seats beneath the canopy, where Sylvia and Mrs Wyndham sat talking together.

Mrs Wyndham had been much gratified by the number of people who now acknowledged her once more, news of her wealthy brother's return having quickly spread throughout society. She was delighted to have already received several noteworthy invitations, especially one from the Duke of Devonshire. So pleased was she with the way the day had gone so far that she had quite forgotten her much-dreaded inclination toward *mal de mer*, indeed, it hadn't even crossed her mind. Wearing sky blue, which became her plump rosiness very well, she was enjoying her interesting conversation with Sylvia, who was dressed in pure white and looked very beautiful indeed. They were discussing the forthcoming ball, a subject that was causing Sylvia a great deal of difficulty because it seemed that every arrangement she made was destined to fall through in one way or another. Gunter's, the fashionable caterers of Berkeley Square, had that very morning informed her that they couldn't provide precisely the menu she had requested, and barely an hour after that she had learned that the orchestra she wished to engage was not available on that particular day.

It really was too much, she declared with great feeling to a sympathetic Mrs Wyndham, and there were times when she wished the annual Parkstone ball had never been thought of.

Charlotte sat apart from them, lounging on comfortable cushions at the prow. She had no wish to be drawn into their conversation and so sat slightly turned away from them, gazing out across the water, her thoughts elsewhere. She wore a lilac silk gown and a white pelisse handsomely adorned with military frogging, so very appropriate for Waterloo Day. Her hat was trimmed with tassels and braid, and there was even dainty braiding on her gloves; she could not have been more fashionable or exquisitely turned out, but she took no pleasure from knowing this; she was too miserable on account of Max Talgarth.

She and Sylvia had not spoken again on the subject of the IOU, or indeed about anything else connected with Max. It was as if there was some tacit agreement not to raise the subject again. Outwardly they seemed as friendly and close as before, but Charlotte knew that her confessed love for Max had alienated Sylvia, whose own confessed loathing for him placed her on the other side of an invisible line. Charlotte was saddened by the situation, but she couldn't lie about her feelings; she had to be honest. She wished to be honest with Richard too, but knew that in this instance it would be wiser not to be, for he might feel honor bound to confront Max, and so she had been avoiding him or, when cornered, had so far managed to avert his questions. He had tactfully declined to press her too much, but she knew that he was very concerned about the quiet, withdrawn mood that had overtaken her since the visit to Kimber Park.

She was just beginning to wonder when the official ceremony would begin when there was a momentary hush as a detachment of Horse Guards arrived to take up positions on the bridge. It was three o'clock precisely, and a salute of cannon announced the approach of the royal party. There were two-hundred-and-two guns, in honor of the number taken at the Battle of Waterloo, and as the booms rang out over the river, a flotilla of barges, headed by the royal barge itself, appeared in the distance. The spectators began to cheer, the cheers becoming louder and louder as the crimson-and-scarlet royal barge slid beneath the center arch of the bridge and landed on the Surrey bank. The Prince Regent alighted, accompanied by his brother, the Duke of York, and by the hero of Waterloo himself, the lean, angular Duke of Wellington. The prince was very fat and had been tightly corseted into a flamboyant uniform he had designed himself. He was hardly an inspiring figure, nor was his equally rotund brother, and the cheers of the crowd were directed at the Duke of Wellington, who alone of the three was not acknowledging the adulation.

To the accompaniment of the military band, the royal party took their place at the head of the procession that had formed in readiness, and then they proceeded across the bridge to the Middlesex side, followed by a train of noblemen, gentlemen, ministers, and members of both houses of Parliament.

The pomp and ceremony continued for some time before the royal party reembarked to sail back to Whitehall. The official side of things over, the crowds remained to enjoy the day, and the armada of little boats still bobbed on the water as the tide began to turn. The change in the river made the admiral's barge sway a little more than before, and Mrs Wyndham suddenly felt decidedly unwell. The admiral, most concerned and anxious, immediately brought the vessel to the shore, assisting her quickly onto the steadiness of dry land, where he led her to a bench.

As Charlotte prepared to step ashore, something made her turn to look back at the river. A very large barge was anchored close to the bank, and on it there were many elegant guests. It was the Earl of Barstow's private vessel, and Charlotte found herself looking straight into Judith's cold green eyes. Wearing a vibrant yellow gown, the matching ribbons of her straw bonnet fluttering loose in the breeze, she stood by the railing watching the small party alighting from the Parkstone barge. For a long moment the two women looked at each other, then Judith turned slowly away and mingled with her father's guests. Charlotte glanced at the gathering, but there was no sign of Max. Then Richard spoke to her and she turned quickly toward him.

He smiled. 'Are you going to hover there for the rest of the afternoon, or are you going to take pity on the aching arm I've been holding out to you for the past minute or more?'

'Oh, I'm sorry, I was just thinking.'

'So I noticed.' His fingers closed around hers as he assisted her onto the bank. 'Charlotte, you'd tell me if there was something very wrong, wouldn't you?'

'There's nothing wrong.'

'Don't fib. I've been watching you since you came back from your day at Kimber Park, and I can tell that all is far from well. Is it something to do with Talgarth?'

'No,' she said quickly. 'Truly, Richard, there's no need to worry.'

'Did he. . . ?'

'No! Please, Richard, don't worry about me, I'm perfectly all right.'

He studied her. 'Well,' he said wryly, 'if this is how you are when you're perfectly all right, I'd hate to see you when things aren't going well.'

He said nothing more, escorting her to the bench where her mother was still looking a little pale.

Charlotte took her hand. 'How are you feeling now?'

'A little better. Oh, dear, how foolish I feel, losing my sea legs on a day as calm as this, and I was doing so well too. I do hope I haven't ruined things for everyone.'

'Of course you haven't,' replied Charlotte, smiling.

The admiral was anxious to reassure her as well. 'We've all had more than enough of water for one day,' he said, 'and that's the truth, even from this old naval man.'

Mrs Wyndham smiled up at him. 'You're being kind to me, Henry.' She looked past him then as a face in the crowd caught her attention. 'Isn't that Sir Maxim over there? Yes, I'm sure it is. Oh, I do believe he's going to speak to us.'

Charlotte's heart seemed to miss a beat. He was walking toward them. He wore a maroon coat, brown waistcoat, and fawn trousers, and a dark, silver-handled cane swung gently in his hand. She stared at him, unable to believe he was going to have the effrontery to speak. After all he'd done, he was surely not going to utter empty civilities! But then, why not? He'd spoken before and couldn't know his dark deeds had been uncovered.

Sylvia glanced at Charlotte's suddenly still face and then turned quickly to Richard, asking him to accompany her to find a glass of water for his sister. They'd gone when Max reached the bench and bowed to Mrs Wyndham and the admiral, subtly contriving to completely exclude Charlotte from the greeting. 'Good afternoon. I trust you are enjoying the occasion.'

Mrs Wyndham, who hadn't noticed her daughter's recent odd mood, smiled at him. 'Good afternoon, Sir Maxim. Yes, we have indeed been enjoying the day; at least, we were until I disgraced myself by feeling seasick.'

'That is surely not a disgrace, madam, since Lord Nelson himself suffered greatly from the same indisposition.'

Charlotte watched him. How cool and gallant he was, so polished and agreeable . . . and so false. He was so believable that it was hard to remember that he was addressing the widow of a man he'd deliberately set out to ruin.

The admiral, meanwhile, was all smiles at seeing his former son-in-law again. 'Max, my boy, it's good to clap eyes on you again. How's life treating you these days?'

'Life?' Max's glance moved fleetingly toward Charlotte's stony face. 'It's treating me tolerably well, I suppose.'

'No more duels in the offing, I trust?'

'I sincerely hope not.'

Mrs Wyndham sat forward a little. 'Sir Maxim, how are you liking it at Kimber Park?'

'I like it very much indeed, Mrs Wyndham. It is indeed the most beautiful estate in the realm.'

Charlotte couldn't endure it anymore and turned angrily away, afraid that the outrage she felt would spill over into words.

Max saw her action. His eyes darkened a little and he turned suddenly to Mrs Wyndham. 'Madam, would it be possible for me to speak with Miss Wyndham?'

'Why, of course,' replied Mrs Wyndham. 'Charlotte?'

Charlotte had no option but to turn back and face him again. She forced a stiff smile to her unwilling lips. 'You wish to speak to me, sir? I cannot imagine why.'

His smile was equally frozen as he offered her his arm, speaking in such a low tone that only she could hear him. 'Don't conduct yourself with such a bad grace, Miss Wyndham. You're supposed to know how to go on in society.'

She was furious, but still managed to conceal it from the others as she put her hand over his sleeve and walked a little way along the embankment with him. The moment they were out of earshot, however, she turned coldly toward him. 'As I said, sir, I cannot imagine why you wish to speak with me, for I have absolutely nothing I wish to say to you.'

'No? You do surprise me, for looking at you right now I'd say there was a great deal you seem to wish to say to me. '

'I don't want to waste my breath on you, sirrah, for you're not worth the effort.'

'No, but I'm worth your fury, it seems. One kiss would appear to have had a diabolical effect upon your temper.'

'Your kiss was eminently forgettable, sir, so don't flatter yourself that my temper now is due to its effects.'

'Then, what exactly is it due to? Surely you aren't still listening to silly whispers?'

'No,' she breathed, 'this time it's much more serious than mere whispers, sir. This time I've seen proof of your misdeeds.'

A cold veil slid across his eyes. 'Have you, indeed?' he said softly. 'Are you going to elaborate upon that statement?'

'Do I really need to? Surely you aren't still acting the outraged innocent?'

'Have a care, Miss Wyndham, for we may be in a public place but I will not put up with endless insult at your caprice. Either explain yourself or have the courtesy to keep a civil tongue in your head, and in future conduct yourself with some semblance of refinement.'

'Considering what I now know of you, sir, I feel that today I've acquitted myself with admirable restraint and decorum, for if I was a man I'd—'

'Yes?' he interrupted in a voice that was dangerously soft. 'What, exactly, would you then do, Miss Wyndham?'

'I'd call you out,' she whispered.

'Indeed? And no doubt your fate would be the same as my previous opponents: you'd either be dead or steeped in ridicule. Now, then, madam, I'm still waiting for your explanation. What do you now think you know about me?'

She raised her chin defiantly. 'You ruined my father, Sir Maxim, you ruined him so that you could force him to sell Kimber Park to you. That didn't succeed, so you resorted to other foul means to dispose of him. I despise you, sirrah, I despise you with every fiber of my being. You had the gall to tell me I was beneath your contempt; well, you're so far beneath mine that I would gladly tread on you for the loathsome insect that you are.'

Close to tears and trembling still with fury and emotion, she turned on her heel and walked away. She struggled to compose herself as she returned to the bench where Sylvia and Richard had rejoined the others. She managed a smile, brushing aside their curiosity about the purpose of the interview by saying that Max had merely been inquiring if a scarf found at Kimber Park was hers. To her relief, at that moment the band on the bridge began to play again and attention was diverted. She took a deep breath to steady herself, for she was still trembling like a leaf, conflicting emotions tumbling through her in bewildering succession. She had told him she despised him, and she knew that that was what she should do, but in the very depths of her heart she knew she still loved him. What did he have to do before she was released from his spell? Why, oh, why, did her heart have to rule her head, and her conscience?

125

15

IT WAS PROPOSED THAT they all go to the Clarendon Hotel that evening for a French dinner, but Charlotte cried off, knowing that in her present mood she would almost certainly be a blight on the proceedings. The house was very quiet after they'd gone, for both Mrs White and Polly had the evening off. After a while the quietness became almost oppressive, for it allowed too many unwelcome thoughts to intrude, and so as it was a very fine evening, she decided to go for a walk.

Regent's Park was very lovely in such weather, and a great many people were to be seen strolling along the paths and among the trees. There were long shadows across the grass when at last she turned back again, and the sun was sinking beyond the groves in a blaze of glorious crimson and gold that was reflected like molten gold in the waters of the lake.

She paused at the entrance of the park to look back again at the sunset, and so didn't notice the carriage that had been waiting at the curb nearby for some considerable time now. Its blinds were down as it moved slowly forward toward where she stood, and as it halted almost alongside, there was a commotion nearby. A young blood driving a curricle far too fast around the curve of Park Crescent clipped the wheel against a bollard and was flung into the road as the vehicle toppled over. Thus everyone's attention was diverted from Charlotte as the door of the mysterious carriage opened and a gentleman stepped silently down. No one saw as he came up stealthily behind her, putting a hand over her mouth and dragging her back to the carriage. It was over in seconds. He thrust her inside and climbed quickly behind her, slamming the door. The coach immediately drove off, the team's hooves clattering on the cobbles as they were brought quickly up to a very smart pace, entering Regent Street and mingling anonymously with the traffic that constantly thronged the fashionable thoroughfare.

Dazed, frightened, and too shocked to scream for help, she lay motionless where she had fallen on the seat. It was so dark inside that her captor was only a shadowy shape as he sat opposite. He didn't say anything, and for a moment the noise of the carriage seemed very loud. Trembling and afraid, she sat slowly up, pushing a stray curl back beneath her bonnet. 'Who – who are you?' she asked at last, still unable to see who her abductor was. 'Why are you doing this?'

He held a blind aside so that the fading evening light fell across his face, revealing the scar on his cheek and the streak of gray in his hair.

She stared at him. 'You!'

'The same.' His hand dropped from the blind, and darkness returned.

'How *dare* you do this!'

'I thought it necessary, if disagreeable, to talk with you again, and when I saw you walking in the park, I decided this was the only way to achieve the desired result, since I doubt very much if you would have come willingly.'

'Come? Come where?' she asked quickly.

'To my apartment at the Albany.'

'I have no intention of submitting to this treatment,' she breathed, 'and I'm certainly not going there with you. Other women may be amenable to your every whim, sirrah, but I certainly am not!'

'The thought of you submitting to my every whim is extremely pleasant, but unfortunately this doesn't happen to be a mere whim. And if you fear for your virtue, let me assure you that I still have no designs upon it.' He glanced away then. 'Beautiful as your face and no doubt your body are, it so happens that right now I'm more interested in your mind.'

'I don't understand.'

'You're an extremely exasperating woman, Miss Wyndham, and I really don't know why I bother with you, but it so happens that your accusations today were far too momentous for me to even begin to ignore. I'm going to prove to you that I did not ruin your father.'

'I've already seen proof that you did.'

'What did you see? An IOU? Ah, I see from your reaction that that is precisely it. You've misunderstood the significance of that little piece of paper, madam, as you'll know well enough before much longer. I leave for Chatsworth in the morning, and I don't wish to leave knowing that you are still under dangerous illusions to which you are only too likely to give voice. I've been accused of many things, Miss Wyndham, but never *ever* of ruining a friend, or indeed of ruining anyone.'

'How very righteous you are suddenly! You've evidently quite put your poor wife from your mind.'

Even in the darkness she saw the anger leap into his eyes. 'And what would you know of that?' he asked softly.

'Enough.'

'You know absolutely nothing,' he snapped.

'I've been told—'

'Damn what you've been told. Were you there? Did you witness what passed between Anne and myself? No, you weren't. You know as little as my sister-in-law, who has presumed to set herself up as judge, jury, and executioner. She didn't know her sister at all, Miss Wyndham, and if she had, she would have come to dislike her as much as I did.'

Charlotte stared at him, but he looked away again, holding the blind aside to see where they were. The carriage had left Regent Street behind now and was driving west along Piccadilly.

The great house known simply as Albany, had once been Melbourne House, and had then become the home of the Duke of York and Albany, from whose title it took its present name. Turned into exclusive apartments for single gentlemen, it was a very sought-after address, and rooms were seldom vacant for long. The house, built of brown brick with stone dressings, was approached through a courtyard, the entrance of which was set between elegant shops in the French style. Eagles supported the balconies of the windows above the shop fronts, and a watchman's box by the opening into the courtyard saw to it that undesirable persons were kept out of this expensive, superior retreat.

The carriage echoed in the courtyard as it came to a standstill before the main door, and as Max flung open the door to alight, the dim evening light seemed almost bright. He turned to look at her. 'The truth awaits you, Miss Wyndham, if you dare to face it. Shall we go in?' There was a mocking smile on his lips as he held out his hand to her.

She ignored the hand, gathering her skirts and stepping down into an area that was strangely quiet considering the noise and bustle of Piccadilly only a few yards away. She walked past him and into the great house.

His apartment lay at the rear of the building, overlooking the famous covered walk that led north into Vigo Street. A very discreet manservant opened the door to them and then silently withdrew, leaving them alone. The rooms were gracious and furnished with impeccable taste. In the drawing room huge marble-topped console tables were built against the wall on either side of the gilded fireplace, and above them were mirrors framed by garlands of fruit and flowers carved most exquisitely by the finest craftsmen. Before the fireplace there was an arrangement of four chairs and two sofas, all upholstered in gray-blue velvet, and the same color was echoed in the niches in the otherwise clear cream walls. There were paintings and beautiful porcelain figurines, and a priceless collection of jade ornaments in a tall display cabinet. The only sound came from the elegant long-case clock standing in the corner. As Charlotte took a seat, it chimed nine o'clock.

Max went to a fine desk decorated with intricate inlaid work, unlocked it, and took out a letter, its seal broken. He held it out to her. 'My loving sister-in-law missed this when she was searching. It's from your father.'

Charlotte's eyes widened. 'Are you suggesting that Sylvia—'

'Broke in here to search my property? Yes, Miss Wyndham, I'm rather afraid that I am. She *was* the one who showed you that IOU, wasn't she?'

'Yes.' What point was there in denying it?

'It disappeared from here the day you and I went to Kimber Park, and my manservant reported seeing a lady answering Sylvia's description hurrying away that evening along the covered walk.'

Charlotte looked away. That was the day Sylvia had had a 'headache' that prevented her from going to the theater. . . .

'Please read the letter, Miss Wyndham.'

As she began to unfold the piece of paper, he went to the fireplace, standing with his back toward her. He leaned one hand on the mantelpiece and rested a foot on the gleaming fender. Silence fell, broken only by the gentle ticking of the clock.

A pang of sorrow passed over her as she gazed at the familiar, untidy scrawl his long-suffering correspondents had likened to the meanderings of a spider that had been unfortunate enough to fall in the inkwell.

My dear Talgarth,
    You cannot imagine with what relief – and with what deep affection – I received your letter, the letter of a true friend and gentleman. It is because I recognize in your actions the

concern of a friend that I will accept the returned IOUs, especially as I know that to refuse would cause you deep offense. But know this, there will come a day some time in the future when I will repay your kindness, for I know how deeply I am in your debt. No, my friend, I cannot brush my obligations aside, even in the face of your express command that I do so. Would that I had not allowed myself to fall into such a hopeless position, but I have, and now my burden has been considerably eased by your exceedingly thoughtful actions. I value your friendship, Talgarth, and trust that one day I might have the opportunity to prove worthy of it. I wish only that others appreciated your qualities as much as I do, for you are sadly misrepresented.

I am, sir, your grateful and loving friend,

George Wyndham

Charlotte's hands shook as she slowly folded the letter again. She felt utterly dreadful. 'It – it seems I owe you an apology, Sir Maxim.'

He turned with a derisive laugh. 'Is that the best you can manage? You were much more liberal and forthcoming with your accusations.'

Her cheeks were hot with shame. 'Forgive me, I—'

'No, madam, I will *not* forgive you, for the simple reason that you don't merit it.'

'I thought . . . believed—'

'Yes, you did, didn't you? You *much* preferred Sylvia Parkstone's jaundiced view of me, even though her own father doesn't support her, and I've little doubt that you'll see fit to do the same thing all over again. That IOU was overlooked when I sent the others back; it had fallen to the back of the drawer and was only found a short while ago, and that is the only reason it was still in my possession. I don't know why I just left it in the drawer when I rediscovered it, but I did, and you may believe, Miss Wyndham, that I heartily wish

131

I'd burned the damned thing the moment it resurfaced. So, that disposes of the matter of the IOU, but there are other things of equal importance, aren't there? I'll warrant you still believe I murdered my wife, for that's surely Sylvia's most favorite crusade of all, the one she rides into battle over time after tedious time until I do indeed sometimes have murder on my mind – hers! Well, I didn't murder Anne, Miss Wyndham, even though I quite openly admit that I wished myself free of her. She was an unreasonable, jealous woman, accusing me of bedding every maid in the house, and nearly every maid in everyone else's house as well. She was convinced that I kept mistresses, when I didn't. Judith came very late on the scene; indeed, she didn't become my mistress until after Anne's death, and she isn't my mistress anymore, no matter how much she may pretend otherwise to the world.' He looked away for a moment. 'I endured a great deal from my wife, Miss Wyndham, and although I loved her when I married her, by the time of her death I virtually loathed her.'

'And yet you gave her a horse and gig?'

He gave a faint smile. 'It was her birthday and I thought perhaps . . . I thought perhaps a conciliatory gesture might melt a little of the ice. It didn't. She accused me of giving it to salve my conscience because I'd slept with another woman the night before. I tried to feel compassion for her, because surely such jealousy is as much an ailment as the ague, but where people recover from the ague, Anne simply remained entrenched in her suspicion and mistrust. A man would need to have the patience of a saint to withstand such endless, unreasonable resentment, grudge-bearing, and imagined grievances and I most certainly cannot claim to be a saint.' Again the faint, wry smile touched his lips. 'I realize that this version of events is far less exciting and titillating than my sister-in-law's, but like my side of the Westington duel, it happens to be the truth. Miss Wyndham, I trust I don't have to remind you that events at the duel vindicated me completely.'

132

Her voice was very small. 'I believe you, Sir Maxim.'

'Do you? Oh, how magnanimous.' He sketched a scornful bow.

She got up a little agitatedly then. 'I can understand your anger, and I know I deserve your sarcasm and derision, but I don't deserve to be spoken to so very harshly when I've admitted to being in the wrong and have asked you to forgive me.' She was struggling to keep her voice level, for she was close to tears.

'But such an empty admission isn't enough, for there are still things I know damned well you doubt. The horse your father won from me, for instance. Well? Do you still wonder if I lost it to him in the hope that it would kill him? Look at the letter again, Miss Wyndham. There's a postscript you haven't read yet.'

She opened the letter again. The postscript had been hastily written on the back.

P.S. Be warned, dear boy, that friendship is one thing, the acquisition of your damned unmanageable nag quite another. Foul-tempered and unridable it might be, but I'll win it from you yet. GW

She looked at him. 'What do you want me to say?'

'Oh, I don't exactly want my pound of flesh; I just want to know beyond any doubt whatsoever that you know the truth, and that means the truth about everything. We'll begin with Kimber Park. I admit to having on more than one occasion offered your father a handsome price for it, but he refused – not because he was inordinately attached to the place himself, but because he said you and your mother were and he could not bring himself to sell it, knowing how deeply upset you would be. That I acquired the property in the end doesn't stand in any doubt, but nor is there any doubt that I offered a very sound bargain indeed, leaving you with enough to purchase another small property and to provide you with an allowance upon which to live. I'm not according myself any laurels, Miss Wyndham, I'm just stating the facts. So, we've covered the subject of your father's debts and death, of my designs upon Kimber Park, and of my parody of a marriage. What's left? Ah, yes, the duels, for there I am undoubtedly responsible for the deaths of others. I've fought four duels in all, Miss Wyndham, resulting in four victories – or three deaths and a considerable humiliation, depending upon which way you look at it. The Westington farce you know already; the others are perhaps not so well-known to you. My first opponent accused me of cheating at cards. Someone was cheating that night at Brooks's, but it most certainly wasn't me, and when he repeated his accusation, I had to defend my honor by calling him out. As he was an excellent shot, I had to be accurate or pay the ultimate price myself. The second man accused me of seducing his daughters – all three of them, would you believe? A busy and virile fellow I might be, Miss Wyndham, but I'm not a fool, and only a fool would attempt to meddle with three very jealous sisters who were always trying to outdo one another. They stuck together in their story of vile seduction, until one of them saw how neatly she could demolish her sisters' reputation by admitting the truth, that I hadn't seduced any of them. By then it was too late, the duel had been fought and their father lay dying of a septic wound.'

He paused for a moment, his eyes lowered. 'The third duel,' he went on, 'resulted in the death of a former friend; he accused me of spreading malicious rumors concerning his financial affairs, rumors that resulted in the bankrupting of two of his business ventures. How the stories got about I've no idea; I only know that I wasn't the perpetrator. He was quite distraught, however, forcing me into a duel, which was the last thing he needed with all his other problems. He gave me no choice but to kill him, for he fired once and prepared immediately to fire again, and as he'd nearly disposed of me with the first shot, hence the scar on my cheek, I wasn't about to be a sitting target the second time. It was kill or be killed, Miss Wyndham, and I'm as eager to continue in this world as the next man. So there you have it, the true story of

Max Talgarth, or is there perhaps something still niggling away at your righteous little conscience?' His blue eyes rested coldly on her.

She shook her head. 'No.' Her voice was barely audible, she felt so wretched.

'Are you quite sure?' he taunted. 'You have a horrid suspicion that I'm planning to assist Bonaparte to escape from Saint Helena? Or that I have designs upon the crown jewels? Maybe it's that I'm really Princess Charlotte's lover and that I'm not really going to Chatsworth at all tomorrow but am going to a secret rendezvous with her instead?'

'Stop it! Oh, please, stop it!' Tears were visible in her eyes now. 'I believe everything you've told me, and I'm deeply ashamed of having doubted you so much. I'm sorry for everything I've said to you, Sir Maxim; I'm truly sorry and I really don't know what else I can say.' She tried to blink the tears away, but they welled hotly from her eyes.

Her distress seemed to take him by surprise. Then he closed his eyes for a moment and stood motionless with his head bowed. The silence hung; then he came to her, taking a handkerchief from his pocket and gently wiping her tears away. 'There is one thing you can say,' he said softly, holding her gaze, 'and that is that you forgive me.'

'F-forgive you? But—'

'No buts. I've behaved monstrously again and I know it.'

'I shouldn't have accused you as I did,' she whispered, acutely aware of the touch of his hand against her cheek.

He smiled a little, his thumb moving softly over her skin. 'You didn't deserve such treatment, nor did you deserve all that happened at Kimber Park that day; it was my fault, not yours. I behaved badly when Judith arrived, dispatching you to the garden and then not offering you anything by way of explanation, and my subsequent behavior at the picnic left a great deal to be desired. You've managed to get under my skin, Charlotte Wyndham.

135

You've a way of looking at me sometimes that plays havoc with my equilibrium, for you seem able at a glance to dispose of any claim I might have had to sangfroid. I've tried to ignore your existence; indeed, for almost a year I did my damnedest to keep you at a safe distance, but it was impossible to forget you or put you from my thoughts. You've come to mean too much to me, Charlotte, and that's why it's so very important to me that you, of all people, believe in the truth about me.'

The air seemed suddenly very still, almost muffled. She could no longer hear the clock or the distant music of a pianoforte drifting in from the darkness outside. The wild beating of her own heart seemed the only sound as she stared at him. 'Wh-what are you telling me?' she asked hesitantly, conscious of every gentle movement of his caressing thumb, of the warmth that darkened his eyes now.

'Don't you understand why I've broken off my relationship with Judith? Didn't you have any inkling that day at Kimber Park? How could I maintain a liaison with her and do right by her when all the time I could only think of you? Since the day I came to Kimber Park to sign the deeds, I haven't been able to think of any woman other than you, Charlotte, and I've been endeavoring to let Judith down as lightly as possible. My feelings for her were very transitory. I never loved her, and I never pretended to her that I did, but she loved me and wouldn't accept that it was over. But it is over, Charlotte, because it's you that I love, and have loved for so long now.' He smiled a little wryly. 'I'll warrant that that was the very last confession you ever expected to hear from me.'

She felt weak. Was this another dream? Would she suddenly awaken?

Her silence made him uncertain. 'Haven't you anything to say? Maybe a suitably crushing rebuff escapes you for the moment.'

Her fingers were over his then, curling urgently around them. She smiled through her tears. 'Oh, Max,' she whispered. 'Max, I love you so very much.'

She could say no more, for he swept her into his arms, stopping her words with a kiss. There was no harsh brutality in him now, but there was a passion that seemed to melt through her, drawing her inexorably toward an ecstasy that threatened to rob her of consciousness. She had dreamed of a kiss like this; now it was happening, possessing her very soul. Her whole body was alive to him, the blood coursing through her veins as if it were on fire. It was a moment she wanted to go on forever.

16

THE BELL OF A nearby church was striking midnight as Max's carriage drew up outside the house in Henrietta Street. The Parkstone barouche was still there and so Max declined to go in, not wishing to risk an unpleasant scene with Sylvia that might ruin this very special evening.

They lingered in the carriage for a moment, and he cupped Charlotte's face in his hands, kissing her on the lips once more before alighting and assisting her down. His fingers were warm and firm around hers as he drew her closer, his lips so very near as he looked down into her eyes again. 'You're sure of your feelings?'

'Very sure.'

'And you know that Judith no longer has any place in my life?'

'Yes.'

'It never mattered in the past that I'd acquired the reputation I had, but then you came along and suddenly it mattered a great deal.' He smiled at her, his eyes almost black in the slanting light of a nearby streetlamp. 'I wish I wasn't going away for the next month, but I must.'

'I'll miss you so very much.'

'And I you.'

'I'll write to you.'

He hesitated then. 'Yes,' he said softly, 'for it is surely expected that a lady should write to the man she is to marry.'

Charlotte stared at him. 'Are you asking me. . . ?'

'To be my wife? Yes, Charlotte, for I can't imagine any other woman at my side, nor any other woman as mistress of Kimber Park.' He touched her hair with his fingertips. 'Will you accept me, my love?'

'If you're sure you want me.'

'Do you need more proof than tonight?'

She smiled then. 'No,' she whispered.

'Then will you marry me, Charlotte?'

'Yes. Oh, yes.'

He drew her into his arms again, his lips lingering on hers for a final time. She didn't want him to leave, for that would mean the end of a day that had started in the depths of despair but that was finishing at the very peak of enchantment and joy. But then he was gone, stepping quickly back into the carriage, which almost immediately drove away, the team's hooves clattering loudly in the quiet darkness.

'It would seem that your problems with Talgarth are more than resolved, Charlotte.' Richard spoke from close by.

She turned quickly to see him standing on the pavement, having just returned from a walk. 'I didn't know you were there!' she cried.

He grinned. 'That much was obvious, even to me.' He stubbed out the Spanish cigar that was the reason for his walk, his sister refusing to countenance tobacco smoke in the house. 'So, that was the reason for your strange mood. I confess I hadn't thought that to be the way of it. Against all the odds, you appear to have snapped up one of England's most eligible men.'

'I love him, Richard.'

'I sincerely trust you do, for I wouldn't approve at all if my niece was as intimate as that with a man she cared little for. Why didn't he go in?'

She hesitated then. Richard, like her mother, still knew nothing about Sylvia's loathing for Max. To spare her mother distress, it had been agreed between Sylvia, the admiral, and Charlotte herself not to mention the matter; now that situation could no longer continue, not if Max was to become part of the family. She went slowly to him. 'Richard, there's something you should know, something that can no longer be left unsaid, even though it will undoubtedly cause more than a little discord.'

'Discord? In what way?'

'Max has asked me to marry him and I've accepted, but Sylvia will not approve at all; in fact, she's bound to be very upset indeed.'

Richard stared at her. 'You're not saying that Sylvia is secretly in love with him herself? Is *he* the one who's always stood between me and happiness?'

'No, far from it. No, Richard, Sylvia doesn't love Max, she loathes him.'

'But she never mentions him!'

'No, we agreed not to, because it might upset Mother. Oh, dear, it's so very hard to explain, especially as I know you love her so very much. Things have to be resolved somehow, Richard; they have to be if I'm going to marry Max and if you are to stand any chance at all of marrying Sylvia. Can we walk for a while?'

'If you wish, but first I must tell Sophia that you're with me. She thinks you've retired to your bed, and if she should go up to find you not there, she'll be frantic with worry.'

He went briefly into the house, emerging again almost immediately. Offering Charlotte his arm, he paused for a moment. 'Is this going to be serious enough to warrant my needing another cigar to soothe my shattered composure?'

'I don't know.'

'That means it is.' He took out a cigar, the lucifer he lit it with flaring brightly for a moment, illuminating his face. The sweet smoke threaded away in the light night breeze, then he offered her his arm again and they walked slowly in the direction of Cavendish Square. 'Now, then, what's all this about?'

She began to tell him everything, leaving nothing out. They made a complete circuit of the square, where the silence was punctuated by the occasional rattle of a passing carriage, and by music and laughter emanating from the Duke of Chandos' mansion on the north side.

When she had finished, Richard was silent for a moment. 'You're right,' he said at last, 'your match with Max Talgarth *is* going to cause discord.'

'Max is innocent.'

'And Sylvia is going to say with equal conviction that he's guilty.'

'She's wrong. I've seen proof of his conduct toward my father.'

'In that respect then, I must agree with you, but have you equally seen proof of his conduct toward his wife?'

She looked away. 'No,' she admitted, 'but I still believe him. And so does the admiral.'

He nodded. 'Yes, there's no gainsaying that the admiral does indeed still hold Max in high esteem, which he would hardly do if there was any doubt in his mind. Charlotte, all this places me in a damnably difficult position. I love Sylvia so very much.'

'I know.' She squeezed his arm. 'I'm sorry to be the cause of all this.'

'*You're* hardly the cause.'

'Everything would be all right if I hadn't fallen in love with Max, and he with me.'

'It can't be helped.'

'Sylvia's bound to be desperately upset, and that will mean my mother having to be told everything I've just told you. It's going to be very difficult and disagreeable, Richard. I don't want to quarrel with anyone. I want us all to be happy: you and Sylvia, my mother and the admiral, and Max and myself.'

He put his arm quickly around her shoulder. 'It may yet be resolved.'

'That can happen only if Sylvia admits that Max is innocent,

141

and I don't think she's prepared to do that.'

'Well, there's no point in postponing the moment. Shall we go back now and tell them what's happened?'

'I don't want anything to spoil tonight.'

'It's been spoiled already, by your having to tell me all this.'

'Yes, I suppose you're right. Richard, I love you very much, and whatever happens—'

He kissed her on the cheek. 'Whatever happens, I'll still love you too. It's going to be the proverbial bumpy ride, but we'll survive.'

'It means so very, very much to Sylvia,' she warned.

He took a deep breath. 'I know, that's why I want to face her with it all now. Waiting would simply make it worse. Come on, let's get it over with.'

Charlotte's heart felt very heavy as they walked back to the house, for she knew that a most dreadful scene was bound to ensue. Sylvia wasn't open to reason at all where Max was concerned, and she wouldn't receive the news very well.

Everyone was seated in the drawing room, discussing the merits of the Clarendon Hotel's fine French menu. Dinner had gone very well indeed; they had enjoyed themselves to the full and were still imbued with a slightly rosy glow after indulging in some excellent iced champagne. Their chatter and good humor faded almost immediately at the serious expressions on the faces of Charlotte and Richard as they entered.

Mrs Wyndham sat anxiously forward. 'Is something wrong? What's happened?'

Richard didn't beat about the bush; he sat on the arm of Sylvia's chair, his hand resting lightly and protectively on her bare shoulder. 'Charlotte has some news for you all,' he said.

Everyone looked at Charlotte. She hesitated. How could she say it without hurting or provoking Sylvia? 'I. . . .'

Sylvia was now as anxious as Mrs Wyndham. 'What is it, Charlotte? You look so dreadfully pale.'

'I'm going to marry Sir Maxim Talgarth.' The words came out in a rush, allowing no room for misinterpretation and sparing Sylvia nothing. Charlotte could have bitten her tongue for inadvertently being so insensitive, but it was done now and there was no going back.

Sylvia was suddenly very still.

Mrs Wyndham was delighted. 'Oh, Charlotte, my dear! You sly minx, I had no idea at all. Oh, what a catch, what a very, very fine catch!' She turned excitedly to the admiral, who didn't know quite what to say. He was quite obviously pleased for Charlotte and Max, but he knew his daughter's reaction.

Mrs Wyndham stared at him. 'Henry? Aren't you pleased?'

'Yes, of course I am, it's just. . .' His glance slid unhappily to Sylvia.

At last Mrs Wyndham looked at her too, her eyes puzzled. 'Sylvia? Whatever is it?'

Sylvia shook off Richard's hand and rose slowly and quiveringly to her feet, her eyes ablaze with furious disbelief. 'Charlotte! How could you? How can you accept him when you know what he's done?'

'I don't believe he's done anything of which he should be ashamed, Sylvia,' replied Charlotte gently. 'Please don't be angry, for I don't want to be at odds with you.'

Sylvia gave a mirthless laugh. 'At odds? Charlotte, it's far more serious than that.'

'I don't want it to be, and there really isn't any need for us to fall out.'

'I can't be friendly with someone who gives her hand to the man who ruined and probably killed her own father and who definitely murdered my sister.'

Mrs Wyndham swayed weakly, her face draining of color. The admiral immediately put a reassuring hand over hers, fixing his daughter with an angry look.

'Sylvia! That's quite enough; your conduct at this moment is

143

beyond belief and quite unforgivable.'

'*My* conduct is unforgivable?' she cried. 'I'm the only one who's right in all this.'

Richard got up and went to her. 'Please, Sylvia, don't distress yourself anymore—'

She still looked accusingly at Charlotte. 'I shall never forgive you for this, Charlotte Wyndham. Never!'

The admiral got up as well. 'Sylvia, it's time we left, before you say anything more you'll regret in the morning.'

'I won't regret any of this. I *know* I'm right, and nothing you say will convince me to the contrary. That Charlotte, of all people, should cleave to that man. . .' She stepped closer to Charlotte then. 'You're making a dreadful mistake and I'm soon going to prove to the world what a monster Max Talgarth is; indeed I've already set about exposing him. Before long everyone who matters is going to know the truth about him, and I only hope by then you will have come to your senses.' Snatching up her reticule and shawl, she hurried from the room and out of the house.

The admiral looked apologetically at them. 'Please forgive her, she's very upset.'

Charlotte managed a smile and Richard nodded. 'Of course.'

The admiral went to Mrs Wyndham then. 'Will I still be welcome here tomorrow, Sophia?'

She patted his hand and nodded, although she was still evidently very shaken. 'Of course you will be, Henry. Let us hope it will be over and forgotten by then.'

'I wish I could think that it would be,' he said heavily, raising her hand to his lips and then departing.

Richard went to the door with him, and Mrs Wyndham immediately spoke to Charlotte. 'Young lady, there appears to be rather a lot of which I've been left in woeful ignorance. Don't you think it's time you did me the courtesy of explaining?'

Slowly Charlotte turned to face her. 'Yes. I'm sorry, Mother.'

'So you should be, missy. So you should.'

144

17

WHATEVER IT WAS THAT Sylvia planned to do to expose Max to the world, it was not revealed over the next month while he was away at Chatsworth. Her initial angry reaction became less bitter, though, and within days of her furious departure she was again calling at the house in Henrietta Street. Her relations with Charlotte fell short of their former intimacy, and she declined to speak of Max at all, which made for a very difficult atmosphere, but one with which Charlotte was more than prepared to put up for everyone else's sake.

Mrs Wyndham's mood alternated between an almost dizzy delight and pride in Charlotte's undoubted coup and moments of grave anxiety that Sylvia might prove right in the end after all. The admiral, decidedly displeased with his daughter, was very open about his delight in the forthcoming match, making no bones about his happiness for both Charlotte and Max.

Richard walked a delicate tightrope, trying to placate Sylvia on the one hand and determined to be fair to Charlotte on the other. It was a very difficult act, but he accomplished it sufficiently well, for his efforts were rewarded by a slight softening in Sylvia's manner toward him. His resoluteness at a time of great difficulty made her look at him with new eyes, and everyone began to hope that this new development might see an end to her opposition to Max Talgarth.

Whatever was going on around her, Charlotte remained secure

in her love. Each letter she wrote to Max, and each one she received in return, made her love him all the more. She could hardly believe that it had happened, and there were times when she was afraid that it was a dream after all, and that soon she would wake up and find herself in her bed, gazing at the morning shadows on the ceiling. . . .

The days seemed to pass on leaden feet, and she felt that the date of his return to London would never come. He was due to arrive on the day before the Parkstone ball, an event he had always attended in the past for the admiral's sake. He was due to attend this year, but Charlotte wondered if he still would. She had told him all about the upset with Sylvia, and knew that he now had grave doubts about going. That remained in the balance, but what was in no doubt at all was that on the evening of his return from Chatsworth he was taking Charlotte to the theater. It would be their first appearance in public together, and she was looking forward to it immensely, just as she looked to so many social events now that her feelings about such things had changed so much. The visit to the theater was, of course, a very important occasion for them both, for although there had obviously not been any formal announcement of their betrothal, or even of their understanding, news had nevertheless somehow leaked out. Society was astonished to learn that Max Talgarth, who could have had his pick of brides, had chosen George Wyndham's unlikely daughter, and everyone was agog for his return so that it could be seen if the rumors were true or not. The house in Henrietta Street received a great many visitors, and almost without exception they managed to bring conversation around to the rumors, which Charlotte neither confirmed nor denied, since she didn't think it right that she should say anything when Max was away. These visitors departed convinced that the whispers were absolutely true, and they in turn spread it all still further.

Sylvia wasn't alone in wishing to stop the match proceeding. Judith hadn't yet given up her efforts to win Max back, and one morning, when she somehow seemed to know that Charlotte was alone in the house, she paid an unwelcome visit.

Charlotte was seated in the garden reading, and looked up with startled surprise when Mrs White announced the caller's name. Judith's tall, yellow figure looked particularly striking among the soft greens of the garden, and her fringed parasol twirled determinedly above her head. Her eyes were alight with unpleasantness and loathing, and the sympathy Charlotte had hitherto felt for her evaporated immediately. Judith halted before her. 'Good morning, Miss Wyndham.' The Devonshire House drawl was almost too much.

'Good morning, Lady Judith. You'll understand if I don't invite you to sit down.'

'Manners were never your forte.'

'I have no wish to remain at odds with you, but it's quite obvious from your bearing now that your visit isn't all charitable, so I suggest that you say what you came to say and then leave.'

'On the contrary, Miss Wyndham, my mission is very charitable indeed.'

'We're all in need of charity, my lady, but yours is a variety I would prefer to forgo.'

Judith gave a cool smile. 'No doubt, but I shall offer it to you anyway. I've come to warn you against Max Talgarth.'

'Again? How very dull and repetitive of you.'

'Well, since you wouldn't listen the first time, I thought it only Christian to give you a second chance.'

'I'm overwhelmed, but since you mean nothing to him, I fail to see why I should be expected to pay any more heed to you now than I did then.'

'I've taken pity on you. You've made such a fool of yourself, letting the *monde* learn how neatly you've been hoodwinked. Really, it's too ridiculous for words. You see, my dear Miss Wyndham, I'm still his mistress, no matter what he might have told you to the contrary. I've returned from Chatsworth this very day, so I should know what I'm talking about, shouldn't I? He's deceiving you, and when he's enjoyed to the full the charms he admittedly finds alluring enough for the moment, he'll leave you.'

Charlotte didn't flinch. 'You're deluding yourself if you think he's going to return to you. I don't believe a word you've said. You certainly haven't been at Chatsworth, and you're most definitely not his mistress. You don't fool me in the slightest; all this is simply an attempt to drive a wedge between Max and myself, and I can tell you that it won't work. You've lost him and nothing is going to change that.'

A dull flush had crept into the other's cheeks, informing Charlotte that she was right. 'I warned you before that you'd made an implacable enemy in me, Charlotte Wyndham, and now I warn you again. I'll get back at you for all you've done, I'll ruin your happiness and I'll ruin your reputation as well. Don't be sure of anything, especially not Max Talgarth, for his heart is very fickle.'

Charlotte picked up her book again and made as if to continue reading. 'Please leave, my lady, I don't think you and I have anything more to say to each other.' She heard the yellow skirts swishing angrily away across the grass.

At last the day of Max's return to London arrived, and as evening approached, Charlotte dressed for the theater. She wanted to look her very best, and so she chose one of Madame Forestier's very finest gowns. It was made of the sheerest white silk, with an overgown of elegant, fashionable plowman's gauze, a rich material that in no way merited its rather rural name. The gauze was transparent and sprinkled with pale-blue satin spots, and the gown's neckline was deliciously low, revealing to perfection the creamy curve of her bosom. Her dark-red hair was dressed up in a knot on the top of her head, and several long curls trailed down from it, entwined with blue ribbons and sprigged with tiny artificial flowers. She wore a faint touch of rouge on her lips and cheeks, and a dab or so of Yardley's lavender water behind her ears. There was a glow about her, a shimmering excitement at the prospect of seeing him again and of being in his arms.

Sylvia had been at the house for some time, having arrived to discuss the ball the next day. She and Mrs Wyndham were so deep in last-minute details – catering, orchestras, floral arrangements, and so on – that they didn't realize how time had passed. It was almost eight when Max was due to call, and Sylvia ran the risk of coming face to face with him.

Richard went into the drawing room to disturb the two women. 'Sylvia, I think such a very fine evening cries out for you and me to take an airing in Regent's Park.'

She looked up, still wrapped in the ball and all its problems. 'Take an airing? But I've far too much to talk over.'

'Nevertheless,' he replied firmly, 'you and I are going to go out. There will be time enough for you and my sister to talk afterward, but for the moment you will put on your bonnet and shawl and come with me, unless you *wish* to cause a scene, of course.' He spoke a little harshly because he half-suspected her of deliberately setting out to engineer a confrontation with Max, and when he saw the quick flush touch her cheeks, he knew his suspicions were correct.

Mrs Wyndham looked reproachfully at her brother. 'Richard, your manner isn't exactly—'

'Sophia, my manner is exactly what this moment requires.' He looked angrily at Sylvia again. 'Put on your bonnet and shawl, and do it quickly. I warn you, I'm quite capable of putting you over my knee and spanking you.'

His sister was appalled. 'Richard, how *could* you!'

He ignored her, still looking at Sylvia. 'Do as you're told, madam.'

She stared at him, her lovely eyes huge. Then, without another word of protest, she got up and picked up her things.

149

He took a deep breath. 'If you'd done that in the first place, there wouldn't have been any need for me to raise my voice.'

'No, Richard,' she said meekly.

'You're the most exasperating minx it's been my misfortune to meet, and there are times when I can't believe I'm fool enough to love you.'

She raised her big eyes to his face in a way that twisted at his very heart. 'I'm sorry, Richard,' she said contritely, slipping her little hand through his arm. 'Do you forgive me?'

He gazed at her. 'I don't know,' he said unconvincingly, for it was quite obvious he'd forgiven her already. 'I'll think about it while we're walking.'

'You've been very masterful recently,' she said, 'and not at all as I'd come to think you were.'

'Masterful? Me?'

'Yes,' she declared, smiling a little, 'and I find I like it very much. Very much indeed.'

They'd gone when Charlotte at last came down. Her mother looked proudly at her. 'My dear, you look very beautiful.'

Charlotte smiled almost shyly. 'Do you know, tonight I actually *feel* beautiful.'

'Love is a sovereign remedy for everything, from low spirits to a stubborn determination to believe oneself ugly. And talking of love. . . .'

'Yes?'

'I rather think Richard has at last turned the corner with Sylvia. He was quite odiously overbearing a moment ago, ordering her about as if he owned her, and she actually melted to him. I declare I've never seen her look so soft and yielding. They've gone for a walk now, and it wouldn't surprise me if things didn't develop very handsomely in the meantime.'

Charlotte looked hopefully at her. 'Do you really think that? I'd be so happy for Richard.'

'So would I. From the outset they've seemed made for each

other, but she didn't seem to feel the same way. Now, though. . . .'

'If she could fall hopelessly and completely in love with Richard, I'm sure she'd forget her battle with Max. I hope so, anyway.'

'So do I, my dear. So do I. But, Charlotte. . . ?'

'Yes?'

'Are you quite, quite sure that Sylvia is wrong about everything?'

Charlotte looked quickly at her. 'Yes, I'm quite sure.'

Her mother nodded. 'I worry so, because I'm such a hopeless judge of character. I want to feel at ease about it all, and my heart tells me that poor Sylvia is mistaken; indeed, Henry and I have talked *ad infinitum* about it all. He assures me that Sir Maxim is the finest of gentlemen and quite worthy of aspiring to your hand. Anyway, enough of such maudlin talk, this is a happy evening and we must talk of other things than doubts and anxieties. Have you heard about the new book that came out today?'

'Book? No.'

'Another *roman à clef*, it seems, and set to be even more outrageous than *Glenarvon*.'

'Really?' Charlotte was very interested.

'No doubt you'll want to read it, but at least now you'll be able to purchase it for yourself instead of having to wait an eternity for your name to reach the top of Wyman's list. I gather that although it only came out this morning, it's already causing a storm second to none.'

'Who is it supposed to be about?'

'I've no idea.' Her mother was a little disapproving then. 'I can't imagine why you find such horrid books so very absorbing.'

'It's the odious, scandalmongering side of my nature. What's the book called, do you know?'

'No. Listen, isn't that a carriage outside?'

Charlotte hurried to the window and looked out, her heart giving a leap as she saw that it was Max. He alighted from the

151

carriage, looking very distinguished in black velvet, but as always there was something about him to prevent him looking too formal; this time it was the way his top hat was tilted almost rakishly back on his dark hair.

She was trembling a little as Mrs White admitted him, and then he was there. He didn't see Charlotte by the window as he bowed over her mother's hand. 'Good evening, madam,' he said, smiling.

'Good evening, Sir Maxim. I confess I don't quite know how to greet you, for when last we met you were a virtual stranger, but now. . . .'

'Now I hope to become your son-in-law?'

'Well, yes.'

'I trust that we will soon become close, Mrs Wyndham, for I love your daughter very much indeed.'

She succumbed to the charm of the smile, falling under his spell and eliminating Sylvia's charges against him once and for all. 'Perhaps, sir,' she said softly, 'you would like to say that to Charlotte herself.' She nodded toward the window.

He turned, a light passing through his blue eyes as he saw Charlotte standing there. He came quickly toward her, taking her hands and drawing them both to his lips. 'Charlotte,' he murmured, 'you're more beautiful than even I had thought.'

She felt very warm suddenly. 'Max, I'm so happy to see you again.'

Mrs Wyndham watched them for a moment. 'I'm sure you will be late if you delay here, and carriages can be so very private, don't you agree?'

'Mother!' Charlotte felt hot color rushing into her cheeks.

'I may be getting on, my dear, but my memory isn't failing me yet.' Mrs Wyndham smiled at Max. 'I understand you're going to the Italian Opera House?'

'We are.'

'What is being performed tonight? Only an opera, or a ballet as well?'

'I gather Von Winter's *Zaira* is the opera, and I'm told the ballet is to be *Gonsalvo de Cordova*.'

'What a very agreeable program.'

'Please, come with us.'

'And be a gooseberry? Sir, that wouldn't suit me at all. Now, then, don't let me detain you a moment longer, for I'm sure you have a great deal to talk about. Oh, and Sir Maxim?'

'Madam?'

She looked earnestly at him. 'Charlotte has told me what you did for my husband. Thank you for being so honorable, and for being such a friend.'

'He was my friend, Mrs Wyndham, and I liked his society very much.'

She smiled, tears in her eyes. 'Thank you again, sir. If Mr Wyndham was alive now, I know that nothing would delight him more than knowing that you are to be Charlotte's husband.'

He went to her, kissing her lightly on the cheek. 'And nothing pleases me more than being able to say to you that Kimber Park is no longer lost to you. It's there for you to enjoy whenever you wish.'

She nodded, her eyes very tear-bright now. She searched for her handkerchief. 'Hurry along, sir, I'm sure you don't wish to see me sniffle.'

He paused for a moment. 'Mrs Wyndham, will you do something for me?'

'Do something?' She wiped away the tears. 'If I can, then of course.'

'I realize that my coming on the scene has caused difficulty with my former sister-in-law. It is my earnest wish to resolve our differences and I'm more than prepared to extend an olive branch to her. I know how she feels about me, and although I know she's wrong, I respect her feelings because I know they are due to the very noblest of causes. Would you tell her what I've just said?'

153

Mrs Wyndham smiled. 'Of course, sir, nothing would please me more. I only hope she meets you halfway, for then we could all be so happy.'

The evening was warm and clear as they stepped out of the house. Another carriage was driving past, the team of grays kicking up their heels in almost sprightly fashion. There were a number of people out enjoying the end of such a grand July day, but Max paid them no heed as he took Charlotte in his arms and kissed her on the lips in front of them all. She drew back, glancing around in embarrassment, and he smiled. 'I've missed you so much that I'm damned if I'm going to wait a moment longer.'

'I've missed you too. Max, I'm so very happy.'

'And so am I. Damn it, why have you got to look so particularly beautiful? My baser instincts are threatening to get the better of me. Perhaps we'd better go before I succumb.' He handed her into the carriage.

The Italian Opera House in the Haymarket was a very fashionable attraction, and the *ton* flocked there during the Season to see and be seen in their private boxes. The street was almost solid with fine carriages, and there was quite a delay before Max's carriage reached the curb by the arcade that encircled the base of the building. There were wrought-iron lamps suspended in these arches, and the windows of the little shops behind looked very charming and bright as the lengthening evening shadows made the arcade almost dark.

Charlotte felt nervous as the door was opened and Max assisted her down. Her gown rustled and the satin spots on the gauze shone as if polished. It was warm and she could smell the lavender water she'd used earlier. It was clear, light, and fresh.

As Max put her shawl about her shoulders, a man walking past caught his eye. 'Bob?' he said. 'Bob Westacot? I trust you're not about to violate the sanctity of the opera by wearing that atrocious peacock garb.'

Charlotte turned to see whom he was addressing, and she saw

a tall, foppish young man dressed in a very tight pea-green coat and very full dark-green cossack trousers gathered at his ankles. He had a mop of contrived Apollo curls that seemed to tumble in all directions at once, and his waist was so tightly laced that it was very waspish indeed. He was evidently a dandy of the first order, his cane adorned with at least five golden tassels and his shining top hat worn forward at such an acute angle that it was necessary for him to raise his head and look down his rather questing nose in order to see who was speaking. It seemed to Charlotte that something rather akin to embarrassment passed fleetingly through his pale eyes before he managed a smile. 'Max! By all that's holy! It's been a long time since I last saw your phiz.'

'It seems not long enough since last you offended my eyes with your so-called taste in clothes.'

'Come, now, my dear boy, there's no need for that. It so happens that I'm just passing by, and the Italian Opera House is to struggle along without me to brighten its portals.' He paused. 'So,' he murmured then, 'here I am, face to face with the man of the moment.'

'Man of the moment?' Max raised an amused eyebrow. 'No doubt I'd have a suitable reply to hand, if I knew what you meant.'

'You mean you don't know?'

'No.'

The other looked a little uneasy. 'Well, far be it from me to be the one to enlighten you.'

Max was a little perplexed now, but then suddenly realized that he hadn't introduced Charlotte. 'Bob, allow me to present Miss Wyndham. Char—'

He got no further, for Mr Westacot interrupted in surprise. 'Miss *Charlotte* Wyndham?'

Charlotte was a little taken aback. 'Yes. Sir, is something wrong?'

He didn't reply, but glanced around as if he wished himself anywhere but where he was.

Max frowned then. 'Yes, Bob, is something wrong? Your manner is, to say the least, odd.'

'Forgive me, it's just that I'm a little surprised, that's all.'

'Perhaps you'd be good enough to explain why?'

'Look, Max, I just don't want to be the one to tell you. Now, if you don't mind, I'll toddle along and mind my own business.' Touching his hat, he turned on his heel and hurried away through the crowds, some of whom were already glancing toward Max's carriage.

Charlotte sensed that there was a little more to their interest than curiosity about a possible match. Her hand crept a little nervously over Max's arm. 'What's happened? Why are they looking at us like that?'

'It's as much a mystery to me as it is to you. Don't let it spoil our evening.' He smiled, his fingers warm and reassuring over hers. 'Shall we go in?'

She nodded and they proceeded into the theater, conscious all the while of the stares and whispers that followed them.

18

T HE RICH RED AND gold of the opera house glowed in the light of the chandeliers. There were five tiers of boxes encircling the huge, horseshoe auditorium, most of them occupied by ladies and gentlemen of rank and fashion. Their servants and other persons sat in the gallery high above, while down in the pit was Fops' Alley, where dandies displayed themselves in noisy splendor, rattling their canes and snuffboxes and talking in drawling, affected tones that almost resembled the braying of donkeys.

Max's box was directly opposite that of the Prince Regent, although the prince wasn't present tonight. From her gilded chair, Charlotte had a commanding view of the stage and the audience. The curtain trembled now and then, as if someone was moving behind it, and as the orchestra took up its position and began to tune up, there was a momentary hush of expectation before conversation began again. She gazed at the sea of faces all around, the gentlemen in dress uniform or dark, formal velvet, the ladies in silk and satin, their hair adorned with jewels and tall ostrich plumes. There was a great deal of shuffling and clearing of throats, with the occasional louder voice emanating from the more vulgar element high in the gallery.

Charlotte had forgotten the strange incident outside with Mr Westacot. She was too intent upon watching the orchestra as it continued to tune up, one violin evidently having a little difficulty, but Max hadn't forgotten, especially as he swiftly realized that he and Charlotte were receiving far more attention than rumors of their forthcoming betrothal would seem to warrant. That there would be interest he did not dispute, for his reputation alone would have assured them of that, but not this veritable stir, a wave of raised quizzing glasses and lorgnettes, and a constant fluttering of fans, behind which lips were murmuring secretly. Too many glances were directed toward their box, and as he watched, he became aware of the hiss of whispering beyond the general drone of conversation.

Looking across at the boxes opposite, he saw the Earl of Barstow and his family and friends, including, of course, Judith. The earl was a thin, hook-nosed man, made even thinner by the tight fit of his evening clothes. He too was intent upon Max and Charlotte, his quizzing glass swinging idly on its ribbon between his bony fingers. Judith was leaning close to the lady at her side, pointing across with her fan and evidently having a great deal to say. The lady's reaction to whatever she said could only be described as shocked, her lips pursed, her eyes widened, and she began to waft her fan to and fro as if suddenly very hot. After a moment she leaned forward to touch a gentleman on the shoulder, whispering in his ear and pointing across the auditorium. He seemed taken aback, staring at Max and Charlotte, and then he too spread the whisper, whatever it was, to his neighbor. So the buzz spread from person to person, box to box, each new recipient seeming shocked, intrigued, and determined to pass the whisper on.

By now Charlotte was aware of the stir. 'Why are they so interested in us? Surely we aren't *that* noteworthy.'

'That's just what I was thinking.'

'I know there's bound to be a certain amount of interest, but not this much.'

He put his hand over hers. 'If it bothers you, we can leave.'

'It doesn't bother me. I just want to know what's going on. I feel rather too conspicuous, as if there's some dreadful sign above my head that only I know nothing about.'

At that moment the orchestra began to play the overture to *Zaira*, shortly after which the curtain rose, and all attention was temporarily diverted to the stage. But if Max and Charlotte hoped that that would be the end of the unwelcome stir, they were soon disabused of the notion, for the ripple of interest continued, circulating the auditorium surreptitiously, as if sheltering behind the screen of music.

As the first act ended, a positive buzz of chatter broke out, and Charlotte was now very uneasy and uncomfortable. She had been so looking forward to her first appearance in public with Max, but this wasn't how she wished it to be.

Max turned to her. 'I think we should leave. I don't like you being exposed to such unwarranted . . .' He broke off as there was a cautious tapping at the door of the box. In no mood to be particularly polite, he turned sharply. 'Yes? Who is it?'

An elderly gentleman peered in almost apologetically. 'Max, my boy, there's no need to snap my head off.'

Max's eyes cleared. 'Randall. Forgive me, I didn't mean to be rude.'

'May I have a discreet word with you?'

'Of course, please come in. Allow me to present Miss Charlotte Wyndham. Charlotte, this is Sir Randall Hopson, my neighbor at the Albany.'

Charlotte smiled at him. 'Sir Randall.'

'Miss Wyndham.'

He was a dapper, slightly built man, looking almost fragile in an indigo velvet coat. An immense diamond pin nestled in the lace-edged folds of his neckcloth, and there were a great many rings on his slender fingers. He wore heavy cologne, which wafted over her as he drew her hand to his lips. Then he turned a little uneasily to Max. 'May we speak in private?'

Max's eyes became suspicious then. 'I take it that it has something to do with all this damned whispering?'

'Well . . .' The other's glance slid awkwardly toward Charlotte. 'Look here, Max, I can't possibly say anything in front of, of—'

'I rather think you'll have to, Randall, since whatever it is evidently concerns her as well.'

'If you insist.'

'I do.'

'I don't relish saying this, Max, but I don't think you can possibly know about it yet.'

'Know about what? Damn it, Randall, will you get to the point?'

'The book, dear boy, the book. It was published today by that scurrilous wretch Horace Wagstaff of Covent Garden, and already, as you can see, it's causing a stir and a half. Damned reprobate you may be, but—'

'What *are* you talking about? What have I got to do with this book?'

'It's a *roman à clef*, just like Caro Lamb's masterpiece, and the key's just as pathetically easy to understand as hers. For the princely sum of fifteen shillings, anyone who wishes can read your supposed escapades, for you're quite obviously meant for the monstrous villain of the piece. Why, the wretched character's name even sounds like yours.'

Charlotte felt suddenly ice-cold. She felt the color beginning to drain from her face. Surely it couldn't possibly be . . . She thrust the dreadful thought away. No, it couldn't be, it mustn't be!

Max was staring at his friend. 'I'm meant for someone in this book?'

'A damned demon of a fellow, cheating his friends, tormenting and murdering his wife, ruining and conniving at the death of a chap who won't sell him his house, and then seducing the wretched man's daughter. I could go on, Max, but that's the general way of it, and anyway, I've already said far more than I should in front of Miss Wyndham, don't you think?'

Max was very still. 'Randall, if this is some kind of jest. . . .'

'Sweet Lord above, do you think I've taken leave of my senses?

160

Courage ain't exactly overpresent in my makeup, and the last thing I'd want to risk is becoming your fifth opponent. Of course it isn't a jest; it's only too true, and when I saw you both sitting here so evidently unaware of what was going on, well, I couldn't let it continue without warning you. I know you, Max, and many a thing you'd do, but not these things. I don't know who the author is, but whoever it is has seen to it that you're in for a very rough time socially.'

Max nodded. 'So that was why Bob Westacot behaved as he did earlier.' He looked quickly at Charlotte's pale face, taking her by the hand. 'I'm so very sorry you've been subjected to this, this . . . Well, words fail me, I'm so very angry that someone has seen fit to write and publish such a despicable book.'

She couldn't reply, she was too shocked. It all sounded so horridly familiar, and yet it didn't. In her book she had accused him of a great deal, but not seducing her; apart from that, it could have been *Kylmerth* Sir Randall had described. . . .

Sir Randall looked anxiously at her. 'Forgive me, my dear, for no lady should be exposed to such infamy.'

'That – that's quite all right, sir,' she said a little shakily.

'Perhaps now is hardly the time, but I gather that congratulations are in order.'

'Thank you.'

He glanced at Max. 'I'll make myself scarce. I'm sorry to have been the bearer of such ill tidings.'

'Thank you for having the goodness to tell us.'

'Think nothing of it, I regard you as a friend.'

As he went to the door, Charlotte suddenly spoke again. 'Sir Randall?'

'Yes?'

'What is the name of the book?'

'Name? I can't recall it for the moment. No, wait a second, it's *Kylmerth*. Yes, that's it, *Kylmerth*.'

The name seared through her like a hot knife. She felt faint, clinging to the arms of her chair to prevent herself from swaying. No, it couldn't be true, it simply couldn't! She closed her eyes for a moment. She couldn't pretend, it was her book; someone had stolen it, altered it a little, and had it published. But who would do such a thing? Her eyes flew open then and she stared across the auditorium at the Barstow box. Judith sat there gazing back, a spiteful little smile curving her rosebud lips. Suddenly Charlotte remembered Polly, the little maid who had been so unexpectedly accosted in the street by a lady who answered Judith's description only too closely. Polly cleaned the bedroom at Henrietta Street, maybe she'd discovered the manuscript hidden away so carefully at the back of the wardrobe. It was the only explanation; by pure chance, Judith had discovered about the book and had had it stolen. This was her revenge.

The second act of the opera had commenced, but the buzz of conversation scarcely died away, droning busily on as the music played. Max took his seat again, his eyes cold and dark, his lips a thin, bitter line. Charlotte sat miserably at his side, her mind spinning at the quandary in which she now found herself. Should she risk telling him and alienating him forever? He had placed such importance upon her believing in his innocence, so how was he going to feel when he discovered that she had so deliberately written all those lies? Would it be wiser to remain silent and hope with all her heart that her guilt was never discovered? This she discarded almost immediately, for the manuscript was hers and if, as was bound to happen, he went to see Mr Wagstaff at Covent Garden, he would recognize her writing if he saw any of the pages. It was possible, of course, that Judith had had the manuscript copied – after all, she had apparently changed the ending – but there seemed too little time for everything. No, her guilt was bound to be revealed in the end, and so she had to tell him; to say nothing would anyway be the grave betrayal of love. She steeled herself. 'Max. . . .'

He didn't hear, for abruptly he got up. 'I've had enough, I'm beginning to feel like an inmate of Bedlam.'

Slowly she nodded, slipping her chill hand into his and rising to her feet. As they left the box, a veritable storm of chatter broke out behind them. She felt quite numb, searching for the right words for her confession as they walked along the silent passage behind the boxes. Liveried footmen bowed, having evidently learned the story, for their curious eyes followed as the two began to descend the grand staircase.

Halfway down, Max halted, taking her hands and turning her to face him. 'I swear to you that I'll seek out and punish whoever did this, I'll show no mercy.'

'Max, I—' Again the awful confession hung trembling on her fearful lips.

He put a finger against them, stopping her words. 'It must be done, sweetheart, for whoever has done it has insulted my honor beyond all endurance, and has hurt you, which last I shall never forgive. I won't let it pass unchallenged, you may be sure of that, and I won't rest until the guilty have been made to pay my price for this monstrous libel. Unfortunately I have a vital appointment in the morning, but my afternoon is free enough. I'll show Wagstaff no quarter until he tells me what I want to know.'

Her heart twisted with guilt, pain, and dread of losing him, but her confession died unsaid. His bitter anger was too much, and she simply couldn't bring herself to face him.

Their carriage was at last brought to the door and they emerged into the night, where the air was blessedly cool against her skin. She sat back against the coach's soft velvet seat, her head leaning wearily against the glass. She had amused herself by writing a silly book, and then she had forgotten about it; now it had come out of the shadows to haunt her and she would have to face the consequences.

As the carriage pulled away down the Haymarket, she struggled again to find the right words, to soften the blow her confession would deal him, but the words wouldn't come. She sat in stricken silence, an almost overwhelming sense of sick apprehension flooding secretly through her. Courage was something she had never lacked before, but now it deserted her completely. By the time they reached Henrietta Street it was too late.

19

RICHARD AND MRS WYNDHAM were alone in the house, and it was immediately apparent that they too had learned about the book. They expressed their sorrow at what had happened, assuring Max that they did not for a moment give credence to the lies printed in *Kylmerth*. He stayed for a time while they discussed the situation, and Charlotte sat miserably with them, not saying anything and wishing that she could find the courage to tell the truth. But her tongue seemed frozen, turned to ice by the bleakness of Max's cold fury at what had been done.

How she endured the remainder of that dreadful evening she didn't know. She moved in a dream, as if she wasn't really there but was observing everything from afar. She felt utterly devastated, plunged into the depths of despair by the actions of a jealous, discarded mistress who bore her only malice and who had undoubtedly succeeded in what she had set out to do.

When Max had gone, having again promised her that he would leave no stone unturned in his quest for the culprit, she went back in to the drawing room, knowing that she must tell Richard and her mother what she had been too afraid to tell Max.

Richard had already observed that there was more to his niece's strained silence than just upset at being the focus of so much unwelcome attention. He went to her as she came back into the drawing room, put his arm around her shoulder, and squeezed her gently. 'Are you going to tell us what's really wrong?'

Mrs Wyndham smiled anxiously as well. 'Yes, Charlotte, are you? It's obvious even to me that there's something very distressing on your mind.'

Tears suddenly flooded into Charlotte's eyes. 'I wrote the book,' she whispered. 'I wrote it, and it was stolen from my wardrobe.'

They both stared at her.

'Oh, please don't look at me like that,' she pleaded. 'I'm so miserable I wish I was dead!' Flinging herself onto a sofa, she hid her face, her shoulders shaking convulsively with her sobs.

Mrs Wyndham went hurriedly to comfort her. 'Charlotte, Charlotte my dear, please don't cry.'

'I don't know what to do. I feel so wretched. I wanted to tell him, but he was so cold and angry that I just couldn't. He's bound to find out, and then he'll hate me. He set such store upon my believing in him, so what will he feel when he discovers that I wrote all those things?' Charlotte's heart was breaking; happiness was fleeing from her outstretched fingertips, and try as she would, she knew she couldn't cling to it or gather it back safely again.

Mrs Wyndham was almost in tears herself at seeing her daughter so distraught. 'Please, Charlotte,' she begged, 'don't take on so. You'll make yourself ill. Richard, bring a glass of cognac.'

He had been standing there, not knowing what to do. 'Yes. Yes, of course.' He hurried out.

Mrs Wyndham shook Charlotte's shoulders gently but firmly. 'Charlotte,' she said a little sternly, 'take a grip on yourself immediately. This won't do at all and it just isn't like you. Now, then, sit up and take this handkerchief.'

The firm tone had a calming effect, and taking gulping breaths to try to steady herself, Charlotte sat up, taking the handkerchief.

Richard came back in. 'It seems the admiral had the last of the bottle earlier. Mrs White's sent Polly down to the cellar to bring another one. It won't be long.' He went to Charlotte, taking her shaking hand. 'Are you feeling a little better now?'

She took another deep, tremulous breath. 'Yes,' she said almost inaudibly, 'at least, I think so.'

At that moment Polly came hurrying in with a tray on which stood the decanted cognac and several glasses. Seeing the maid, whom she suspected of assisting Judith, Charlotte rose swiftly to her feet, fixing the startled maid with a furious gaze. 'You did it, didn't you, Polly? You saw that manuscript in my wardrobe and knew what it was, so that when Lady Judith approached you and offered you money if you could tell her anything to harm me, you took my book and gave it to her. Didn't you?'

Polly's eyes were as round and frightened as a rabbit's and she began to shake so much that she would have dropped the tray had not Richard rescued it. 'M-miss Charlotte? I d-don't know what you're talking about!'

'I heard Mrs White talking to you about seeing you with a lady in a yellow carriage.'

'But I didn't tell her ladyship anything,' wailed the maid. 'I said that there wasn't anything to know and that she shouldn't ask me. Please, Miss Charlotte, you must believe me.'

Charlotte was shaking with distress again. 'I can't believe you when I know you spoke to her. You have access to my room every single day. Do you really expect me to believe you didn't know the manuscript was there?'

Polly was distraught too. 'I saw it – of course I saw it – but I didn't know what it was.'

'I don't believe you!'

'But, Miss Charlotte,' whimpered the maid, her cheeks wet with tears, her little apron crumpled between her trembling hands, 'the manuscript could have been anything. I can't read.'

Charlotte stared at her.

'I can't read. I saw only sheets of paper with writing on, that's all. You must believe me. I wouldn't do anything to hurt you, truly I wouldn't.'

'Oh, Polly,' whispered Charlotte, conscience-stricken. 'I'm so sorry, please forgive me. I could only think that you gave it to Lady Judith.'

'I wouldn't do that, Miss Charlotte, nor would Mrs White. Whoever took your book to her ladyship, it wasn't anyone in this house; it was an outsider.'

Charlotte lowered her eyes and nodded.

'Can – can I go now please?'

'Yes, of course.'

The maid scuttled out thankfully.

Mrs Wyndham took a deep breath. 'Charlotte,' she said reproachfully, 'you should be a little more sure of your facts before you accuse someone like that.'

'I thought I *was* sure, now I just don't know. Someone took the manuscript and gave it to Judith.'

'Are you even sure that Judith is responsible?'

'She promised to have her revenge, and if you'd seen her at the theater tonight, well, you'd have seen that she'd done it. She was like a great yellow cat, licking its paws after the finest dish of cream ever set before it.'

Richard led her to a chair. 'Sit down and tell us all about it, from the very beginning.'

In halting tones she told him how the story of Rex Kylmerth had come into being, starting with the inspiration she'd been given by *Glenarvon* and ending with the last time she'd put the manuscript away in the wardrobe and forgotten all about it. 'The book that has in so short a time set society by the ears is mine,' she finished. 'It's the same in every detail except that Judith has altered the ending to include my seduction. Apart from that, I recognize my work only too well.'

Mrs Wyndham looked sadly at her. 'Oh, my poor dear,' she murmured, 'what a fix you've got yourself into.'

'What am I going to do? I know that I should have told Max the moment I realized, but I just couldn't. I tried, more than once, but I simply couldn't put it into words. I love him so much, but he's going to hate me when he finds out. He's going to the publisher in Covent Garden tomorrow afternoon, and he'll recognize my writing, I know he will. I'm going to lose him and I don't think I can bear it.'

Richard put a firm hand on her shoulder. 'Max may be angry now, but when he realizes that you wrote the book before there was anything between you, and when he understands that you never had any intention of having it published—'

'He'll still despise me. He went out of his way to convince me of his innocence, Richard. He told me that it mattered more than anything to him that I believed in him. He's going to see this book as a betrayal of everything.'

'It's a risk you're going to have to take if you're to have any chance of salvaging your love.'

'I know.'

'If he's going to this Mr Wagstaff tomorrow afternoon, I strongly suggest you and I go there in the morning. You must have all the facts, there's no other way.'

'What point is there?' she cried despairingly. 'The book is mine, there's no gainsaying it.'

'Maybe, but *you* didn't take it to be published; someone else did. We'll go in the morning and find out if it was Judith.'

She nodded wearily. 'If you think it best.'

'I do. And when you've found out what you need to, you must go to Max immediately. There's to be no more dilly-dallying, Charlotte.'

'Very well.'

'It isn't lost yet, you know,' he said softly.

She didn't reply.

'You mustn't give up, Charlotte.'

'I don't think you understand the depth of his feeling about these lies, Richard,' she said emptily. 'They've taken on a significance that once would never have existed.'

He glanced sadly at his sister and fell silent.

Mrs Wyndham got up then. 'Do you know, in the heat of all this, we've quite forgotten to tell her your good news, Richard.'

'So we have. Somehow, now doesn't seem the right time.'

Charlotte looked at him. 'What good news?'

'Sylvia accepted me tonight.'

She managed a smile, because she was genuinely pleased. 'I'm so glad for you, Richard, you and she were meant for each other.'

Mrs Wyndham nodded. 'They were indeed, so it wasn't before time tonight that he took a firm line with her. She positively basked in his masterfulness.' Her smile faded then. 'Oh, dear.'

'What is it?' asked Charlotte.

'I was thinking of how this wretched book is going to affect Henry and Sylvia, for it resurrects all the whispers about Anne's death. The ball tomorrow night is going to be a dreadful strain for us all.'

'I won't be going,' said Charlotte quickly. 'I could possibly have endured it if the book wasn't mine, but not now, when I know that it is and that by this time tomorrow night Max will hate me.' Her voice broke on a sob, and gathering her skirts, she got up and hurried out.

Mrs Wyndham made to follow her, but at that moment someone knocked at the front door. Charlotte had fled up the stairs to her room when Mrs White emerged from the kitchens to admit Sylvia and the admiral, who had come the moment news of the book reached them.

Sylvia looked very pale and shaken as she sat down, and the admiral looked distressed. 'Sophia,' he said straightaway, 'what can I say? It's too dreadful. Poor Max and poor Charlotte, what an infamous ordeal for them both.'

Sylvia clasped her trembling hands in her lap, her eyes lowered to the floor. 'It wasn't me,' she said suddenly. 'You must believe that it wasn't me. I didn't write it. I know I've said all those things about Max, but I didn't write it. Tonight I'd decided never to accuse him of anything again. I was so happy because Richard and I are to be married that I wanted everything to start anew. I was going to tell Charlotte that, I was going to say that I would be a changed person where Max was concerned and that I would do my best to put the past well and truly behind me. You must believe me,' she pleaded again, her eyes bright with unshed tears.

Richard went to her quickly, sitting at her side and drawing her close. 'We know you didn't do it, sweetheart,' he said gently, 'because Charlotte wrote it herself, she told us so.'

The admiral was so startled that he almost jumped. 'Eh? What did you say? Charlotte wrote it? That can't possibly be so!'

Mrs Wyndham gave a wan smile. 'But it is, Henry.' She explained everything, just as Charlotte had done earlier. 'So you see,' she finished, 'someone stole the manuscript from Charlotte's wardrobe and took it to that horrid man in Covent Garden. Charlotte says that Lady Judith Taynton is the one responsible, and it seems that this must indeed be the case.'

The admiral nodded. 'The wretched wench may be related to me, but I have to confess to thinking she probably did do it; it's just the sort of thing she would do. She was a loathsome brat of a child; now she's still the same, only bigger and more venomous than ever. Where's poor Charlotte now?'

'In her room, crying her heart out,' replied Mrs Wyndham. 'I feel so desperately sorry for her.'

'Does Max know yet?'

'No. That's the real problem. She tried to tell him but he was so very angry about the whole business that she simply couldn't. I've never seen her so distressed before, it's quite out of character, she's usually so strong. She's been my strength in the past, anyway. Now I wish I could be strong for her. Oh, how I despise those Tayntons! I've never liked any of them; they're as poisonous a nest of vipers as anywhere in England, and Judith is the worst of them all. I've done my best to ignore her malice in the past, but if she was here right now, I swear I – I'd choke her with my bare hands.'

Richard nodded heavily. 'To have done the foul thing she's done, she doesn't deserve anything else. She's ruthlessly and contemptuously destroyed Charlotte's happiness. I feel only revulsion for anyone who could do such a thing.'

At his side, Sylvia found it all too much. She began to cry, hiding her face against his shoulder, her arms around him, clinging tight. He held her close, gently stroking her short dark hair.

20

A<small>FTER WEEPING BITTERLY UNTIL</small> well toward dawn, Charlotte at last fell into a fitful sleep, only to be wakened by the murmur of voices in the street outside. She lay there for a moment, fleetingly forgetting all that had happened the night before, but then memory returned, sweeping through her with a swingeing force that made her sit up with a gasp of utter wretchedness. It wasn't a nightmare, it was all real. . . .

The voices intruded into the room once more, and she got up from the bed, putting on her wrap as she went to the window to look out. A small crowd had gathered there, vulgar persons who were staring curiously at the house, pointing and talking. So, the book's fame had already passed beyond fashionable drawing rooms. Looking up toward Cavendish Square, she saw that there was a little gathering outside the Parkstone residence as well.

With a heavy heart, she sat before her dressing table, brushing her long red hair. Her head ached, her eyes were sore and tired, and she felt spiritless. She wished she had never read *Glenarvon*, never paid foolish heed to her mother's chance remark, never spent all those hours writing by candlelight. But it hadn't meant anything; it had been an idle exercise, an amusing way of passing the time. There was nothing amusing about it now.

Pinning her hair up into a knot, which made her head ache all the more, she put on a neat pink-and-white-striped lawn gown and draped a plain white shawl around her shoulders. Looking in the mirror, she saw how dark the shadows were beneath her salt-stained eyes, and how empty and desolate the expression on her tense face. She was defeated before she began; she saw no hope of surviving this day and retaining Max Talgarth's love, or even his lingering respect.

Slowly she went down to breakfast. Her mother and Richard were sitting silently at the table, their food untouched, and only cups of strong coffee before them. The morning newspaper was folded by Richard's plate, and as Charlotte sat down, he pushed it toward her. 'I think you'd better read this.'

Her heart sank still further as she saw that he'd marked a piece in the fashionable but rather scandalous column of *on-dits*, a page rarely missed by anyone who was anyone in the *beau monde*. She read aloud. '*Kylmerth*, a fellow betrayed for a publisher's fee, is perhaps known more by a name commencing with T. Scandal once again resumes her place in the public mind, for a tale is very prevalent in first circles that the identity of the villain, Kylmerth, in the wicked anonymous tidbit of the same name is none other than Sir M———m T———h. To go into more detail might spoil the fun, but the appetite should be whetted to think of the delicious smell of bacon carrying on the breeze.' Bacon on the breeze. Wind ham. Wyndham. She closed her eyes. 'Is there anything more?' she whispered.

'Not in that newspaper,' replied her mother, reaching over to pat her hand for a moment.

'But in all the others?'

'Maybe. We don't know.'

'And we don't want to know,' said Richard. 'Have – have you seen Sylvia this morning?'

'Yes,' Richard said.

'How is she? I – I heard her crying as she and the admiral left last night.'

'She's not feeling exactly sparkling; in fact, she wanted to cancel the ball tonight, but her father wouldn't hear of it. He said

174

that to do that would be to give in to gossip, and he wasn't prepared to do that. He says we must all cock a grand snook at society by carrying on as if the book didn't exist.'

Mrs Wyndham nodded approvingly. 'And quite right too.'

Charlotte gave a humorless, ironic laugh. 'Would that it was that easy.'

'But, Charlotte,' said her mother earnestly, 'by far the most sensible thing would be to carry on as if nothing had happened.'

'I agree, except that for me that is quite impossible.'

'I want you to be brave and come to the ball tonight. Please, Charlotte, for your own sake.'

'I couldn't.'

'Please. You must try to find the strength, for to stay away will serve only to give credence to the book's claims. Society knows you too well, Charlotte; it knows your character and spirit and it will *expect* you to attend the ball and fly in the face of adversity. Under any other circumstances, you wouldn't hesitate. At least give the matter proper consideration, try to see beyond the immediate.'

Charlotte looked away. 'I've already seen beyond the immediate and it's a very lonely view.'

Mrs Wyndham lowered her eyes and said nothing more.

Richard's carriage had been ordered promptly for ten, and before it was due to arrive, he sent for the parish constables to move the crowd on from outside the house. They did their best, but even so there were still a number of staring faces as he and Charlotte emerged from the house. She wore a veil over her face, but they still seemed to know instinctively who she was. Pressing forward, they jostled her as Richard did his best to fend them off. At last they were in the carriage, which pulled swiftly away. She was trembling and more than a little shaken, and she was glad of Richard's comforting presence at her side. He held her hand and tactfully said nothing at all.

The premises of Mr Horace Wagstaff, bookseller, print seller, and publisher, stood adjacent to one of the more notorious coffee houses in Covent Garden, a place where at night madams openly paraded their charges and where usually the only carriages were those of gentlemen seeking such pleasures. Today, however, there were many other carriages thronging the street; indeed, there was a considerable crush as society converged upon the bookshop, eager to acquire a copy of the volume that was so very much the rage.

The shop was dingy, with bottle-glass bow windows and a door sadly in need of a fresh coat of paint. A creaking, faded sign swayed in the light breeze, the sound barely audible above the babble of conversation and the clatter of horses and carriages. The windows displayed open books and a number of prints, including, Charlotte saw to her dismay, a clever, cutting caricature of Max, executed by none other than the great Mr George Cruickshank himself. Above the doorway was pinned a notice announcing that copies of *Kylmerth* could be purchased within, price fifteen shillings.

A number of ladies and gentlemen were waiting for the crowded shop to clear so that they too could purchase the book, while those who didn't wish to be seen in such a disreputable area on such an errand sent their footmen instead – in plain clothes, of course, not identifiable livery.

It was some time before Richard was able to usher Charlotte into the low-ceilinged shop, where the cluttered, small-paned windows let in only a little light. There was only one counter, with upon it a steadily diminishing stack of *Kylmerth*. Charlotte stared at the volumes as she waited her turn. How handsomely bound it was, its leather cover embossed in gold. It was the usual practice for books to be sold without covers, the pages merely stitched together so that the purchaser could bind it as his personal taste directed, but shrewd Mr Wagstaff had been so sure of this book's success that he had lavished a great deal upon its presentation.

Just as she and Richard reached the counter, she heard some-where behind her a voice she knew and loathed, a Devonshire House drawl that carried so clearly that everyone in the shop must have heard it. 'My *dear*, if the book's claim that George Wyndham's daughter was seduced is true, it doesn't surprise me in the slightest, for she never was the lady she pretended to be.'

Charlotte glanced around, angry color flushing hotly to her cheeks. Judith was with some friends and hadn't seen her. Richard put a warning hand on his niece's arm, and with a great effort she turned back to the counter again. The man behind it, a rather untidy, dusty fellow in an old-fashioned coat, a quill behind his ear, looked inquiringly at Richard. 'Yes, sir?'

'We wish to speak with Mr Wagstaff.'

'He's very busy, sir, a great many people have wished to see him since yesterday.'

'I don't care how many he's seen. Will you simply inform him that Miss Charlotte Wyndham wishes to see him immediately.'

The man's mouth dropped open. 'M-miss Charlotte Wyndham?'

His voice carried, and the room fell suddenly silent. Even Judith had nothing to say for a moment. Everyone stared at Charlotte's veiled figure by the counter.

Without another word, the man hurried through a door at the rear of the shop, and a minute later Mr Horace Wagstaff himself appeared. He was a very fat man, with heavy jowls falling over his high, tight collar and cravat. His light-brown wool coat wasn't particularly well-cut, and his green waistcoat was strained across his immense paunch. The hands that he placed very daintily and precisely on the counter were soft and pink, the nails scrupulously cleaned and manicured. His chestnut hair was too neatly curled and simply had to be a wig, and his mouth was small and almost prim, as if he had but a moment before sucked upon a very sour lemon. His eyes were very shrewd and clever, however, their blue-ness almost pretty, but so very cold and calculating as well.

177

Charlotte disliked him on sight.

He was all agreeability, giving them both a beaming smile. The shop was still quiet as he spoke. 'Why, Miss Wyndham, what a pleasure it is to see you again. Have you come to see how well your masterpiece is going?' He waved a languid hand toward the copies of *Kylmerth.*

Charlotte was stunned, her heart almost stopping within her. She heard the shocked gasps rippling through the onlookers, and she felt Richard's start of astonishment.

The publisher was still smiling. 'As you can see, I shall soon have to bring out a second edition. You write very well, Miss Wyndham, and I do trust you will not retire from the literary scene too soon.'

She found her tongue at last. 'Why do you say you've seen me before, sir? You know perfectly well that you and I have never met.'

He gave a slight laugh, as if vaguely surprised. 'Well, if that's how you wish it to appear, madam, that's your own affair. All I know is that in recent weeks you've been here on any number of occasions, reading through proofs and making slight alterations here and there.'

Richard looked angrily at him. 'I don't know what clever game you're playing, sir, but you and I know perfectly well that my niece has never met you and certainly has never visited these premises before.'

'That simply isn't so, Mr—?'

'Pagett.'

'Mr Pagett. She has come here frequently, as I said but a moment before. Maybe she kept her activities a secret, even from you.'

Richard took a step forward at this, but Charlotte held him back. 'Don't, Richard. Please!' She looked imploringly at the publisher then. 'Sir, you know that you're not telling the truth. Why are you doing this to me?'

He smiled sleekly. 'Are you saying that you didn't write the book, Miss Wyndham?'

The shop was so quiet that a pin could have been heard dropping. Whispers had spread out into the street as well, and everyone waited in hushed astonishment for the seduced heroine of *Kylmerth* to deny her hand in its publication.

Charlotte stared at him, guilty color staining her cheeks.

He grinned then, producing a sheet of her original manuscript from beneath the counter. 'Do you deny that this is your writing, madam?'

She could only look helplessly at the paper.

'There,' he cried triumphantly. 'You can't deny it! Come, now, Miss Wyndham, don't try at this late stage to play the innocent. If you'd really wished to remain anonymous, as you said originally, then you wouldn't have come here so openly today.'

'I came here to find out who stole my manuscript and rewrote part of it before giving it to you.' She watched him closely, but his eyes didn't flicker once toward Judith, whose figure was so prominent among those watching.

'Madam,' said the publisher wearily, 'this is getting us nowhere. You wrote *Kylmerth* and you brought it to me.'

'I may have written it,' she replied icily, 'but Lady Judith Taynton stole it and gave it to you.' There were more shocked gasps as she whirled about to point an accusing finger at Judith.

Judith seemed absolutely nonplussed for a moment, a myriad expressions flitting across her lovely face, but then she swiftly regained her composure, a smooth if somewhat bemused smile curving her sweet lips. 'My dear,' she drawled, 'would that I could indeed claim responsibility, for I'd adore the kudos of having given your horrid little exposé to the world, but since I've never exactly been *persona grata* at – where is it now? Henrietta Street?' She paused, a cool eyebrow raised disdainfully, as if the utterance of such an address was definitely beneath her. Then she went on. 'Since I've never been welcome at your house and since I'm not your bosom friend, I fail to see how I was supposed to know your tawdry scribble ever existed.'

'I don't know how you found out, but you did.'

'Many qualities and accomplishments I've claimed in the past, my dear, but not clairvoyance.'

A ripple of laughter greeted this, and Mr Wagstaff looked on with delight, for such an entertaining confrontation would spread interest in the book still further. He could almost have rubbed his hands with glee.

Unhappy tears pricked Charlotte's eyes as Richard steered her toward the door. The crowd parted for them to pass. Outside everyone seemed somehow to know what had passed in the shop. The tears were wet on Charlotte's cheeks as she climbed into the anonymity of the waiting carriage, which pulled quickly away into the busy streets beyond Covent Garden.

For a long while neither Charlotte nor Richard spoke, but then she looked at him. 'What am I going to do?' she whispered. 'Now Max will *never* believe what I say. The last thing I expected was for that man to point a finger at me like that. I should have guessed. I should have realized that Judith wouldn't leave any trace of her involvement, she's too clever for that.'

'There's nothing for it now but to go to Max and tell him the complete truth.'

'I can't!'

'You have to, Charlotte.' He leaned from the window and directed the coachman to drive to the Albany.

The front of the great house was impossible to approach, for the crowds gathered there hoping for a glimpse of Max were far greater than those outside her house. The coachman had no option but to drive on, approaching the Albany from the rear, drawing the carriage to a standstill on the corner of Vigo Street. Richard left Charlotte there, walking along the pavement to the entrance of the covered walk, where yet another crowd was being moved on by irate constables and wardens. No one gave Richard a second glance as he went inside.

Charlotte closed her eyes as she waited. Her heart seemed to be rushing so much that she could no longer count its beats. She felt cold and sick, an awful apprehension holding her in a relentless grip from which she felt she would never again be free. Please let Max believe her, let him forgive her.

Richard returned and sat opposite, shaking his head. 'He wasn't there, he had an appointment this morning from which he hasn't returned. He isn't expected to go back there, he doesn't wish to inflict the crowds and furore on the other residents. I left a message with his manservant that if Max should return, he was to be told to contact you urgently. That was all I could do, Charlotte. I'm sorry.'

She received the news resignedly. The moment was postponed, that was all. Now she would have to steel herself still more, knowing that in the end all would be lost.

21

SHE WAITED ALL DAY for word from Max, but none came. His silence became ominous. Had he already been to Covent Garden and been told all those clever lies about her? Had Judith succeeded in everything she'd set out to do? The hours crept by on leaden feet, convincing Charlotte that this was indeed what had happened.

The crowds still gathered in Henrietta Street and outside the Parkstone residence, where preparations for the ball that evening were still going ahead. The parish constables tried time and time again to clear the streets, but each time they did so, after an hour or so the crowds returned. If it was this bad here, thought Charlotte, gazing from her bedroom window, what must it be like outside the Albany now? The home of Rex Kylmerth himself would be bound to be subjected to even more unwelcome attention, more so as the day wore on and word of the book spread ever further.

The admiral sent a note to Mrs Wyndham, begging her to come and help with the arrangements for the ball, as Sylvia was still so upset that she frequently burst into tears. Mrs Wyndham and Richard immediately set off, finding the way momentarily clear as the constables had only just succeeded in moving the onlookers away for what seemed like the hundredth time.

The afternoon gave way to evening and Mrs Wyndham and Richard were still at the Parkstone residence. Charlotte was alone in the house, and as the minutes dragged by, her misery intensified. There was no distraction now, no mother to keep telling her that all wasn't yet lost and that she must be brave and face the fashionable world at the ball, and no Richard to give her that silent, comforting support that gave her more strength than anyone else.

The evening shadows were creeping across the garden now and Charlotte sat beneath the cherry tree. She knew as she sat there that her courage wasn't up to the ball, no matter how much her mother told her it was. Oh, why hadn't Max come? Why hadn't he at least acknowledged the message that had been left? Surely he owed her that . . . She lowered her eyes then. Did he owe her that? Did he owe her anything at all? She'd appeared to him to have stabbed him in the back by writing the book, and he probably had no wish to have anything further to do with her. She blinked back the fresh tears that again stung her eyes. Doubt flooded miserably through her, draining her of everything but a despair that seemed to tighten its hold upon her more and more as the hour of the ball crept ever closer.

Charlotte still sat beneath the cherry tree, the hem of her beige muslin gown lifting now and then in the light evening breeze, and the lemon ribbons tying her hair fluttering prettily at the back of her neck. Her face was pale, with no soft color to warm her cheeks, and no brightness to put a sparkle in her sad gray eyes. The onus was upon her to go to Max and tell him the whole truth. Maybe he'd refuse to receive her, maybe his love had already been transformed into the most bitter of hatreds, but she had to go to him and risk whatever form his hurt and resentment took. He didn't owe her anything, but she owed him a great deal.

Getting up, she went back into the house, where she encountered Mrs White by the kitchen door. 'Mrs White, will you do something for me?'

'But of course, Miss Charlotte.'

'My mother and Mr Pagett will return shortly to dress for the ball, and I want them to think I shall be going too, but a little later because I'm feeling slightly indisposed. A headache. I shall go to my room and stay there until they've left. I want you to procure a cab for me, to wait around the corner by the chapel.'

'I'll do that, of course, but, Miss Charlotte, where are you going?'

'To see Sir Maxim.'

The cook nodded understandingly. 'I'll do all you ask, Miss Charlotte.'

'Thank you.'

Hearing a stir in the crowd which had returned outside and Richard's rather angry voice demanding that a way be cleared, she hurried on up the stairs to her room and was safely inside with the door firmly closed when her mother and uncle came into the house. Charlotte quickly took out a silver tissue ball gown she had intended to wear, laying it carefully over a chair beside her silk stockings, satin slippers, and black-and-silver lace shawl, then she drew the curtains and lay down on the bed in the semidarkness.

A moment later her mother tapped anxiously at the door. 'Charlotte? May I come in?'

'Yes, of course.'

Her mother came quietly to the bedside. 'My dear, I do hope your headache isn't going to stop you from attending the ball, for I'm convinced that going there would be the wisest thing you could do under the circumstances.'

'If I rest for a while, I'm sure it will soon go. It's just been such a strain today.'

'Yes, it most certainly has. Mrs White tells me that there's still been no word from Sir Maxim.'

'No. Nothing.'

'Then I suppose we must conclude—'

'That he believes Mr Wagstaff? Yes, I think we can.'

'I'm so very sorry, my dear.'

'I'll be all right. You attend to your dressing, otherwise Muriel simply won't have time to put your hair up the way you like it.'

'I don't like to go when you're so upset and unwell.'

'I'm all right,' replied Charlotte firmly. 'Go on now.'

Mrs Wyndham bent to kiss her daughter's white cheek and then hurried out, closing the door softly behind her.

It seemed an age before at last Richard's carriage was brought to the door and the crowd became more pressing as it awaited Charlotte's emergence. Lying on her bed still, she heard the disappointment ripple through them all as only Richard and Mrs Wyndham came out to climb into the carriage, which drew away as swiftly as it could through the crush of people. Ahead, in Cavendish Square, it was noisier than ever, as everyone waited to see who arrived at the ball. The Parkstone house was bright with lights and already a number of elegant carriages had begun to arrive.

Charlotte slipped from the bed and held the lace curtain slightly aside so that she could watch for a moment. She saw the crowds milling around and the carriages conveying the more exclusive to the ball, but even though they were two different worlds, she knew that their sole topic of conversation was the scandalous publication of *Kylmerth*.

Lowering the curtain, she went to the wardrobe to select a pelisse to put on over her beige gown, but then she hesitated, glancing at the silver ball gown. A little latent spirit stirred within her suddenly. She'd wear her ball gown and fly dazzlingly in the face of adversity! Taking a deep breath, afraid that this morsel of courage would slip away again, she unbuttoned her gown and stepped out of it, picking up the beautiful silver tissue gown and putting it on. She brushed her dark-red hair up into a light, shining knot and pinned to it the intricate black-and-silver satin bow she had so painstakingly made during Max's absence at Chatsworth. It was a very pretty ornament, with trailing ribbons and silver spangles, and it sat perfectly on the side of the knot of hair at the back of her head. She could feel the ribbons resting

185

coolly against her skin. Several minutes later her hasty preparations were complete and she was ready to go down. Selecting the most voluminous and concealing hooded cloak in the wardrobe, she donned it over her evening finery before going down the stairs to find Mrs White waiting anxiously in the hall, Polly beside her.

'The crowds are so very bad, Miss Charlotte, I'm not sure it would be wise to go.'

'Have you procured the cab?'

'Yes, I sent Polly out. It's waiting outside the chapel, as you asked. Miss Charlotte, you must let me go with you, you shouldn't go on your own.'

The cook was right, and Charlotte knew it. 'Thank you, Mrs White, I would be most grateful.'

The cook nodded with relief, waving Polly quickly away to fetch her best mantle. 'I took the liberty a little earlier of looking out into the disused alley at the bottom of the garden, and it was deserted. I don't think they realize it's there because its entrance in Vere Street is closed by such heavy gates. Anyway, I thought if we went that way, we'd come out close to the chapel and be able to slip away without anyone being any the wiser. Of course, if you'd prefer to run the gauntlet of the front way. . . .'

'No,' said Charlotte quickly. 'No, I'd prefer to slip out the back way if possible.'

Polly brought the cook's mantle and a moment later they were hurrying down through the quiet garden to the narrow gate that opened onto the alley separating the properties of Henrietta Street from those in parallel Oxford Street. They looked out carefully first, for fear that its existence had been discovered after all, but all was quiet and so they crept secretly from the garden and along the dark, overgrown way toward the entrance in Vere Street, to the west. Cool leaves hung over the way, brushing their faces, and tall heads of stinging nettles swayed almost seductively in the light breeze, as if inviting them to touch and be stung. A black tomcat melted away before them, vanishing between an elderberry bush and a tangle of brambles.

They reached the gates into Vere Street, listening for a moment as they heard a carriage pass. For a heart-stopping moment of wild hope, Charlotte wondered if it could be Max coming to see her at last, but as she listened, the carriage turned the corner of Henrietta Street, driving away to the west, not to the east and the door of her house. The bolts on the gates were rusty from never being used, and it was some time before they could be shifted. With a grinding, complaining resistance, they at last gave way and the cook dragged one of the gates back, crushing the weeds and brambles that had so determinedly grown against them.

Vere Street was quiet – almost deserted, in fact – and they stepped quickly out and pushed the gate to again. It was as if they had never been moved, for on this more public side there were no weeds to tell the truth with their bruised and broken leaves.

The rather ancient cab waited patiently outside the red-and-gray-brick chapel on the corner. The coachman slouched on his seat, a blanket over his knees even though it was a fine, warm July evening, and his horse held its head very low, as if too weary to lift it up. Seeing the two women hurrying toward him, the man stirred himself a little, picking up his whip and reins as he recognized the cook.

'Where to, ma'am?'

'Albany, Piccadilly,' Mrs White replied, but Charlotte spoke up quickly. 'No, not Piccadilly, go to the rear entrance in Vigo Street.'

'Yes, ma'am.' The man looked curiously at her, catching a glimpse of silver tissue and silk stockings. This was no serving girl or even a governess, this was a fine lady.

They climbed into the unlovely vehicle with its straw-covered floor and drab upholstery, and as the coachman whipped his unfortunate horse into action, the whole vehicle shuddered, making the glass rattle. It drove down Vere Street and across bustling Oxford Street into the more elegant confines of New Bond Street, where the dandies were to be seen strolling in their finery in this almost exclusively male domain. At the commencement of Old Bond Street, where the narrows almost reduced the way to little more than a single track, they turned east into old Burlington Gardens, drawing to a sudden standstill before reaching Vigo Street.

The coachman leaned down to speak to them through the slightly open window, 'I can't go on, ladies, Vigo Street's almost completely closed, the constables are turning away anyone they don't want going near the Albany. Do you want me to try the Piccadilly entrance?'

Mrs White looked quickly at Charlotte. 'Surely that way will be even worse.'

'Yes, we must try this way.'

'But those constables won't let us in.'

Charlotte thought for a moment. 'They might, if they think I'm related to someone residing there.'

'But who? You can hardly use Sir Maxim's name. . . .'

'No, but I can use Sir Randall Hopson's.'

The cook stared at her. 'Who?'

'Oh, it doesn't matter who he is. It only matters that I know him and he has an apartment in the Albany, close to Max's. Come on, we'll walk the last few yards.' She smiled a little wryly. 'It's as well I put on my finery, isn't it? Now we look just like a lady and her maid, which is just the thing if we want to get past the constables.'

They alighted and paid the coachman; then, with Mrs White walking a respectful distance just behind Charlotte, they walked along the pavement toward the beginning of Vigo Street. Two burly parish constables immediately placed themselves in their path. Charlotte tossed her hood back, looking as indignant as she could. 'What's the meaning of this?'

'No one's to pass this way unless they've good cause.' The taller of the two glanced swiftly over her, taking in the glitter of her silver gown and the costliness of her satin slippers and silk stockings. 'Begging your pardon, ma'am,' he added prudently, 'but we're only carrying out orders.'

'I quite understand.' She began to walk past, but his companion wasn't entirely convinced, having seen the two women alight from a less-than-elegant cab.

'Could you identify yourself, ma'am? And maybe state your business?'

She gave him an affronted look, but did as she was requested. 'My name is Miss Hopson, I'm the niece of Sir Randall Hopson, who resides at the Albany. He's expecting me.' She saw his glance move back toward the cab. 'If you're wondering about my less-than-agreeable model of transport, sir, it's because my own carriage has met with a mishap and the cab simply happened to be passing. Now, then, will you allow me to pass, or must I send word to my uncle that you have refused to let his niece keep her dinner appointment with him?' She held his gaze, marveling that she could behave so calmly and resolutely when all the time she was dreading what her reception might be if she managed to get inside the Albany.

Her manner convinced the man. 'Please go on in, ma'am. I'll escort you if you wish.'

'There won't be any need for that, it all seems admirably quiet.'

He took this last as praise. 'We've had a job of it today, ma'am, but in the end we managed to move on all those who shouldn't have been here. It's all on account of this book, you know.'

'Yes, so I understand.' She walked on then, Mrs White hurrying behind.

At the opening into the covered walk at the back of the Albany, they were halted again, this time by the vigilant porter, who emerged from his little lodge like a guard dog from a kennel. 'Good evening, ma'am,' he said suspiciously, not trusting any face he didn't know.

'Good evening.'

'May I have your name, ma'am?'

She took a deep breath, hoping that she remained convincing. 'Miss Hopson. Sir Randall is my uncle and he's expecting me for dinner.' She looked him squarely in the eye.

'Sir Randall? Oh, yes, ma'am. I'll send word to him that you're here.'

Her heart sank, but before she could protest that she'd just go in on her own, he'd diligently dispatched a boy on the errand. She watched as the boy almost ran along the covered walk, past the cream-painted stucco of the new apartments that had been built overlooking the little garden on either side. These buildings were three stories high, with plain, large-paned windows and balconies of the same design as those on the shops by the entrance from Piccadilly.

There were lights at a number of windows, including the drawing room of Max's apartment. Her heart began to beat more swiftly as she stared at that light, and the sick apprehension seized her more strongly. Would he agree to see her? Would she even get as far as his door?

The boy was returning now, followed by a rather puzzled-looking Sir Randall, resplendent in evening attire and evidently just about to go out. She seized the initiative, gathering her skirts and almost flying along the walk toward him. 'Uncle Randall,' she cried.

Startled, he halted, but then his eyes cleared as he recognized her. 'Why, my dear young lady—' he began.

'Please, Sir Randall,' she begged urgently, 'you *must* help me! Say that I'm your niece, it's very important.' She glanced anxiously back at the suspicious porter, who was quickly approaching now that the boy had reported Sir Randall's puzzlement when told of his 'niece's' arrival.

Sir Randall hesitated, having already heard all about *Kylmerth* and the story Mr Wagstaff was putting about concerning her involvement, but when he saw the desperate anxiety in her large gray eyes, he relented. 'Very well, my dear, but if this is any further trickery, I swear that—'

'It's not a trick, I promise you.'

The porter reached them. 'Shall I have this person ejected, sir?'

'Eject my niece? Good heavens, man, what can you be thinking of?'

The man's jaw dropped. 'You mean, she *is* your niece?'

'Of course.' Sir Randall looked him straight in the eye and then offered Charlotte his arm. 'Shall we go in, my dear?'

She gratefully accepted and they proceeded back along the walk toward the house, Mrs White once again respectfully bringing up the rear.

Once inside, Sir Randall turned a little sternly to face Charlotte. 'Now, then, Miss Wyndham, perhaps you would be good enough to tell me why you are resorting to this subterfuge.'

'I must speak to Max.'

'With all due respect, my dear, I very much doubt if he wishes to speak to you. He knows all about your book and—'

'But I must explain to him.'

'Explain what? That you didn't write it? If that is your intention, perhaps I should warn you that he has seen the original manuscript, and the writing is indubitably yours. Now, then, I've saved you from embarrassment in front of the porter, but I really think you should now leave.'

'But, Sir Randall, I love Max with all my heart and have never set out to hurt him, you must believe me. I know that Mr Wagstaff is saying that I took the book to him, but it isn't true. I admit to having written the book; I did it before Max and I came to mean anything to each other and I'd forgotten all about it. Someone else took it from my room and saw to its publication. I had nothing whatsoever to do with it. Please believe me.'

He hesitated then, swayed by the honesty in her eyes and voice. 'I don't know—' he began.

Another voice broke the silence then. It was Max. 'It's all right, Randall, let her come through.'

She turned with a quick gasp to see him leaning against the wall by the door of his apartment. His arms were folded and his expression was very cool and guarded. There was something very distant about him, something that told her once and for all that he believed what Mr Wagstaff was saying about her.

Leaving Mrs White where she was in the passageway, Charlotte went slowly toward him. He avoided her glance, remaining where he was as she walked past him into the apartment, then he followed her inside and closed the door. 'Well? What is it you wish to say?' His tone offered no encouragement whatsoever.

She turned to face him, her heart pounding with a rush of guilty desperation. 'I know what you think, Max, but I didn't take the book to Mr Wagstaff, I swear that I didn't.'

'Ah, yes, this mysterious but highly convenient unknown person did it,' he replied dryly, going to pour himself a glass of cognac. 'I was rather under the impression that this unknown person was not so unknown after all, since you saw fit to accuse Judith.'

'I believe she is the one, yes.'

'She denies it.'

'She would, wouldn't she? She isn't going to admit to such a crime when she still nurses a hope of winning you back again.'

He held her gaze. 'I spoke to her earlier today; I asked her point-blank if she'd done it, and she denied it. I know her too well, Charlotte, well enough to know when she's lying and when she's telling the truth. I believe her when she says she didn't take the manuscript to Wagstaff.'

'But she *has* to be the one,' cried Charlotte. 'I saw her at the theater, she was—'

'Gloating?'

'Yes.'

'That's hardly the same thing as being guilty, is it? Of course she was pleased, she'd revel in anything that might put my, er, romance with you in jeopardy. She'd have been positively jubilant if she'd known then that you yourself had written the wretched book. I've been the original fool, haven't I? You've made a laughing stock of me, holding me up to ridicule for having believed in you. Being subjected to ridicule is a salutary experience, madam, it brings one to one's senses more swiftly than anything else.'

She stared at him. 'Please, Max,' she whispered, 'I admit to having written the book, but it was some time ago now, and I didn't mean to—'

'Didn't mean to write it? Spare me such transparent lies, for you must have sat for many hours writing that vitriolic list of lies.'

'I don't deny writing it, but I most strongly deny ever intending to have it published!'

'How ardently you implore, I swear I could almost believe you,' he said dryly.

'I'm telling you the truth.'

'No, Charlotte,' he replied softly, 'you're lying. You wrote the book because you believed all Sylvia Parkstone had told you, and still believed it when you were confessing your love to me. You decided that since you could never prove my guilt where your father was concerned, you'd punish me in another way. Even when you read the letter your father sent to me, you were still convinced of my guilt. You've made a fool of me, Charlotte, and I think you've come here now to try to continue the farce for as long as possible. It won't work, madam, I see through you now and I wonder that I could ever have been so blind as to trust and love you.'

'Nothing you say about me is true,' she whispered, tears leaping into her eyes.

'Pray spare me another display of feminine tears, I'm immune to your tricks.'

She struggled to retain her composure. 'I'm not resorting to trickery and I'm not lying to you. If I'm close to tears now, it's because of my utter misery at being disbelieved and even hated by you. I love you, and I want with all my heart to hear you say that you believe me.'

He gave a scornful laugh. 'Just as *I* wanted you to believe what *I* said? My, my, how the tables do turn.'

'I say again that I've been telling you the absolute truth. If I'm wrong about Judith, then I must concede to having made an error, but that doesn't change the fact that someone stole the manuscript and took it to Mr Wagstaff. I didn't do it, Max, and I'd swear it upon my father's memory and honor.'

He put his glass down slowly. 'You should have been on the stage, Charlotte, for you're undoubtedly the most consummate actress I've ever come across.'

'I'm *not* acting,' she cried. 'I'm telling you the truth! I didn't do it!

His glance was thoughtful as it rested upon her anxious face. 'Very well,' he said abruptly, 'we'll put your protests to the test; we'll go to Wagstaff and face him together. Either he'll come across with the name of the real culprit, or he'll merely cling to his original story. Are you prepared to come with me now?'

'Yes.'

'But remember this, Charlotte, even if you're vindicated from having taken the manuscript to him, you're still, on your own admission, guilty of having written the book in the first place. For that I can never forgive you.'

He called for his manservant and sent him to see that a carriage was brought to the Vigo Street entrance immediately, then he went to put on his evening clothes. Charlotte waited miserably where she was. There had been such ice in his glance and words, as if his heart was frozen against her; now she felt as if a sliver of that ice had entered her own heart and was slowly freezing her very soul. She'd lost him forever, and the realization was numbing. No matter what happened now, even if the real malefactor was exposed, Max would still despise her for having put pen to paper in the first place. She had no one but herself to blame, she had by her own foolish actions forfeited her right to his love.

22

THE COFFEEHOUSE NEXT DOOR to Mr Wagstaff's bookshop was bright with lights as the carriage drew up at the curb, and there was laughter and jaunty music coming from the open doorway. The bookshop was in darkness.

Mrs White remained in the carriage as Max and Charlotte alighted. Charlotte's spirits had sunk still lower on seeing no lights in the bookshop, for if there wasn't anyone in, then her claims couldn't be confirmed. Max went to the door, rapping his cane upon the glass. There wasn't any response from within. Peering inside, he saw a thin line of light around the door at the rear of the shop. Someone was there. He rapped more loudly, and after a moment the line of light became brighter as someone looked cautiously into the shop. Seeing Max's face at the outer door, whoever it was swiftly withdrew, extinguishing the light. Another door slammed somewhere at the back of the building.

With a curse Max glanced along the street a little way, and seeing an arched alleyway, he went swiftly toward it. Instinctively, Charlotte followed, ignoring Mrs White's anxious call. The alley was dark and cobbled, and she could hear Max's spurred boots as he gave chase to someone in the gloomy shadows ahead. She went hesitantly into the narrow way, turning a corner into a second alley, which passed directly behind the bookshop. A door still stood open, and she knew that whoever had been in the shop had escaped this way. She heard a sudden thump ahead and then a gasp, and she virtually flew toward the sounds, halting with relief when she saw Max standing there, pinning a terrified Mr Wagstaff to a dark wall with one furious hand.

The publisher, his wig awry to reveal a completely bald head, was as white as a sheet. 'Wh-what do you want with me?'

'The truth. Now, then, did Miss Wyndham bring that manuscript to you?'

The man's eyes were still sly as they slid toward Charlotte. 'Yes.'

Charlotte could have wept with anger and frustration. 'You *know* that I didn't,' she cried desperately. The man was lying, and yet it seemed there wasn't anything she could do to disprove his charges.

Max glanced at her. Something in her tone struck an undeniable note of truth. His grip tightened inexorably on the publisher's cravat. 'If you're still lying, Wagstaff,' he said, his voice low and menacing, 'you'd better beware, for in future you'll be a fool to ever walk down dark alleys. I'm not a man to stand idly by and let others escape retribution. Do I make myself quite clear?'

The man swallowed with difficulty, for his cravat was now so tight that it was cutting into his throat. 'All right,' he said quickly, 'all right, I'll tell you what really happened. It wasn't Miss Wyndham who brought it to me; it was Miss Parkstone, Miss Sylvia Parkstone.'

Charlotte stared, horrified. 'No,' she whispered, 'no, that cannot be so.'

'I swear I'm telling the truth,' cried Mr Wagstaff. 'She brought it to me, said that it was yours but that you didn't know it had been taken. She said the book should be published, for the world should know the truth about the deaths of her sister and Mr George Wyndham. She paid me well to keep her name out of it and to say nothing about the real author, but then on the night of the first publication day, she came to try to stop me selling any more copies. She said she'd suddenly realized how many people were being hurt by what she'd done and she wanted it to stop. It was too late by then, and I told her so. Besides, the book was a gem; it was selling like the tastiest of hot cakes, and I'm a businessman, not a saint. She was upset when I refused to withdraw the book, but there wasn't anything she could do about it. It would have been left there, but when you came to the shop the next day, Miss Wyndham, it was obvious to me that there was going to be trouble of some sort unless I put the blame fairly and squarely on you. And so that's what I did, I accused you in front of everyone and there wasn't anything you could do about it because I could prove that you'd actually written the book. That's the truth, I swear it is.'

'And there's nothing more?' demanded Max, his grip still almost choking the man.

'Upon my honor!'

'Honor? You haven't any!' Max flung him contemptuously aside.

Mr Wagstaff almost fell, but saved himself by snatching at a grimy wooden post. Breathing heavily and still terrified that Max hadn't yet finished with him, he leaned weakly back against the wall, straightening his wig, his frightened eyes shining in the silver light that suddenly bathed everything as the moon slid from behind a cloud.

Max turned slowly toward Charlotte. 'It seems that you were telling the truth.'

She said nothing.

'What now?'

She thought of Sylvia's tears on the night the book was published, tears that were so explicable now the full truth was known. Two things had happened to Sylvia that momentous day: she'd realized the dreadful consequences of what she'd done, and she'd finally fallen in love with Richard. She'd wished with all her heart that she had never taken the manuscript, never sought her revenge this way, but by then there was no going back.

Charlotte looked at Max. 'Can't we just leave the matter as it is?

If we point a finger at Sylvia then a number of innocent people will suffer as well. Richard will, my mother will, and so will the admiral.'

He met her gaze for a long moment and then slowly nodded. 'I agree that they've done nothing and therefore don't deserve to suffer, but I don't agree that everything can be left as it is. You and Sylvia between you have brought my honor into very severe and very public question, and I'm not prepared to let that situation continue when there's maybe a way that something can be done about it.' He gave an ironic half-laugh. 'A man could reasonably be expected to see the writing of such a book by his fiancée as a forgivable sin, but he could hardly keep smiling if she'd gone to the length of having it published as well.'

'And is it a forgivable sin?' she inquired softly.

'No, Charlotte, it isn't, but I'm prepared to pretend for a while that it is. Do you wish to salve your conscience? And do you think Sylvia wishes to salve hers?'

Charlotte closed her eyes for a moment, but she nodded. 'Yes, of course I do, and I believe Sylvia would agree if she were here. If there's anything I can do to help put all this right, then I'll willingly do it. You must believe me, Max.'

'Oh, I believe you, since you're so very anxious to protect everyone else and since what I'm about to suggest will do just that.'

'What is it?'

'I'm willing to go to the ball with you tonight as if nothing has happened, and I'm prepared to pretend to them all that nothing has changed between us, that I still love you and that the book is a nine days' wonder that hasn't made the slightest difference to anything. Your presence at my side will give the lie to the book's claims concerning my dealings with your father, and if Sylvia conducts herself agreeably toward me as well, then that should greatly assist in scotching the charge that I maltreated my wife and brought about her death. I'm determined to put an end to the whispers once and for all, Charlotte. I've had more than enough of it, and since you and Sylvia have been instrumental in focusing public attention upon these lies, I think it only right that you should exert yourselves to undo all the damage you've done.'

She was silent for a moment, then she nodded. 'I'll do as you suggest and I'll speak to Sylvia the moment we arrive and tell her what's happened.'

'There's just one thing more.'

'Yes?'

'As I said earlier, a man can reasonably be expected to gloss over a certain amount of foolishness from his future wife, but not as much as you are at present presumed by the world to be guilty of. You must be publicly absolved of blame concerning having the book published, and Wagstaff here can stand up in front of them all at the ball and say that the manuscript was sent anonymously to him.'

'But—'

'No buts, Charlotte. Either you agree to everything, or you don't.'

She looked away. 'Very well, I agree, but I must tell Sylvia first.'

'I see no reason to object to that.'

'How – how long do you intend keeping up the public pretense of affection between us?'

'Just as long as it takes for the fuss to die down. Believe me, I've no wish to continue seeing you for any longer than absolutely necessary.'

He was a stranger. It was as if there'd never been any tenderness or understanding between them, never been the sweetness of a shared kiss or glance, never even been the warmth of a fleeting touch. There was no kindness in him at all, and he cared nothing for the hurt he inflicted with each deliberately cruel word. She wanted more than anything to reach out to him, to stretch her fingers toward his and breach the awful chasm that yawned between them both now, but his rejection of her was complete.

He spoke again. 'Are you still prepared to go through with this?'

'Yes.' Her voice was very small.

'I trust that you will prove as talented an actress as I think you are, for, believe me, I shall be the finest actor you've ever seen.' He turned back to Mr Wagstaff then. 'No doubt you heard all that, so you know what's expected of you now.'

The man nodded. 'I'm to go to the ball with you and tell them all that the manuscript was sent anonymously and not by either Miss Wyndham or Miss Parkstone.'

'You're not to mention Miss Parkstone's name at all; you're merely to exonerate Miss Wyndham from blame, is that clear?'

'Yes, Sir Maxim.'

'And if one further word leaks out about what you've heard here tonight. . . .'

'I won't say anything, Sir Maxim, you may count upon it.'

Max gave a thin smile. 'Yes, I'm sure I can.'

Mrs White was peering anxiously out of the waiting carriage, and she smiled with relief as the three figures emerged from the archway. Max assisted Charlotte into the carriage, releasing her hand as quickly as possible, as if he loathed even this small contact. Charlotte was glad of the semidarkness, for it hid the tears shining in her eyes.

With Mr Wagstaff sitting uncomfortably in one corner, the carriage pulled swiftly away from Covent Garden, setting off at a spanking pace for Cavendish Square and the Parkstone ball.

23

THE SQUARE SEEMED TO be filled with waiting carriages. All around the railed garden in the center there were landaus, barouches, and town coaches, their attendant coachmen, postilions, and grooms standing in quiet groups, some talking and joking, others more intent upon the serious business of dice or cards. The other crowds had at last been moved on, thanks to the efforts of constables as determined as those in Vigo Street.

The Parkstone residence was ablaze with lights, every curtain and shutter having been opened and every room illuminated with as many lamps and candles as possible. Lanterns had been placed along the balconies and the iron railing separating the house from the wide pavement, and the colors were a vivid blaze of red, green, and blue. Music drifted from the open windows, and so did the sound of laughter and conversation as the many distinguished guests indulged in the pleasures of dancing, display, and critical observation of their fellows.

Footmen with flambeaux accompanied the carriage the final few yards to the gaily decorated porch, where garlands and ribbons adorned the columns, and moss, sweet-smelling flowers, and herbs had been carefully strewn over the steps. The music was louder now and the babble of voices almost deafening as the carriage doors were flung open and Max alighted, followed by a sweating, very nervous Mr Wagstaff, who continually mopped his forehead with a large handkerchief.

The chandeliers in the house cast their warm glow over Max's face from the open doorway as he turned to hand Charlotte and Mrs White down too. The diamond pin in his neckcloth flashed brilliantly, but his eyes were still veiled and cold. He beckoned to a nearby footman, instructing him to escort the cook safely back to the house in Henrietta Street, then he turned to Charlotte. 'Remember,' he said softly, 'from this moment on we'll merely be acting the part of two people in love, for I no longer feel any love for you.'

She couldn't meet his eyes, the heartbreak was too great. She didn't know how she was going to carry this night off successfully. She felt too wretched to conduct herself with the style she knew was necessary, but as she slipped her cold hand over his arm and they proceeded up the flower-strewn steps, with Mr Wagstaff dutifully following, she felt a sudden strength come to her from somewhere deep within. Was it strength? Or was it a spark at last of the spirit for which she had hitherto been known? Whatever it was, it gave her the courage to face what lay ahead.

The whole house had been opened up for the ball, and the guests were at liberty to stroll wherever they pleased. It was a glittering gathering, the ladies in exquisite silks and satins, with plumes and precious stones in their hair; the gentlemen very dashing and elegant in the finest clothes London's tailors could produce. There seemed to be music everywhere, echoing around the marble-columned hall with its pale-pink walls and grand double staircase, and lingering sweetly in every anteroom, as if trapped by some invisible force. Everything had been decorated with flowers, garlands, ribbons, and streamers, and there were so many leaves and branches that it was like a sylvan bower.

Entering the crowded hall, Charlotte felt as if she were about to run the gauntlet of the whole of high society, for all eyes swung immediately toward the new arrivals, and she heard one word being whispered, 'Kylmerth.' To her intense dismay, the first people to come toward them were Judith and her escort, Mr Bob

Westacot, the dandy who had been outside the opera house the evening before. Had it really only been then? It seemed a lifetime ago now. . . .

Judith wore a spangled gown of the richest yellow-gold silk, with diamonds at her throat and in her hair. A fragile cashmere shawl trailed with careful nonchalance along the floor behind her, and a fan and a lozenge-shaped reticule stitched with golden threads dangled from her elegant, white-gloved wrist. She had halted in quick dismay on seeing Max enter with Charlotte and Mr Wagstaff, and for a moment she'd seemed undecided what to do, but that moment had been very fleeting and now she and her companion were almost upon the trio by the doorway. She opened her fan and her cold glance took in Charlotte and Mr Wagstaff before she spoke to Max. 'Good evening, Max,' she said in her affected voice, 'I must say that after your visit earlier today I find your arrival with Miss Wyndham, of *all* people, something of a surprise.'

'A surprise? Why do you say that?' Max's hand moved to rest tenderly over Charlotte's, but it was an empty gesture for the benefit of others, nothing more.

The fan began to move more swiftly. 'Don't toy with me, Max. You know perfectly well that when we last spoke, your opinion of Miss Charlotte Wyndham was exceeding low, to say the least.'

'The heat of the moment,' was the bland reply.

Bob Westacot flicked open a jeweled snuffbox, taking a pinch between an elegant finger and thumb. 'I say, Max, come off it, eh? You can't pretend there ain't the damnedest fuss over this wretched book. It's the only topic of conversation here tonight, and now here you are with the author of the horrid piece. Judith told me what you had to say this afternoon, so this now ain't exactly what folk are expecting.'

'Well, you know me, Bob,' replied Max in an exceptionally agreeable tone, 'I've never been one to do the expected. Besides, what does the book really matter? It's only a lot of foolishness someone anonymous saw fit to steal and have published.'

Judith was staring at him now. 'Someone *anonymous*? Max, only this afternoon you were utterly convinced that it was Charlotte Wyndham and *only* Charlotte Wyndham.'

Charlotte found herself laughing in a tinkling way worthy of Judith herself. 'I'm afraid that I've been exceeding fluff-headed, writing such a nonsensical book, but I have to swear that although I wrote it, I most certainly didn't do anything else with it, as Mr Wagstaff is going to explain to everyone.'

Judith's fan snapped closed. 'How very disagreeable for you, to be sure,' she said sweetly. 'So, now we know why Mr Wagstaff is here; he's to say his lines like a good boy and clear you of the more odious part of the blame. Well, I suppose it's a clever enough ruse and it might indeed fool many, but you and I both know the truth, don't we, *dear*?' She gave a sugary, false smile

'Do we?' replied Charlotte in a like manner. 'I'm told that you didn't steal my manuscript after all, and so I suppose I should really apologize for having accused you, but then I have to remember that you quite openly admitted that you wished you *had* done it, so I don't think an apology would be entirely appropriate, would it?'

A flush touched Judith's cheeks and she looked swiftly at Max, who hadn't heard this part of the encounter that morning. 'I may have said it,' she explained to him, 'but it was simply to get back at her. I'd never really have done it, as I trust you know full well, because I'd *never* be party to such a disgraceful and regrettable affair.' The fan opened once more, moving very busily to cool her suddenly hot face. 'So, whoever it was who took the odious scribble to be published, it still remains that she wrote the thing in the first place, which is why I find it astonishing that you and she are together here tonight. Have you really forgiven her?'

Max met her eyes without a flicker. 'My dear Judith, you know how hasty my temper is,' he said with easy charm, 'and I'm afraid that for a while today I let it get the better of me. Then I had second thoughts and realized that although Charlotte was a little indiscreet to write the book, she hadn't done anything really unforgivable. Besides, when one is truly in love . . .' He allowed the sentence to trail away unfinished as he drew Charlotte's hand to his lips and smiled into her eyes. He was so very convincing that all those watching – and there were a considerable number – could only believe that he meant every word and gesture; only Charlotte could see the shadow across his eyes. The touch of his lips burned slowly against her skin, a sweet pain that seemed to linger for a very long time.

Judith's jealous anger was clearly visible now. 'So, after all this, nothing has changed between you? You're still to marry?'

Max smiled. 'Of course we are. You don't really think I'd let a nine days' wonder like this jeopardize my future happiness, do you?'

Charlotte had to look away. Why, oh, why couldn't what he said be the truth? Why had unkind fate decreed that all of this now was a sham? The hurtful answer came almost immediately: he'd never loved her as much as she loved him; if he had, then he would really be fighting for that happiness, he wouldn't be standing at her side in this false way.

Judith's eyes flashed with fury. She'd never finally accepted that it was over between her and Max, now it seemed that it was. 'Happiness? My dear Max, you'll never know a moment of it with this, this . . .' Words failed her and she tossed a poisonous glance at Charlotte before gathering her skirts and pushing away through the press, followed a moment afterward by a slightly embarrassed Bob Westacot.

There was a buzz of conversation and Max took the opportunity to speak coolly to Charlotte. 'I congratulate you, my dear,' he murmured so that only she could hear, 'you're really doing very well; in fact, you're every inch the magnificent actress I said you were.'

'My talent, sir, is as nothing when compared with yours,' she replied, 'but then you probably already know that. There are flaws in my performance, but yours is quite immaculate.' She looked away again, struggling to conceal her unhappiness in a bright smile as another acquaintance greeted her.

Their progress toward the ballroom was very slow indeed, for they had to stop time and time again to converse, behaving as if nothing of any real import had occurred. They acted their respective parts: she pretending to be merely a little shamefaced for having written the book, he appearing almost amused at her indiscretion, and both of them evincing complete mystification about who it could have been who had really taken the manuscript. Mr Wagstaff, mindful of Max's dire warning, backed them up to the best of his ability, managing to skirt around his own less-than-gentlemanly conduct as he invented a tale of a mysterious parcel being left on his doorstep in the dead of the night.

By the time the ballroom was at last in sight, all those with whom they'd spoken were convinced that the book itself was nothing more than an absurdity that had got out of hand because of someone's mischief-making, and interest was centering now upon who that person might be rather than the contents of the book itself.

Charlotte had been looking all the while for Sylvia, but there hadn't been any sign of her yet, which was a little worrying as she had to be told what was going on before Mr Wagstaff made his public announcement. Charlotte glanced anxiously around, afraid that something might go wrong and Sylvia might think she was about to be unmasked in full view of everyone, but as they reached the wide marble steps leading down to the ballroom, Sylvia was still nowhere to be seen.

The ballroom lay at the rear of the house and was a truly magnificent room. Decorated in gold and white, with two Ionic colonnades running down its considerable length, its ceiling was a rich, deep blue painted with golden stars and moons, and its walls hung with gilt-framed mirrors. There were flowers everywhere, and the orchestra's dais at the far end was decked with so much greenery that it seemed to rise like an island above the sea of people. The great floor-to-ceiling windows stood open on to the lantern-lit terrace and the gardens beyond, where all the shrubs and trees were illuminated, and the fountains lit by concealed lights that made the splashing water seem like cascades of diamonds.

There was a moment, as Max gave their names to the master of ceremonies, when Charlotte could observe the scene below unnoticed. She saw her mother and the admiral, seated with the Duke and Duchess of Devonshire, William Lamb, and Lord Palmerston; and at last she saw Sylvia, looking very pale and strained as she danced with Richard. She wore sky-blue taffeta, with matching ostrich plumes springing from her short, dark hair. There were jewels at her throat and in her ears, and more around the wrists of her white-gloved arms. She looked ethereally beautiful, and so very, very vulnerable. Charlotte's feelings were mixed for a moment. She should despise Sylvia for what she'd done, but somehow she couldn't. Sylvia was suffering an agony of remorse and self-loathing for what she'd done; the fact was written large on her tense face as she tried to smile at something Richard said.

The master of ceremonies' staff rapped peremptorily on the marble floor, and everyone looked toward the top of the steps to see who had arrived so very late. The glances became astonished stares then and a murmur of conversation broke out. The stir was so great that the dancing ceased and gradually the orchestra stopped playing. The staff rapped once more. 'Sir Maxim Talgarth, Miss Charlotte Wyndham, and Mr Horace Wagstaff.' The names rang out clearly, and suddenly there was absolute silence.

Charlotte looked anxiously at Sylvia, who was staring at them, her face ashen and her eyes wide with alarm. There was dread in the way her lips parted on a gasp of utter dismay.

Richard was looking toward them as well, his initial delight at seeing Max and his niece evidently reconciled gradually dying away as he realized instinctively that all was not as it should be. He turned sharply in the direction of his sister and the admiral, and saw that they too were aware of something being wrong. Mrs Wyndham rose anxiously to her feet, the folds of her green silk gown by Madame Forestier spilling richly as she gathered her full skirts to push her way through the gathering to reach her daughter. The admiral followed her.

Mr Wagstaff, anxious to get the business over and done with as quickly and efficiently as possible, thought that the moment was right to make his speech, and before either Max or Charlotte realized it, he had stepped forward to commence. 'Ladies and gentlemen. . . .'

Charlotte gasped, her hand tightening on Max's arm. 'He mustn't begin yet; I haven't been able to warn Sylvia.'

But it was too late, the publisher was saying his piece. 'Ladies and gentlemen, I'm here tonight to clear the name of a lady I have been maligning concerning the publication of the book *Kylmerth*. I've claimed that Miss Charlotte Wyndham not only wrote the book but also brought it to me for publication. This is not so, for the truth is that—'

He got no further, for Sylvia's anguished cry halted him. 'No! Please! Don't say it!' Trembling from head to toe, she looked so afraid and guilty that there was no mistaking that she thought she was about to be exposed.

Charlotte stared at her in dismay. 'Don't, Sylvia,' she whispered, 'please don't say another word.'

Richard put an anxious hand on Sylvia's arm, but she shook it off, pushing her frantic way toward the steps and hurrying up to the trio at the top. She hesitated before them, her whole body quivering and a sob choking in her throat. Her tear-filled eyes were large and distraught. 'Please don't,' she whispered. 'I couldn't bear it.' Then with a haunted glance back at the staring faces in the ballroom, she gathered her skirts and fled toward the hall and the double staircase.

Richard followed her, having paused for a moment to throw an accusing glance at Charlotte that pierced her to the heart.

A babble of conversation broke out then and Charlotte gazed miserably down at her mother and the stricken admiral. Then she looked at Max. Slowly she removed her hand from his arm, turning and walking away from him.

At the foot of the staircase she hesitated, wondering if she should go to Sylvia, but then she heard Richard's anxious voice begging to be allowed in and Sylvia's distressed reply begging him to go away and leave her alone. Charlotte walked on out of the house and into the coolness of the night.

24

THE BALL CONTINUED, BUT the atmosphere was charged with whispers about the startling new turn the *Kylmerth* scandal had now taken.

Sylvia had locked herself in her private apartment and wouldn't respond at all to Richard's desperate entreaties to let him come in. He waited anxiously at the door, agitated and distraught by the heartrending sobs from within. In spite of what she'd done, he loved her still and he wanted to tell her so and comfort her, but the door remained locked and her shame and misery reached out almost tangibly to him. He felt as if his own heart were breaking, and he was angry at the way she had been so publicly disgraced and humiliated. Charlotte and Max may indeed have much to blame her for, but there surely hadn't been any need to expose her so heartlessly in front of the world.

'Pagett?'

Richard whipped around on hearing Max's voice behind him. 'God damn you, Talgarth! God damn you to hell and back for this!'

Max's eyes darkened a little. 'Have a care, sir, for I rather think you're about to say something you'll regret.'

'I won't regret anything,' said Richard furiously, stepping forward rashly.

'One more step and you'll discover the error of your conviction,' replied Max coolly, his blue eyes like ice.

Richard hesitated, aware suddenly of the danger he was courting.

Max relaxed a little then. 'That's better, for, believe me, you're wrong – about everything, as it happens.'

'How can I be wrong about the callousness of your actions tonight? Maybe that's your notion of protecting your damned honor, but I call it the act of a despicable coward.'

'Pagett, I'm fast losing patience with you, for whatever you may feel on the subject, the fact is that you aren't thinking very clearly at all. There was never any intention to accuse Sylvia, even though we knew she was guilty.'

'Then why did Wagstaff say what he did?'

'He spoke before he should have done, and if she'd only let him finish, she'd have escaped all this. He was going to say that the manuscript had been left anonymously with him and that he had no idea who had done it. Her guilt provoked her to react as she did, and that is the truth. Charlotte and I intended smoothing the whole matter over; indeed, we were going to tell Sylvia we knew and say it would be forgotten if she made an acceptable effort to behave sensibly from now on. I didn't do any of the things that damned book accuses me of, and I have no intention whatsoever of allowing the whispers to continue. If Sylvia and Charlotte seemed publicly to accept me, then within a week or so, I believe, the whole affair would be over and done with, leaving you and Sylvia to look forward to a future together and leaving the admiral and Mrs Wyndham to presumably do the same. Ever since my wife's death, Sylvia has taken up this crusade against me; and I'm tired of it all, more tired than you'll ever know, Pagett, for it's cost me very dear. Now, then, if you're still on your high horse and intend to challenge me, then go ahead, but I warn you that I shall take up the gauntlet and I shall do so with every grim intention of seeing the business through to a very final conclusion.'

Richard looked at him and then shook his head. 'I'm not going to issue a challenge, Talgarth, for I know when I'm being told the truth. I thought . . . Well, maybe I don't know you all that well, but Charlotte is my niece and I should have known she wouldn't have been party to all that. I owe you an apology, sir, and I trust that you will accept.'

Max nodded slightly.

Richard glanced at the door again. 'If only she'd let me in . . .' He thought of something then, looking again at Max once more. 'You and Charlotte, there is something wrong tonight, isn't there? You haven't forgiven her.'

'I can never forgive her for writing that book.'

'But, damn it all—'

'The matter is closed, Pagett. Charlotte and I have nothing more to say to each other. She knows that, and what you saw earlier was merely an act, calculated to give the lie to the claims her book made.'

'But she loves you, man,' cried Richard.

'I think not, sir, and what's more, I care not. I've said what I came to say. I've already explained everything to the admiral and Mrs Wyndham, so I don't think there's anything to be gained by continuing with this conversation, do you?'

Richard stared at him. 'No, I suppose not,' he said after a moment, 'except. . . .'

'Yes?'

'Where's Charlotte now?'

'At home. I took the precaution of sending a footman after her.'

'You cared enough about her to do that, it seems,' said Richard quietly.

Max gave a faint smile. 'Don't read anything into it that isn't there, Pagett. I feel nothing for your niece now but a very deep regret that I ever knew her, let alone loved her. Good night.' Inclining his head briefly, he turned and walked away.

From her window, Charlotte saw Max's carriage leave Cavendish

Square. It drove past and she could see him inside, but he didn't even glance at the house. She watched until it had passed out of sight and then she turned away from the window, going to sit desolately on the edge of the bed, her silver ball gown shimmering in the shaft of moonlight slanting into the room. She couldn't weep; she felt beyond that. She was drained of all emotion and so weary that sleep should have come effortlessly, except she knew it wouldn't.

She remained there on the edge of the bed, watching the slow approach of dawn and listening to the carriages departing as the ball ended. She heard the first street cries, and her mother and Richard returning. They came to her door, but she asked them to go away. She couldn't talk to them yet. Not yet. Curling up on the bed, the ball gown crumpling and spoiling, she hid her face in the pillow. And still the tears had not come.

The sun was high in the afternoon sky before she emerged from her room. She hadn't pinned her hair but had just brushed it loose, so that it hung softly to her shoulders. She had at last discarded the ball gown and wore instead a simple white muslin dress with a square neckline, high waist, and little puffed sleeves.

Her mother was alone in the garden and looked up anxiously as she approached. 'Charlotte, my dear. . . .'

'I'm all right, Mother.'

Mrs Wyndham lowered her eyes at the emptiness in the voice. 'Richard, Henry, and I know how it all happened last night; Sir Maxim told us everything.'

'Everything?' Charlotte sat down on the grass, plucking idly at the daisies that were sprinkled everywhere.

'I'm so very sorry, my dear.'

'It was all my own fault.'

'I don't see how you can blame only yourself.'

'Oh, I know Sylvia took the manuscript, but there shouldn't have been a manuscript to take, should there? That's what I mean. It *was* my fault. Now I've lost him, and I love him so much that I don't know how I'll endure.'

'Oh, my sweetheart,' whispered Mrs Wyndham sadly. 'I wish there was something I could say to comfort you.'

Charlotte looked away for a moment, watching a robin hopping along the wall by the alley, then she glanced at her mother again. 'How's Sylvia?'

'Absolutely inconsolable. She hasn't left her rooms yet, and Henry and Richard are almost beside themselves with worry. She cried her heart out all night.'

'I didn't want it to turn out the way it did, Mother.'

'I know. Sir Maxim explained what should have happened, and I wish with all my heart that things had gone as you planned, for this morning it would all have been so different.'

'For the rest of you, maybe.'

'I was thinking that maybe things would have improved for you and Sir Maxim as well.'

'No. He despises me, Mother, he's left me in no doubt of that.'

The sound of voices made them turn. Richard and the admiral came down the garden toward them, still looking pale and anxious.

'Is Sylvia any better?' inquired Mrs Wyndham as they sat down.

The admiral shook his head. 'She opened the door at last, when Richard threatened to break it down if she didn't, but she won't come out. She's so ashamed and miserable, so tormented with guilt and self-reproach, that she just sits there in her rooms with the curtains drawn. She won't talk or eat. I don't know what to do, Sophia, I've never seen her like this before.'

Richard had slumped dejectedly in his chair. 'She did say one thing,' he said emptily. 'She told me that she could no longer contemplate marrying me. She said that what she did was so bad that she would never be a fit wife, and that I should loathe her for ruining Charlotte's life. But how can I loathe her when I love her so very much? I want to comfort her and stand by her, but she

215

won't let me; she's shutting me out and I can't seem to do anything about it. Oh, God, what a mess all this is! So many lives ruined, and for what? A damned scribble!'

Charlotte's breath caught and she bowed her head.

Richard reached out to her immediately. 'I'm not blaming you,' he said gently. 'Please don't think that I am, for you've suffered as much as anyone in all this, more probably. Forgive me for having doubted you last night. I should have known better and should never have looked at you in the way I did.'

Her fingers curled quickly around his. 'I'm so sorry all this has happened, Richard. I know Sylvia shouldn't have done what she did, but I don't hate her for it. What's done is done, and perhaps, in a strange way, it's as well that it did, for me at least.'

'How can you say that, Charlotte?' gasped her mother in astonishment. 'What possible good can there be in all this misery?'

'It proved one incontrovertible fact, Mother, and that is that Max's love for me was a very fragile thing, shattering in a moment and disappearing without trace. Maybe it's better to find that out now, than later.'

The admiral sat forward then. 'Charlotte, my dear,' he said gently, 'Max is a very proud man, too proud perhaps. His love for you hasn't shattered; it's there still, hurting him constantly because he can't shrug it off. I've known him for so long, and I know him well. Don't misjudge him by thinking him shallow, for that is the last thing he is. He'll never love anyone as he loves you, but whether his pride will ever permit him to admit that fact, I simply do not know.'

Tears sprang suddenly into her eyes, winding their silent way down her pale cheeks. Without a word she got up and hurried away, her muslin skirts whispering through the grass.

In the hallway she paused, still trying to fight back the tears that stung so hotly in her eyes. Then, on sudden impulse, she hurried to the door and out into the street, running along toward the Parkstone residence in Cavendish Square. People stopped in astonishment when they saw her, her hair flying loose behind her, her head bare and without a shawl.

She knocked loudly at the door, not stopping until a startled footman opened it and admitted her. She ran into the hall, where the decorations for the ball were still being taken down, and up the staircase toward Sylvia's apartment.

At the door she hesitated once more, but then resolutely opened it. It was dark inside, so dark that for a moment she couldn't see anything, but gradually she made out a shadow moving by the window. It was Sylvia, getting up slowly from a chair.

'Charlotte?' The voice was a tiny whisper.

Charlotte went to her. 'Sylvia, you mustn't spurn Richard now, you mustn't. He loves you. And I don't hate you. I know that you regretted doing it and that you tried to put it right.'

With a sob, Sylvia hugged her close. 'Oh, Charlotte, I'm so very, very sorry. I wish I was dead for having done such a despicable thing to you. I couldn't help myself. I've been a monster, an absolute monster, and I know it. I've been wrong about Max all along, and I admit it, but when I stole your manuscript, I just wanted to save you from him at all costs.'

Charlotte couldn't help an ironic smile. 'You did that all right,' she murmured.

Sylvia drew guiltily away. 'I feel so utterly dreadful about it. I suppose the fact that you've forgiven me like this is going to make it even worse too.'

'Worse? In what way?'

'Max might think it signifies your lingering belief in what I've always claimed about him.'

'But he knows I don't believe it.'

'He might still misunderstand this. You know how important it always was to him that you believed what he'd told you.'

Charlotte turned away. 'There's nothing I can do about it, Sylvia. He's lost to me forever no matter what I say or do now.

Besides, I came here today not for my own sake but because I want my mother and your father, you and Richard, to be happy together, and that won't come about as long as you and I aren't speaking. I had to come and see you, to tell you that I've forgiven you because I knew you'd be wondering if I'd walk from the room every time you entered, or if I'd refuse any invitation that might place me in your company. I don't feel vindictive toward you, because I understand why you did it and because I know that you tried to stop it. Let Richard come to you, and tell him that you'll still marry him; it's what you want, and it will make him very happy again.'

'Oh, Charlotte, I don't know how you can find it in you to forgive me. I ruined your happiness and I shall blame myself forever.' Sylvia hesitated. 'Maybe I'm the last person to advise you on anything right now, but I think you should go to Max and tell him all that you've told me. Don't risk there being any more misunderstanding.'

'It isn't that easy, Sylvia, for I doubt if he would even receive me.'

'In which case there isn't anything you can do about it, but what if he *does* receive you? Might there not be something to gain? Go to him, Charlotte. If you don't you might regret it forever.'

Charlotte turned to look at her. 'I'm afraid to go,' she whispered. 'I'm afraid I'll find only coldness and I don't think I could bear it.'

'You must go, Charlotte,' said Sylvia softly, 'you must.'

Vigo Street was very quiet as Charlotte alighted from the Parkstone landau. Sylvia's maid had quickly pinned up her hair, and now she was much more correctly turned out with a shawl and white-ribboned bonnet borrowed from Sylvia herself. No time had been allowed for reconsidering; the carriage had been ordered straightaway and now the entrance of the Albany was in sight. Her nerve almost failed her as she looked toward the porter's lodge, but his attention was diverted by some street musicians.

Alighting quickly, she slipped quietly past him and along the covered walk, but he saw the white movement and called angrily after her. She heard his heavy steps as he gave chase.

She reached Max's door and knocked frantically upon it. The noise seemed to reverberate through the building, and she glanced anxiously back to see that the furious porter was almost upon her. Suddenly the door opened and Max's manservant looked curiously out to see what all the noise was. He was so startled to see her that he automatically stepped aside for her to enter. She was inside then, the porter's angry protests ringing after her as he took the bemused servant to task for such deliberate flouting of the house rules.

She glanced quickly around the drawing room and then the adjacent dining room, but there was no sign of Max. The manservant came hesitantly back into the apartment, leaving the still-protesting porter at the door. 'Sir Maxim isn't at home, Miss Wyndham.'

She stared at him in dismay, her heart sinking. 'Wh-when will he return?'

'I don't know, madam, he didn't say.'

She was in a quandary then. She had somehow been so sure he'd be there and now she didn't know what to do.

The porter's voice growled from the doorway. 'I think you should leave, miss.'

She retraced her steps, a cold trembling spreading through her, as if she were stepping out into a winter morning, not the warmth of a beautiful summer day. Tears were horribly close as she walked back along the covered way, trying to look as composed and calm as possible. She didn't see another carriage drawing up behind the Parkstone landau; she wasn't aware of anything until a dark shadow fell across the way before her. With a start she looked up, straight into Max's eyes.

219

'Good morning, Miss Wyndham,' he said coolly. 'To what does the Albany owe this honor?'

'I – I came to see you.'

His mouth twisted contemptuously. 'Then you've wasted your time, for I have no desire to see you.'

How hard and unforgiving he was. She stared at him, a disbelieving hurt swathing through her. She couldn't speak, the words died unsaid on her lips. Afraid that the tears, already so painfully close, would reveal to him how deeply and easily he could wound her, she gathered her skirts and began to walk quickly past, her head high and her glance averted to hide the utter desolation his cruel coldness wrought in her.

As she passed, he whirled about, catching her arm almost roughly. 'You must have had good reason to come, so there seems little point in going without revealing what it was.'

She tried to pull away. 'There's no point, sir, no point at all.'

'I was unnecessarily harsh.'

'You were simply being honest. Please let me go.'

'Damn it, stop struggling! I want to know why you came.'

She became still then, trying to conceal her inner trembling as she faced him. Her voice was quiet. 'I came to tell you that I've forgiven Sylvia and that she and I are friends once more.'

His hand dropped from her arm. 'I already knew you'd forgiven her, so why bother to tell me again? It's of no consequence whatsoever as far as I'm concerned, for I haven't forgiven either of you.'

'No, I can see that. I came because I didn't want you to think that the fact that I'm going to be seen in her company meant that I still believed what she's said in the past.'

'Shall I tell you what I think, Miss Wyndham? I think that you're taking the easy way out in all this. It's much easier to be friendly with her than it is to be at odds.'

'That isn't true, and you wrong me greatly by suggesting it.'

'Do I?'

She looked into his cold eyes. 'Yes,' she whispered, 'yes, you do. I came not only to tell you I'd healed the rift with Sylvia, but also to tell you *why* I'd done it. Do you want to know why, Sir Maxim? Or are you going to heap scorn upon my every word?'

He gazed at her pale face for a moment, as if undecided, then he folded his arms and leaned back against one of the posts supporting the roof over the walk. 'Very well, I'm at your disposal, Miss Wyndham. Explain your all-important reasons.'

'Nothing can change things between you and me, Sir Maxim, but if I'd left everything as it was after the ball last night, there would have been four more unhappy people this morning, my mother and the admiral, and my uncle and Sylvia. I could see that as long as I left Sylvia with her shame, everyone would be miserable. She regrets all she's done, and she's so utterly wretched that she'd even told Richard she couldn't consider marrying him now. That would then have placed my mother and the admiral in difficult circumstances, for there would have been so much awkwardness that nothing could ever be the same again. I'm not giving myself a halo, nor am I taking the easy way out. I'm doing what I think has to be done when the happiness of those dearest to me is at stake. Sylvia tried to stop the book, but it was too late. She bitterly regrets what she did, and she doesn't blame you at all now as she once did. Because of this, and for the others' sakes, I had to go to her, to try to make things as much like before as possible. You do understand, don't you, Max?'

He took a long breath and nodded. 'Yes, I understand. You're right, there's no need for the innocent to suffer because of what's happened.'

Tears were bright in her eyes. 'If I could wave a wand and put things right between us too, Max, believe me I'd do it. But nothing can ever be right for us again, you've made that perfectly clear.' She hesitated. Her love was so great that it was an ache deep within her, and she knew she had to tell him one last time how she felt toward him. 'I love you, Max,' she whispered, 'I love you so much I don't know how I shall go on without you, but I *will* go on, because I have to. Please don't think too badly of me anymore, for I didn't mean to hurt or betray you. I *did* believe all you told me, and there wasn't anything false or underhanded in anything I said to you. I meant my words of love with every fiber of my being, and nothing has changed; I love you still, and I always will.' She pulled the shawl more closely about her shoulders, as if to shield herself from his coldness.

He bowed his head and said nothing.

She turned slowly away, walking back toward the waiting carriage, aware that the coachman and the porter had witnessed everything.

'Charlotte?'

She hesitated, looking back.

He raised his head then and she saw that the coldness had gone from his eyes. 'Oh, Charlotte,' he said softly, 'do you really think I find the prospect of being alone any easier or more bearable than you do?'

'I don't know what to think. You've become so distant that I can hardly believe you're the same man who asked me to marry him.'

'Distance is a cloak I've donned, Charlotte, for without it I'm as vulnerable as ever to my love for you.'

She stared at him. The sounds of London faded away and she could only hear the quickening of her heart.

He straightened slowly, his eyes very dark as he looked at her. 'I despise myself for every cruel word I've said to you, especially as today you've shown me that you'll always be the perfect creature I love and need so much that being apart from you is like being cut in two. Can you ever forgive me for hurting you?'

An unbelievable joy was suddenly spinning wildly through her. 'Oh, Max,' she whispered, 'I'd forgive you anything if you loved me still.'

'I've never stopped loving you.'

She ran to him then and he swept her close, crushing her so

222

tightly to him that she could feel the beats of his heart echoing those of her own. He tilted her lips toward his, kissing her at first softly but then more urgently. She was oblivious to everything but the wild desire and happiness coursing wildly through her veins.

He cupped her face in his hands, caressing her with his thumbs. 'If you hadn't come here today, I'd have lost everything which mattered in my life, and I'd have lost it because of bruised pride. I'll never be too proud again, my darling, for I'll never again put our love at risk.' His fingers twined luxuriously in the warm hair at the nape of her neck, and he bent his head to kiss her again.

The tears of happiness were wet on her cheeks as she clung to him, but then she became aware of the astonished stares of the coachman and the porter. She drew back, a little embarrassed. 'We're about to cause another scandal, I think.'

'I don't care, for it's a scandal I approve of if my name is linked again with yours.' He smiled at her. 'Tell me,' he murmured, 'will you be putting pen to paper for this time as well?'

'Never.'

Ignoring the onlookers, he kissed her again, and with such passion that the coachman cleared his throat and shifted his position, and the porter went very pink indeed, finding something of immense diversion to stare at on the roof above them.